W9-CPB-723

TO LOVE, HONOR,
AND DISOBEY . . .

Even in the chill of the night, Ritter felt the heat of her fury.

"Just who the *hell* do you think you are? You made me look like a damn fool! Well, I'll tell you somethin', *Mr. Sloane*, I ain't gonna wear a *one* of them dresses!"

"You will if you plan on going into town again."

"Hah! Not on your life, gunfighter. And there's not a damn thing you can do to make me."

He jerked back on the reins suddenly and the horse reared to a stop. Almost before he realized it himself, he was pulling her to him, wrapping his arms around her and lowering his mouth to claim hers.

There was nothing gentle in his kiss. Nothing soft or seductive. Only a furious need to touch, to quench a thirst that seemed to have been with him a lifetime. He groaned when her lips parted under his and he felt her last token of resistance melt away. . . .

Praise for *Shotgun Bride*:

"Humor abounds. . . . A story that deeply touches the heart." —*The Paperback Trader*

DIAMOND WILDFLOWER ROMANCE

A breathtaking line of searing romance novels . . . where destiny meets desire in the untamed fury of the American West.

*Diamond Books
by Ann Carberry*

FRONTIER BRIDE
NEVADA HEAT
SHOTGUN BRIDE

SHOTGUN BRIDE

ANN CARBERRY

DIAMOND BOOKS, NEW YORK

If you purchased this book without a cover, you should be aware that this book is stolen property. It was reported as "unsold and destroyed" to the publisher, and neither the author nor the publisher has received any payment for this "stripped book."

This book is a Diamond original edition,
and has never been previously published.

SHOTGUN BRIDE

A Diamond Book / published by arrangement with
the author

PRINTING HISTORY
Diamond edition/November 1993

All rights reserved.
Copyright © 1993 by Maureen Child.
This book may not be reproduced in whole or in part,
by mimeograph or any other means, without permission.
For information address: The Berkley Publishing Group,
200 Madison Avenue, New York, NY 10016.

ISBN: 1-55773-959-5

Diamond Books are published by The Berkley Publishing Group,
200 Madison Avenue, New York, NY 10016.
DIAMOND and the "D" design
are trademarks belonging to Charter Communications, Inc.

PRINTED IN THE UNITED STATES OF AMERICA

10 9 8 7 6 5 4 3 2 1

To the Child brothers—

My wonderful husband Mark, Tom, Chris, Steve, and Mike—and to the only other woman smart enough to marry one of them, Steve's wife, Chela.

SHOTGUN BRIDE

Chapter

One

Benteen ranch, outside Stillwater, Wyoming

"WHAT A *stupid* way to die."

Stop that nonsense! she argued with herself. Now was *not* the time to be thinkin' about dyin'!

Hallie Benteen lay on her back in the snow and peered between the bare arms of the surrounding trees at the star-studded black sky above her. The only other sound was the tree limbs as they clicked softly together in the chilling breeze.

She snorted a mocking laugh at her carelessness and aimed another useless kick at the fallen tree limb imprisoning her right leg. Struggling, she managed to lift her head slightly. The heavy branch lay across her like an ancient trap. Hallie ignored the now pounding pressure in her head and tried to think clearly.

"How long have I been layin' here?" she asked aloud, more to hear the sound of her own voice than anything else. She reached up with tentative fingers and explored the knot on her forehead. As close as she could figure, the damned branch had snapped free, clipped her a good knock on the head, then landed across her body.

1

And wouldn't you know it would be the granddaddy of all branches! A *twig* wouldn't be enough by *far* for a Benteen!

Judging from the position of the stars, she must have been unconscious for quite a while. But even if the stars were covered in clouds, she would have known that. The numbness in her body was proof enough that she'd been lying in the snow for far too long. She could hardly feel her right leg anymore, and even through her thick gloves, Hallie's fingers felt lifeless . . . dead.

Oh, no, she told herself firmly. Don't start *that* again. She wasn't about to die, trapped in the snow, under a tree branch, when she could see her own house not more than a couple of hundred yards away! Why, if she ever *dared* to die so stupidly, she had no doubt that her pa wouldn't let Saint Peter open the pearly gates for her, he'd be *that* ashamed!

She shook her wooden fingers madly for a few brief seconds, then gave it up. She was just too blamed tired. Maybe if she rested for just a little bit.

Her head throbbed steadily with a dull pain that pounded relentlessly against her skull. She stared for a moment at the misty fog of her own breath before closing her eyes in disgust. "Damn fool," she muttered aloud. "Shoulda known better than to traipse under old trees laden down with snow."

Well, how was I to know the durned thing'd tear off and thump me?

"And where the hell are the boys?"

Shoot, you know them. If you don't show up on time, they'll be spreadin' out all over the country lookin' for ya.

"Yeah, well," she argued out loud with her own thoughts, "they shoulda *found* me by now." She was suddenly furious at her three brothers.

Maybe they did find ya. Maybe you don't remember 'cause you're already dead.

Her eyes flew open at the wild thought. Her chest heaved with a sudden fright, and she watched her breath mist and dance in front of her. *Not dead yet.*

She licked her lips and smiled halfheartedly. She'd just have to stop thinkin', that was all. Wasn't Jericho always tellin' her that too much thinkin' wears out the brain?

Laying her head back down, Hallie told herself that she'd never known before what a soft, comfy pillow snow could make. She closed her eyes and envisioned the boys. If she knew Shad, he'd be about worried to death by now and houndin' the others something fierce.

They'd find her, sure as shootin'. Wasn't her brother Micah the best damn tracker in the country?

Then where in blazes *are* they? her brain screamed.

Ritter Sloane tugged his fleece-lined collar higher up around his neck, then pushed his dust-colored Stetson lower down over his eyes. Irritably he watched the white clouds of his horse's labored breathing and cursed the late-season storm one more time.

He ducked his head as he rode under another low-hanging branch and told himself that it wasn't the storm to blame. It was Hamilton Butler.

The old bastard had lied to him.

Ritter'd only taken the damn job because it was simple. Straightforward. Squatters on Butler's land needed to be moved.

The horse stumbled, and Ritter patted the animal's neck in reassurance before returning to his thoughts.

Butler hadn't told the whole story. It wasn't squatters on his land. It was a family. A woman and her brothers. A family that had occupied the same land for over twenty years. And now, because Butler got greedy, the wealthy rancher wanted that family run out of the country.

So Butler'd called in a gunfighter.

Well, he'd hired him the wrong man.

Ritter Sloane didn't make war on women.

Frowning into the distance, Ritter spotted a long, low line of darkness silhouetted against the backdrop of the night sky. Once he got this settled, he told himself, he could get the hell out of there. Go someplace warm.

Maybe Mexico. Not too many people knew him down there. Maybe he could find a little peace for a while.

As he drew nearer to the house, he noticed that there was no light showing. No sign of life.

Ritter drew his horse to a stop. He sat perfectly still in the saddle, one hand on his thigh, near the butt of his gun, the other gripping the reins tightly.

Something was wrong. It wasn't *that* late that people would be abed already. Usually, at least *one* member of a household would be up—reading, cleaning, getting ready for the coming day.

Uneasy, Ritter tugged at the reins, and the horse reluctantly turned to the right. Keeping a wary eye on the darkened ranch house, Ritter began a slow, careful circle of the property. In his business, *careful* was the only way to stay alive.

Hallie's eyes opened slowly. The stars had moved again. Time. Too much time. Doggedly she tried to push at the tree limb again. But this time her left leg refused to do as she wanted. It felt almost as though it belonged to somebody else.

The deep, bone-shattering cold had seeped into her body until she no longer ached with it. Her teeth weren't chattering as they were awhile ago. And the damp, icy sensations had completely stopped. In fact, Hallie told herself, she felt downright cozy . . . except for the blasted tree limb.

She wasn't ignorant, though. She knew that the false warmth that flooded her was a bringer of death. But somehow, Hallie didn't mind nearly so much anymore. Though she *did* wonder what had become of the boys. They should have found her long ago.

Then suddenly she remembered. The three of them had gone into town together. Something about poker, she thought idly. No telling when they'd be back. Probably not till morning, at least. Hallie sighed and noticed that her breath made a much smaller cloud than it had earlier.

That was it, then. No one would be comin' lookin' for her. Not till it was much too late.

She shook her head against the pillow of snow and turned her gaze to the stars. It was a shame, she thought, her dyin' like this. Why, she'd never yet been to a big city. Or seen the ocean. She'd always wanted to have a look at the ocean. Why, some folks said that it stretched out clean to forever!

And a baby. Hallie clamped her lips together against a sigh of disappointment. Guess she never would have that baby she'd daydreamed over and planned for.

And the boys. Her brothers. How in the world would they get along without her? A moment of distress pulsed through her as she realized that the boys would find her here, cold and dead, when they returned home. She could almost see their grief-stricken faces and wished she could somehow help them. Let them know that it hadn't hurt any, at least. But there was simply nothing to be done about it. They would have to deal with her death as best they could.

It pained her to think of it, though.

Sadly Hallie pushed all thoughts of her family away. Instead, she narrowed her gaze to a single star and concentrated mightily on the glimmering light so far away. As the cold and exhaustion finally forced her eyes shut, Hallie wondered if a body could see the backsides of the stars from heaven.

Nothing. No movement, no sounds, no light. Nothing. As Ritter completed his circle of the ranch house his stallion suddenly sidestepped nervously. In an instant a smooth, walnut-stocked pistol rested in Ritter's hand.

Alert, wary, Ritter held his breath and waited. He listened, straining for the sound, the hush of movement his horse had reacted to. *Something* was ahead of him, sheltered by the low-hanging branches and the drifts of snow.

Slowly he dismounted, mentally cursing at every creak the leather saddle made as his weight shifted. Knowing his well-trained horse would stay put, he let the reins drop and carefully edged his way into the shadows.

Could be a trap. But who? his mind questioned rapidly. Hell, it could be any one of a hundred people. He ducked beneath a branch and continued on, knees bent, watching where he placed every step.

Butler?

No. Wouldn't have had the time to beat Ritter here. Besides, the old bastard was just greedy. Not vicious. A trap wouldn't be his way.

The Benteen family? Ritter paused and let his practiced gaze move over the darkness surrounding him. Patches of moonlight drifted down over the silent scene, casting weird shadows of light and dark. What if the Benteen family had heard about Butler hiring him? What if they'd decided to rid themselves of the problem? After all, he knew nothing about the Benteens. Maybe they were worse than Butler.

A muffled sound drifted to him, and he spun in a crouch to meet it. The noise was coming from the far side of an ancient tree.

Carefully, quietly, he approached the pine and told himself that he hoped the Benteen family hadn't declared war on Ritter Sloane. He was getting too old for it.

Cautiously he stepped around the wide tree trunk and came to a dead stop. Stretched out in front of him, a body lay in the snow, trapped under a heavy limb. His gaze flicked around the tiny clearing, then, satisfied that it wasn't a trap, he hurried to the still form. He hoped he wasn't too late.

In the darkness Ritter was only able to see how small the body was. As he knelt down beside the poor soul, he heard a faint rattle of breath, and a grim smile curved his lips. "Good. You're not dead, then."

The body's lips moved, and when the soft, breathy voice broke the silence, Ritter started in surprise.

A woman!

"H'lo," she sighed on a soft cloud of mist.

"Hello." His hands rubbed briskly up and down her jacketed arms as his brain raced to decide what to do first. What the hell was a woman doing out here in the snow? Alone?

"You a angel?" she whispered.

He snorted. "Not hardly."

"Mmmm." She sighed and closed her eyes again. "Saint Peter, then." The woman pulled in a shallow, shuddering breath. "You see that Pa lets me in now, y'hear? This wasn't my fault."

Ritter shook his head. She was rambling. Lucky to be alive. Though she was closer to death than life. He frowned. This had to be the Benteen woman. Who the hell else would be here, in the snow, so close to the Benteen ranch house? Well, their first meeting wasn't going anything like he'd thought it would.

He hated to leave her just lying there, but he had to go for his horse. He needed a rope. Blankets. Quickly he stood up, shucked his fleece-lined coat and spread it over her. Probably wouldn't do much good, he thought, but it wouldn't hurt any, either.

Once he'd got everything set up, it hadn't taken long at all to free her. Ritter glanced up at the rope, stretched across a low-hanging branch. One end tied to the limb across the girl, the other tied to his saddle horn, all he'd had to do was back up his horse and lift the dead weight right off her.

He ran his hands over her body impersonally, checking for broken bones. But she'd been lucky. Nothing *too* serious, beyond about freezing to death. His arms beneath her, Ritter lifted her as gently as he could. Shifting her weight, he moved one hand long enough to loosen the rope from his saddle. The heavy branch dropped back to the ground with a muffled thud. He would collect his rope again the next day. The most important thing right now was to get the woman in his arms warm again.

Ritter rode his horse directly into the barn. Once out of the wind the big stallion seemed content to help himself to the feed stacked handily in the nearest stall.

Ordinarily Ritter would care for the huge animal right away. Tonight, though, the best he could manage was to loosen the cinch strap and let his saddle slide off the horse's broad back. He dared not waste any more precious time. Since the few words she'd spoken when he first found her, the woman hadn't uttered another sound. In fact, she hadn't even opened her eyes again.

Hurriedly Ritter tightened his arms around her and crossed the open yard to the darkened house beyond. Awkwardly he managed to pull on the latch string, and when the door yawned open, he stepped inside and kicked it shut behind him. Moonlight peeped through the two front windows, and in the vague half-light Ritter spotted a huge stone fireplace.

He marched across the wood floor and used the toe of his boot to kick a thick bear rug closer to the hearth. He laid the woman down on it, then turned to the cold fireplace. Quickly, instinctively, he laid the fire. Rather than waste time searching for matches in a strange home, he rifled the pockets of his coat, still covering the unconscious woman.

In seconds a tentative curl of flame licked at the kindling, feeding at the dry wood until it was strong enough to accept the thick log Ritter laid across it.

With the firelight, indistinct shapes wavered in the

darkness and slowly took form. His careful gaze swept the huge main room and his knack for lightning-quick observation stood him in good stead.

Several large hide-covered chairs clustered around an overstuffed, fabric-covered settee which faced the prominent fireplace. To one side of the great room, a long, heavy trestle table, flanked by two benches with intricately carved backs, sat beneath three hanging kerosene lamps with shining brass shades. Along the front wall, near a now empty gun rack, a short, wide cabinet rested directly under one of the windows.

Ritter glanced down at the woman. Her flesh was still far too waxy to suit him. He had to get her warmed up quick. With any luck, he told himself, that cabinet just might hold a little something to help him.

He stood and crossed the room in a few long strides. Wrenching open the heavy, swinging door, Ritter squatted down and peered inside. With a grunt of satisfaction, he reached in and pulled out a bottle of whiskey. Knowing that the Benteen family included quite a few men, Ritter'd hoped that he might find some. Hurrying back to the woman, he pulled the cork from the bottle and knelt down beside her.

Gently his palm cupped the back of her neck, and he lifted her head slightly. Pressing the bottle to her lips, he tipped it up and spilled some of the strong-smelling liquid into her mouth. She coughed and sputtered immediately, but he was fairly certain that at least *some* of the whiskey had gotten down her throat.

The fire crackled and spit, and in its light he studied her for the first time. A short crop of auburn curls framed her pale features, ending just below the dainty silver hoops in her ears. He couldn't recall ever seeing such short hair on a woman, and he suddenly decided that he liked it. Dark red eyebrows arched over her closed eyes, and below a small nose her full pink lips moved in whispered mutterings.

A pretty woman, but far too pallid right now to suit him.

He pulled his jacket off her and watched the shallow rise and fall of her chest. Ritter's brows narrowed worriedly. She was too still. Her pale, waxen features looked lifeless, and he knew a moment's panic. She needed warmth and she needed it quick.

And there was only one sure way he knew of to do that.

The man's blue and black checked flannel shirt she wore was damp and tucked into the waistband of even damper, well-worn buckskin britches. Ritter shook his head. She'd never get warm enough in those clothes. They only served to trap the cold next to her still-shivering body.

There was really only one thing to be done. With a silent apology to her sensibilities, Ritter began unbuttoning her shirt.

Surprisingly, his fingers seemed suddenly clumsy as he moved down the row of white buttons. He'd never before undressed a woman who wasn't wide awake and eagerly helping him. He pulled the shirttail free of her britches, undid the cuff buttons, then lifted her to pull the wet flannel off. Her damp, plain white chemise covered, but didn't manage to hide, the deep rose of her erect nipples. Deliberately he looked away and turned his attention to the buckskin pants encasing her curvy hips. Quickly Ritter reached down and tried to pull the laces of her knee-high moccasins. But they wouldn't budge. Wet rawhide didn't move easily.

She moaned softly, and he spared her only a glance before slipping his hand down to his right boot and pulling out the Arkansas Toothpick he carried there. The knife blade, ten inches long and double-edged, was razor sharp. Ritter grasped the bone handle and sliced upward through the rawhide strings on both her shoes, then laid his knife on the stone hearth nearby. Quickly he pulled her moccasins off, then unhooked the waist button on the right side of her britches. He tugged the cold, wet buckskin free of her long legs and, to his credit, hardly blinked when he saw she wore nothing under them.

His mouth suddenly dry, Ritter rubbed one hand across his jaw, moved slightly, and before he could think twice about it, pulled her cotton chemise off over her head.

And still she shook with cold. He turned her toward the blazing fire, lifted the edge of the bear rug, and covered her with it, rubbing his hands briskly up and down the length of the thick hide. After a few long minutes he peeled back the bear hide and lay the flat of his palm against her back. The icy cold of her flesh stabbed at him, and he knew that what he was doing wouldn't be enough to save her.

He *had* to get her warm fast, or she wouldn't survive the night. She'd simply sink lower and lower into the cold until she couldn't be reached again. Flicking the robe over her once more, he stood up. After laying another log across the blazing fire, he leaned back against the river stones and lifted first one foot, then the other, tugging his own boots off. Quickly he stripped out of his clothes, dropping them in a careless heap. He laid his holster and gun within reach on the river-stone hearth.

Once he was completely naked, he pulled the bear robe aside and stretched out beside the nude woman. He turned onto his left side, and pulled her up close to him. Ritter gasped aloud when her cold flesh touched his, but he only wrapped his right arm across her body and pinned her to him. It was like lying down naked in an ice house. Her bone-deep cold seeped into Ritter's body until he felt himself shake in response. He held her tighter. Spoon-fashion, his long, muscular legs curled directly behind hers, and her smooth, icy bottom nestled snugly against his already hardened body.

It was going to be a long night.

She shuddered and scooted closer to his warmth, mumbling incoherently. Ritter rested his chin on the top of her head and mentally willed her to be still. Though he didn't mind saving her from the cold one bit, he didn't relish the idea of being tortured, either.

Ritter shifted uncomfortably in his sleep. Almost immediately a warm, soft body snuggled in closer to him. He tugged on the blanket covering them until it was wrapped around them both like a sheltering cocoon. Without opening his eyes, still more asleep than awake, Ritter smiled and ran one hand up over the curve of her hip and along her side until he cupped her breast gently.

She sighed and nestled up against him.

Idly his thumb circled her nipple, teasing and toying with the tiny bud until it stood erect, demanding attention. He smiled sleepily, then shifted position so that his lips could travel the length of her throat before reaching the nipple waiting for him.

His mouth moved gently over the warm, sweet-scented flesh beneath him. Idly his tongue flicked against the woman's skin, and he swallowed a smile at her sleepy sigh of pleasure. Slowly, slowly, he worked his way down across her chest until he found the bud he sought. He slid his hand aside and took her nipple into his mouth. When his lips closed over the delicate flesh, Ritter's right hand slipped down, over her flat abdomen to the mound of curls at the juncture of her thighs. She sighed softly and opened her legs for him almost hesitantly, but he felt her jump in his arms when the heel of his hand pressed against the hot center of her.

She moaned out loud as the edges of his teeth moved over her sensitive breast, and he felt her fingernails dig into his shoulder. Ritter shuddered and stifled a groan that threatened to choke him. He couldn't remember ever being so ready for a woman. It was almost as though he'd been preparing for this moment for hours. Sweet torture racked his body, and when her legs spread wider to accommodate his seeking hand, he knew that she, too, was more than ready.

He clamped his lips tightly over her nipple and suckled her, drawing out the pleasure for them both. Her sighs and moans fed his own hunger until he couldn't wait another moment for completion.

Ritter lifted his head from her breast and stopped dead.

Something cold and hard lay against the right side of his face. Passion died instantly. He came fully conscious for the first time. In a heartbeat, memory returned. He knew where he was. He remembered how he came to be there in the snug cabin. Slowly he opened his eyes and saw beneath him, her lake-blue eyes still glazed with unsatisfied want, the woman he'd found in the snow.

A familiar calm settled over him. Cautiously, hardly risking a deep breath, Ritter looked out of the corner of his eye and froze.

A bearded man with wild, red-brown hair to match the whiskers on his face stood behind the shotgun that even now pressed against Ritter's cheekbone. Just to the man's left were two more men, each identical to the first . . . each holding an identical shotgun . . . which were also aimed at Ritter's head.

Chapter

Two

"Mornin', boys."

The woman beneath him spoke, but Ritter didn't look at her. Instead, he watched, hypnotized as the double-barreled shotgun moved from his cheekbone to a spot just an inch from his eyes. He stared into the dark centers of the steel barrels and held his breath.

"What the hell's goin' on here, Hallie?" the man behind the gun asked.

"Well, now," she answered slowly, sliding her hand from Ritter's shoulder down the length of his arm. "I ain't really sure. . . ."

With a great force of will, Ritter bit back a groan. His gaze slid carefully from the gun barrel to the man behind it. He found no comfort there.

Tall and thin, the man's wild reddish-brown hair fairly bristled with raw anger. Green eyes flashing dangerously, brows lowered, he glared at Ritter—silently daring him to move.

Ritter mentally cursed himself for a fool. He was well and truly caught. His holster and pistol were too far out of reach, and even his knife still lay where he'd left it on the hearth. Cautiously he glanced out the corner of his eye at the two other men.

The early morning sunlight streamed through the front windows, outlining the intruders in a soft yellow light. Squinting, Ritter tried to focus. They hadn't moved an inch. Their shotguns, though not stuck in his face, were poised for action. He blinked once, twice. He wasn't imagining things. All three men were as alike as bullets taken from the same box. From their hair and eye color to their defensive posture to the grim determination stamped on their outraged features.

Triplets.

Ritter knew he was in deep trouble.

"Micah," the woman said evenly, "put that gun down."

Ritter heartily agreed.

"Not till we know what's goin' on here," the first man answered in a cold, calm voice.

"Well, maybe we can figure it all out if you'll put the danged gun away so's this fella can move."

"Seems to me," one of the others put in, "he done moved enough already."

"Shad," she countered quickly, "you ain't helpin' any."

Ritter hardly breathed. He wasn't going to move an inch until that shotgun did. He sure as hell didn't want to die buck naked!

The three men exchanged a long, silent look. Slowly, reluctantly, the cold steel barrels shifted until they were pointed at the floor. And still Ritter didn't move.

"Mister," the woman said and tapped Ritter's hand, still cupping her breast.

He glanced at her warily.

"You best let me go now so's the boys don't get all het up."

He would've sworn they were "het up" already, but if there was a chance they could get worse, he was all for avoiding it. Ritter shifted position slightly, releasing the woman, yet still managing to hold on to the bear hide that covered them.

"All right," Hallie said firmly. "You boys turn around now until I get myself dressed."

Her brothers looked at one another uneasily, and she could see they had no intention of turning their backs. Well, for heaven's sake! She wasn't about to stand up bare-assed in front of her own brothers! It was bad enough, layin' here in the altogether with a man who seemed only vaguely familiar, she told herself.

Suddenly, in a flash of memory, the night before swam before her eyes. The cold. The fear and loneliness. And then . . . *someone* bending over her. Whispering to her. Carrying her to the house and making the cold go away. She remembered clearly, the almost painful sensation of warmth touching her frozen body and how she'd curled into it instinctively. Slowly Hallie recalled the fire blazing in the hearth and the comfort of strong arms wrapped around her.

Whoever the blond man was, he'd saved her life. He'd held her and warmed her with his own body. And in the first light of morning he'd shown her more heat than she'd ever imagined. Hallie knew she'd never forget waking in his arms with him kissing her breast.

She shivered. Just the memory of his touch brought the same warm rush of pleasure his mouth had. She'd never felt anything like it in her life, and if truth were told, Hallie'd been mad enough to spit nails when the boys showed up and ruined everything.

Of course, she couldn't tell *them* that.

"Micah, Shad, Jericho," she said again, louder this time. "You bunch turn your backs this minute, y'hear?"

"All right, Hallie," Micah answered slowly. "We'll turn around. But, mister," he added, pointing the shotgun in Ritter's face, "you so much as breathe loud, we'll hear ya. Don't you even *think* about movin'."

Hallie saw the red flush creep up the blond man's neck and knew he was mad enough to try anything. Quickly, before he did something stupid, she rolled out from under him, jumped to her feet, and snatched a threadbare quilt off a nearby chair. She wrapped it around her shoulders, letting the excess material pool around her feet. "All right, boys. I'm decent."

They turned as one.

"Now," Hallie continued, her voice purposefully light, "I'm gonna go on in to my room and put on some clothes. Why don't you boys let this fella get dressed before we start talkin', all right?"

The man on the floor shot her a grateful look, then glared at her brothers. This wasn't going to be easy.

Deliberately, Hallie turned her back on the four men and walked to her room, the washed-out flowered quilt trailing behind her like the train of an elegant ball gown.

Once inside her small bedroom, with the door safely shut, Hallie dropped the quilt and hurried to the chest at the foot of her bed. Tossing back the lid, she leaned over the meager contents and began to paw through her clothes. One after the other, she threw moccasins, shirts, and hand-me-down britches over her shoulder into a pile on the floor behind her. At the bottom of the carved cedar chest, she finally found what she'd been looking for.

Two dresses, long hidden and never worn. Tenderly she held one in each hand and lifted them as she stood up. Cocking her head to one side, she studied them carefully.

First, the red and white checked gingham, with a narrow skirt, short sleeves, and a rounded neckline . . . She frowned at it for a long moment, then shook her head. Not right. She'd made it with the leftover fabric she'd had after fashioning curtains for the main room, and there hadn't been enough to make a full, swirling skirt.

The second one, yellow calico with tiny blue flowers, had the same round neckline, but it also had full sleeves and a wide skirt fit to twirl all night at a square dance. She smiled softly, remembering how she'd bought far too much material for bedroom curtains and how the boys had laughed at her for her mistake.

Of course, she'd never told them it wasn't a mistake. And since she'd never worn either dress in front of them, they had no idea that she'd ordered extra fabric on purpose the second time.

And now was the perfect chance to wear one of the dresses she loved at long last. She'd like to watch that good-lookin' blond man's pale blue eyes sweep over her approvingly. She'd even like to see her brothers' surprised faces when she showed up dressed like a girl.

She bit down on her bottom lip for a moment and furrowed her brow thoughtfully. Knowing the boys, she told herself, right now, they were decidin' on one of two things. She pursed her lips as she recalled exactly the scene they'd walked in on such a short while ago. Hallie pondered on the problem for a while, then finally came to what she thought would be the boys' decision.

Deliberately then, she dropped the red and white gown

into a crumpled heap. Hallie closed her eyes and held the yellow calico up against her still-bare flesh. The material caressed her skin, and she imagined that it was the blond man's hands moving over her body. She pursed her lips to taste his again and felt her heart thud erratically in response.

"Oh, my," she said softly, fanning herself with the fingers of one hand. A crash sounded from the main room, followed by a man grunting in either pain or surprise. She held perfectly still and waited. Silence.

From the corner of her eye, Hallie caught sight of her own reflection in the small square mirror hanging on the wall. She quirked her lips slightly and told herself, "You best get dressed and get out there, or the boys just might hurt that fella before you get another chance at him!"

Ritter Sloane sat on the floor, rubbing one hand over his aching jaw. He glared at the man standing over him but made no move to get up. Not with the other two holding shotguns on him.

Slowly he laid both arms across his upraised knees. At least they'd let him put his pants on. He moved his lower jaw tentatively, wincing at the accompanying pain. Nothing seemed to be broken, though it wasn't for the lack of trying. For a fairly thin man, Micah Benteen had quite a punch.

"You gonna get on up here, gunfighter," Micah asked "or are you gonna make me reach down and get ya?"

Ritter sighed heavily. Even explaining who he was hadn't had the least effect on the three men. They didn't seem concerned at all that they were holding a notorious gunfighter in their midst. And his reputation certainly hadn't stopped Micah from handing out punishment.

For the first time in more years than he could remember, Ritter's name hadn't brought listeners to a shuddering halt. Usually people fell all over themselves to stay out of his way. To keep from insulting him. They smiled and flattered him, hiding their distaste and alarm behind a false mask of friendship. All in fear of the gunfighter's terrible retaliation.

The only folks who treated him differently were the young men looking to kill him and build their own reputations as gunmen.

Or fellow gunfighters.

Until now.

"I'm not going to fight you, Benteen," Ritter said softly.

"Why the hell not?"

"Well, for one thing, your brothers over there are holding two shotguns on me!" He shook his head. "I don't go up against a stacked deck."

Micah frowned. "They'll stay out of it. Right, boys?"

The other two nodded solemnly.

Disgusted, Ritter shoved his hands through his hair. "I *told* you already. *Nothing* happened between your sister and me."

"Hmmph! Ain't what it looked like to me," Micah countered, holding his balled fists up and ready.

"I'll say this *one* more time." Ritter glared at Micah, then shot a quelling glance at the other two. "I came out here to tell you about Butler hiring me and me quitting. I figured you should know what the old goat's up to, because he'll probably hire somebody else now I've left." He waited for a response and got none. Shaking his head, he went on tiredly with the story he'd told them only moments before. "I was coming up on the house here and found your sister stretched out in the snow, pinned under a tree limb. She was about frozen stiff. I brought her in here, built a fire, and did all I could to get her warm again."

"Yeah," Micah said. "We saw the limb down. Saw your tracks. Found your horse in the barn. Then we come in here and find you a-cozyin' up to Hallie like you was dyin' of thirst and she was the only water hole for miles around!"

"That's true, mister."

Ritter groaned and looked from one grim face to the next. There was no way to deny it. They'd all seen him "cozyin' up" to their sister.

Shit! How the hell had he gotten into this mess anyway? By doing the right thing, he told himself. If he'd just left this damn valley right after quitting Butler, none of this would have happened. But then, his mind taunted him, the girl would have died. And that would have been a sore waste.

Besides, he thought disgustedly, it wasn't saving her life they were angry about. It was helping himself to her warm, luscious body that had them hopping mad. He couldn't blame them, either. If he had a sister who looked like that, he'd damn sure keep the no-accounts away, too.

A brief memory of her deep blue eyes swam before him. As clear as a mountain lake in summer, they'd stared at him in frank appraisal. There hadn't been a trace of coyness, embarrassment, or shame. Merely the shadows of unfulfilled want. He pushed the vision away deliberately. Idle thoughts about a woman like that could only make this already difficult situation even more complicated.

Yet, even as he gave himself such sage advice, another image of the auburn-haired woman leapt at him. The way she'd jumped up to cover herself before her brothers. The curve of her hip, the smooth pale flesh of her behind, her long legs . . . Stop it! his mind warned.

"Nothing happened," he said aloud, more forcefully than before.

"Now, mister . . ." The third brother spoke for the first time. "We'd surely like to believe ya. Matter of fact, I'm thinkin' that you'd be lookin' a sight worse than you do right now if you'd tried anything that Hallie didn't like."

His brothers nodded.

Ritter felt a swell of hope, but it was dashed almost immediately.

"Howsomever . . ." the same man went on, "it don't really make no difference if somethin' happened or not, now does it?"

"What?"

"Jericho . . ." Micah looked at his brother.

"Now, Micah, Shad . . ." He took a deep breath, set the stock of his gun on the floor, and leaned both forearms on the upended barrel. "You know as well as me what's got to be done."

The triplet in the middle wrinkled up his forehead before turning to his right. "That's so, Micah. Jericho's right. There just ain't no help for it. What's done is done."

Ritter's uneasy gaze flicked back and forth, following the unnerving conversation. After all the years of traveling, selling his gun wherever there was a market for it . . . all the years of shoot-outs, range wars, and lonely campfires, it appeared he was about to be killed by the brothers of a woman he hadn't even been able to enjoy. No doubt somewhere, some of his long-dead enemies were having a helluva laugh.

Micah thoughtfully ran his hand down the barrel of his shotgun. Ritter watched and tried to read the different expressions crossing the man's face as he obviously weighed his brothers' statements. If Ritter could only get hold of his gun, he thought dismally, at least he could make a chance of escaping.

"Well, boys," Micah finally said, "I reckon you're right. There ain't no way outa this here mess but one."

Ritter swallowed, lifted his chin, and glared at each one of the men. He'd be damned if he'd give them the satisfaction of hearing him try to talk his way out of this. If they were going to kill him, he wouldn't make it easy for them. They'd have to shoot down an unarmed man.

"All right, mister"—Micah looked at him—"you can get up now. Shad, fetch the man his shirt and such . . . ."

Confused, Ritter stood up slowly, half expecting to be punched back down. When Shad handed him his shirt, though, the man grinned and thumped Ritter's back companionably. What the *hell*?

"Soon's you're dressed and Hallie gets herself out here, we'll get it done." Micah leaned on his gun, his lean body taking the same posture as his brother.

Ritter pushed his arms into the sleeves of his plain white shirt, then reached for his boots. So that was it. They wanted to shoot him in front of their sister. Make her watch it. He sneered at them. A fine bunch of brothers, indeed. Why, even though he was preparing to die, he could feel a stab of sympathy for the woman forced to live with a crew like that.

He slammed one foot into his boot and stamped loudly on the floor. "Why wait for her? Why not just go outside and do it now? If you've got a problem with me, let's us handle it like men. Just us."

The three men looked at one another in confusion, then turned back to Ritter as he pulled on his other boot.

"It wouldn't be fittin' to go without Hallie," the one called Shad said.

"And hardly worth the trip," Jericho added.

"You didn't seem to mind havin' Hallie around just awhile ago," Micah said, his lips quirking slightly.

"That's got nothing to do with this." Ritter put his hands on his hips. Feeling more confident now that he was dressed and standing on his own two feet, he faced down the three bearded brothers. "Leave her out of it."

Shad snorted a laugh. "Son, we cain't hardly do that, now can we?"

Ritter'd had enough. He felt his temper rising, and that was something he hadn't allowed to happen in years. "If you're going to shoot me, why the hell do you want her to watch you do it?"

"*Shoot* ya?" Jericho's booming laughter echoed around them. "Shit, mister, if we was gonna shoot ya, you'd be dead by now!"

Micah shook his head disgustedly as he stared at the gunman across from him. "We ain't fixin' to shoot you, Sloane."

"Well, *what*, then?"

"Hell, mister," Shad spoke up, his wide grin splitting that red-brown beard right in half, "we're gonna take you and Hallie into town and get you married up."

"*Married!?*"

"Hell, yes!" Micah shook his fist at him. "You think we're gonna let a man nuzzle on Hallie like you done without bein' married to her?"

"I can't marry your sister!" Ritter's mind worked furiously. He'd never expected *this!*

"Why?" Shad asked worriedly. "You hitched already?"

"Of course not!"

"Well, then"—Micah shrugged—"can't see why not."

"Goddammit!" Ritter threw his hands high in the air. He couldn't believe it. They couldn't be serious! But they were. "For the same reason I'm not 'hitched' already! I'm a gunfighter! I *told* you that!"

"Yeah?"

"So?"

"What's that s'posed to mean?"

They all spoke at once, and Ritter could only look from one to the other of them in stunned silence. Good God! What kind of men would want their only sister to be married to a gunfighter?

Calm down, he told himself. Think. That's the only way out of this ridiculous situation. *Jesus,* if he'd just been more awake this morning, he'd never have touched the woman! But it was instinctual, drawing that lovely warm body up close to his own. For God's sake. Any man might have done the same thing!

The woman. Of course. The woman would never agree to this plan of her brothers. Surely *she* would see that it would never work! Yes, he told himself. That's it. She'd seemed perfectly rational when the "boys" came in loaded for bear. But would they listen to her?

"What about your sister?" he asked quickly. "What if she won't have me? Doesn't she have a say in this?"

They looked at one another, then turned back to him, shaking their heads.

Micah spoke first. " 'Pears to me she already had her say."

"When?" Ritter's voice sounded panicked, even to himself.

"Hell, when she let you go on nuzzlin' at her . . ."—he paused and groped for the right word—"*chest* without killin' ya."

"True," Shad and Jericho agreed.

This is absurd! Ritter told himself. For most of his life he'd spent his time being run out of town by the local upright, law-abiding, God-fearing citizens! He'd never been able to *glance* at a so-called "decent" woman in years! No one wanted a dirty gunslinger in their family bosom.

Except, his brain added wryly, the Benteens!

No. No, this wasn't right. He shook his head wildly. Something was very wrong with the whole situation. Maybe the three of them didn't really *understand* exactly who Ritter Sloane was. Maybe, being triplets, he told himself with a wary glance in their direction, they only got one brain to share between the three of them.

That would explain a lot.

Desperate, he tried to reason with them one last time.

"You can't want a *gunfighter* to be your sister's husband!"

Shad smiled and shrugged. "Don't really matter *what* he is. We want the man who seen her *naked* to be her husband!"

Chapter

Three

"HALLIE!" MICAH shouted into the stunned silence. "You about ready?"

"Hold on to your hair," came the somewhat muffled reply. "I'll be out in a shake."

Ritter's eyebrows shot straight up. This was the most infuriating, hardheaded, *outlandish* family he'd ever run across. And for the life of him, he couldn't think of a way out. His only hope lay in convincing Hallie Benteen to make a stand against her brothers.

A fragile hope, but one he clung to resolutely.

The door behind him opened. Even if he hadn't heard the creak of complaining hinges, Ritter would have known by the looks on the faces of the three men facing him. Slowly, almost fearfully, he turned around to meet his fate.

Hallie couldn't have asked for a better response. Her gaze passed over the thunderstruck faces of her brothers and settled on the handsome blond man standing alone in the center of the great room.

He was taller than she'd first thought. Of course, she admitted silently, it was hard to tell lyin' down. Deliberately she let her gaze wander over his broad shoulders, narrow waist and hips, and down his long legs to the elegantly tooled leather boots he wore. Then her eyes moved back up to study his face.

A narrow band of flesh across his high forehead, a shade lighter than the rest of his features, told Hallie that the man wore a hat more often than not. His pale blond hair was disheveled and looked as though he'd jammed angry hands through it more than once. His eyes were a cool blue, and his nose looked as if it'd been broken at one time. Blond whisker stubble along his strong jaw shone in the early morning light, and the soft lips he'd touched to her breast were now curved in an appreciative smile.

Something warm and heavy fluttered in her stomach, and Hallie swallowed nervously.

"*Have* mercy!" Micah muttered wonderingly.

"Ya look real pretty, Hallie."

She smiled at Shad.

"Where'd you find girl clothes?" Jericho asked, his forehead wrinkling.

"I made it," she finally said, looking at no one but Ritter.

His gaze met hers, and she drank in his silent admiration until he looked away to snap at Micah.

"Now, why don't you tell your sister what you have in mind?"

Micah shrugged. "This here's Ritter Sloane, Hallie."

"The gunfighter?" Hallie glanced at her brother, then back to Ritter.

"See?" the gunman exploded. "*She* knows who I am. *She'll* know that your idea is crazy!"

"What idea?" Hallie asked.

"The weddin', o'course," Shad tossed in.

"Oh."

"Oh?" Ritter said, clearly astonished. He gaped at her. "That's all you're going to say? *Oh?*"

"Well," Hallie continued, "there ain't a whole lot *to* say. I figured the boys'd see things that way—"

"I don't believe this is happening!" Ritter shouted, clapping one hand to his forehead. "I thought for sure *you'd* listen to reason!"

Hallie watched him pace back and forth muttering furiously to himself. She shook her head and sighed. She sympathized with him. It was hard enough dealin' with the boys when you were raised up to it. But comin' on 'em all of a sudden like that . . . well, it *must* be the very devil!

"Boys . . ." She waited until all eyes were on her. "Why don't you all go on outside for a minute. Let me talk to him."

"I don't know. . . ." Micah looked at the still-pacing man warily.

"For corn's sake, Micah! You're fixin' to marry me to him!" She put her hands on her hips and leaned toward her brother. "I figure that means you're gonna leave us alone *sometime!*"

"Well . . ." Micah hesitated, but Shad nodded at his sister and headed for the door.

"C'mon, you two," he said quietly. "Let's get the horses ready."

Hallie waited until the boys were gone before she said, "All that walkin' up and down ain't gonna help any, y'know."

He stopped and stared at her. "Do you mean to say you're actually willing to go along with this . . . craziness?"

She straightened her shoulders, lifted her chin, and stared back at him. "It ain't all *that* crazy, Mr. Sloane. Considerin' . . ."

"Considering what?"

"Considerin' what we was doin' when the boys came home."

"Oh." He had the good grace to look sheepish for a moment. "Yeah, well, that was a . . ."

"Mistake?"

"Accident."

"Accident," she echoed softly. "Like shootin' yourself in the foot, or slippin' off a rock?"

"Or getting trapped under a tree limb."

Hallie's lips quirked slightly. He had a point.

"Hallie," he said quietly, "don't you see? This couldn't work out. I'm just not husband material."

"Why not?" She took a step closer. "Ya look healthy enough. You're sure old enough." Another step. "Don't ya *like* girls?"

His jaw worked nervously, and he stepped back a pace. "Of *course* I like girls. It's not that."

"Then why?"

"Because I'm a gunfighter, dammit!" Suddenly he came toward her and grabbed her shoulders in a steely grip. "Gunfighters don't have wives, families. They live alone, they work alone, and they damn well *die* alone."

"Is that a rule y'all have?"

His breath left him in a rush, and his fingers loosened their hold. "No, it's not a rule. It's just the way it is."

"Just like this here."

"Huh?"

"I *said*," Hallie continued firmly and looked him straight

in the eye, "just like this here." She watched him and saw that he still didn't understand. "This marryin' idea just *is*. Nothin's gonna change it."

His hands dropped from her shoulders. "You can't *want* to marry me. You don't even *know* me."

She smiled softly. "Don't matter. See, I've known the boys my whole life. Ain't nothin' I can say to make 'em back off. Arguin' with them was always a waste of good breath and too much time. It's easier by far to just do it their way and be done with it. Besides, after what they saw this mornin', there's only two things they *could* do. . . ."

He waited.

"Fix up a weddin'—or a funeral."

His eyebrows lifted slightly. Clearly, Hallie told herself, that's exactly what he'd been expecting.

"Now, maybe I ain't no fine lady," she told him, "but I expect I'm at *least* as good as a first-class wake."

His posture softened and he lifted one hand to cup her cheek. She watched his lips quirk to one side in a lopsided grin. "*I* think you're quite a lady, Hallie Benteen. And much better than a wake . . . first class or not." His hand dropped to his side again. "It's only that—you know nothing about me . . . what kind of man I am—hell, my profession *alone* should scare you off!"

A slow smile curved her lips. He may not think so, she told herself, but she was willin' to bet she knew a helluva lot more about him than he did about her!

He turned away from her and walked to the closest window. Standing in the sunshine that poured through the sparkling-clean glass, his blond hair shining, he stared blankly at one of Hallie's favorite views. Quietly she stepped up beside him.

Her fingers touched the opened red and white curtain and pushed it farther aside. Her eyes moved over the familiar landscape, the white pines, the larches, the tall spruce trees that littered the edges of the clearing surrounding the Benteen cabin. In the near distance the craggy mountain peaks jutted up into a sky trying to decide whether to snow or shine.

Across the yard the boys stepped out of the barn, leading five saddled horses. It was almost time.

"If you're thinkin' 'bout me," she said softly, "don't bother yourself. I'm used to the boys' ways." She shifted her gaze from the cabin yard to the tall man standing so close to her that she could feel the heat of him.

He continued to stare unseeing out the window. "Hallie, I can't stay. There're people waiting on me . . . jobs."

"Well . . ." She thought for a moment. "You could send 'em a wire. Tell 'em you won't be comin' for a while."

"A while?" He snorted a choking laugh. "I think those brothers of yours have more than just *a while* in mind."

"I been thinkin' on that." She nodded slowly and waited for him to look at her. "And I believe I know what to do."

Ritter smiled and shook his head. "What?"

"We go ahead on and get hitched like the boys say." She paused and tapped her finger against her front teeth. *"And . . ."*

"And"—she grinned at him suddenly and took a deep breath—"in six weeks the boys'll take off on their yearly huntin' trip. Winter provisions are about used up. They always go off about that time to get fresh meat."

"So?"

"So, after they leave, so can you!"

He rolled his eyes and let his head drop back on his neck. Blowing a stream of air up toward the beam ceiling, he said harshly, "No good, Hallie. First, they prob'ly won't leave if they think *I* will. . . ."

"That's easy," she countered, laying one hand on his forearm. "If you act all sweet and nice to me for six weeks, they'll figure you're good and truly caught and won't want to leave. Hell, they'll prob'ly be so sick of seein' you act all funny like, they might even leave early!"

"Nope." Ritter shook his head. "Still wouldn't work."

Hands on hips, she cocked her head and stared at him. Wasn't he gonna help *a'tall*? "Why the hell not?"

"Because"—he chuckled at her, which only served to feed her ire—"once they get back and find me gone, what's to keep them from coming after me and hauling me back here to my *lovin'* wife?"

"Hmmm . . ." He was right. Come hell or high water, the boys wouldn't take to *no* man desertin' their sister. They'd hunt him down if it took 'em *years*. And, she told herself grimly, once they found him, there wouldn't be enough left of him to bring back to her! Still . . . there *had* to be a way.

"Sure!" Hallie grinned, grabbed his hand and held on tight. "I got it! I know what we can do!"

His fingers curled around her hand, and she felt his thumb move over her flesh as surely as if it were a red-hot branding iron. She drew in a shaky breath, ran her tongue over suddenly dry lips, and blurted out, "When the boys come back from huntin', I'll just tell 'em you *died*."

"WHAT?"

Ritter stared down at the woman's upturned face and couldn't believe it. She was happy with her plan. Happy?

No. *Proud.* What the *hell* kind of family was this, anyway?

"You'll tell your brothers I died?"

"Sure. That's the only way I know of keepin' 'em from trackin' you down like a dog."

He shook his head, as if the action might clear away the cobwebs. "And what makes you think they'll believe you?"

Ritter watched, speechless, as she began to think. He could almost see the convoluted wheels of her brain thrashing and turning together. His breath caught when she turned that dazzling smile on him again, even though he'd already learned what it meant.

She'd had an idea.

"I'll bury ya."

Shortly after dawn, huddled into their coats, the Benteen family and Ritter Sloane rode their horses quietly down the one and only street of Stillwater. An outhouse door slammed shut, breaking the eerie silence as effectively as a gunshot, but none of the riders seemed to notice.

Homer Triggs studied them curiously as he pulled his suspenders up and walked from the convenience to the front door of his barbershop.

Elmira Huggins watched the strange, early morning parade from the warmth and comfort of her second-story bedroom above the general mercantile.

Dixie Weaver held bright red draperies aside with one hand and held a match flame to the end of a long, slender cigarillo with the other. She took a deep drag on the tiny cigar and waved out the match as she watched the small group of people pass the Silver Spur Saloon. Surprised to see the Benteen boys out and about so early, one of her finely plucked black eyebrows arched delicately.

Ritter felt the curious stares. Without looking, he knew that there were curtains parted all up and down the narrow street—and behind every set was a pair of nosy eyes.

Grumbling to himself, he leaned his weight on his crossed wrists, tied to the pommel of his saddle. The Benteens were taking no chances on the bridegroom escaping before doing his duty. His fingers clenched and Ritter tried to shrug deeper into his coat. A sharp, bitter wind blew down the street, dusting up fresh snow and teasing the already near-frozen faces of the small mounted group.

He cast one wary glance toward the woman who rode beside him. She sat astride, her back straight, chin lifted, eyes straight ahead. With the collar of her coat turned up and her hat pulled down low on her forehead, he couldn't make out much of her expression, but he had a feeling it hadn't changed. She was as set on this wedding as her brothers.

If there was only some way out of all this. Ritter tore his gaze away from Hallie and looked from one to the other of the three men. No. He didn't have a chance. Not one of them was willing to let the marriage idea go.

And if he was any other man, maybe he wouldn't be so dead set against it, himself. He remembered clearly her flesh beneath his fingers. The warm compliance of her mouth. The incredible deep blue of her eyes, shining with desire.

He groaned and tried to shift to a more comfortable position. Impossible. He hadn't been comfortable since he'd ridden into the Stillwater valley, and he was beginning to doubt he'd ever know comfort again.

Still, he told himself, if she was right . . . if the boys did go off on their hunting trip, and he *could* leave safely without worry of them tracking his every step for the next twenty years . . . Ritter's brow furrowed and he turned to glance at Hallie again.

What had she said? That she would *bury* him? Now, what the hell did she mean by that? And why had her damn brothers picked *that* moment to burst into the cabin and end their conversation?

Besides, did it really make any difference? Could he really walk away from the responsibility of a wife once he'd taken it on? He didn't know. Hell, he didn't know anything anymore. He was sure of only one thing.

Ritter would give anything to have his fingers curled tightly around Hamilton Butler's thick neck.

"It's right up yonder," Micah said suddenly, nodding his head at the tiny church with the steeply pitched roof. "You bunch tie up your horses and go on in." He urged his horse to the left. "I'll go fetch the parson and be right there."

As the others started for the hitching rail at the front of the whitewashed building, Micah called out warningly, "You boys keep a handy eye on that fella, now. Don't want no *terrible* 'accidents' on Hallie's weddin' day."

Ritter turned his head slightly and glared at the bearded man. But he'd already turned his horse toward the small house to one side of the church.

A shattering silence hung in the frigid morning air. No one spoke to break it, and as they dismounted, the crunch of their feet in the fresh snow came as loud as a gunshot.

Ritter hadn't moved. Until the Benteens untied his wrists, he was trapped in the saddle. When one of the men stepped up and deftly undid the knotted rope, Ritter turned a fierce stare on him.

"Now," the man said slowly, "don't take on so. It's just a weddin'."

Ritter swung down from the horse, keeping an eye on the slightly shorter man.

"You ain't the first been caught dallyin' where he shouldn't ought to be." The reddish beard split into a wide grin.

"I already *told* you. *Nothing* happened."

"Uh-huh. But I figure if we'd a been a mite later gettin' on home . . ." His eyebrows wiggled and he let his words trail off.

Ritter sucked in a deep breath through clenched teeth and turned his gaze to the young woman waiting on the porch steps. Now that she'd dismounted, she'd let her bunched calico skirts drop to hide her buckskin britches. Swallowed up as she was by the too big fleece-lined coat, Hallie Benteen looked small. Fragile. Her finely drawn features were a shade paler than they'd been a short time ago, and her deep blue eyes shifted away from Ritter's uneasily.

Immediately a disconcerting stab of shame swept through him. He was only making this whole mess worse for her. Wasn't it bad enough that he'd disgraced her in front of her brothers? That he'd taken advantage of a situation that should never have happened in the first place?

Good Lord. After rescuing her, he'd helped himself to her charms as though taking a justly owed reward.

Never mind that he hadn't been thinking clearly. The point was that he'd done it—and, as one of her brothers had thoughtfully pointed out, been caught at it.

None of his complaining and arguing was going to change the Benteen brothers' minds. She'd been right about that.

Ritter slowly rubbed the chafed skin on first one wrist, then the other. He felt the men's watchful stares, but he kept his gaze trained on Hallie. She'd already been through enough embarrassment due to him. The least he could do was go through with this wedding with as much dignity as possible. She didn't deserve to be the brunt of any more pointed barbs. And she *certainly* didn't deserve to hear her bridegroom continually trying to talk his way out of a marriage.

Slowly, deliberately, he stepped around the man in front of him and walked to the foot of the steps. There he stopped and waited for her to look at him. It seemed to take forever. And finally she turned hesitant eyes to him.

Ritter's lips curved in a slight smile, and he reached up to pull off his hat. Quietly their gazes locked, and he climbed the steps to her side. He reached for her hand and tucked it into the curve of his crooked arm.

"Let's go inside, out of the cold, to wait for the preacher." His voice soft, Ritter waited again.

She tilted her head back to study him carefully. He kept his features blank, a useful trick he'd learned long ago. The gentle pressure of her hand on his arm was the only indication of her nervousness. Her cheeks were once more a soft, peachy hue and her eyes were steady.

"All right, Mr. Sloane," she said finally.

"Ritter," he corrected.

"Ritter."

The blond man gave the door a yank and ushered his bride into the church. When the door swung to behind them, Jericho turned to his brother.

"Now, what d'ya suppose come over him?"

Shadrack shrugged his shoulders and scratched at his bearded jaw. "Don't rightly know. You figure this could be a trick?"

"Nah . . ." Jericho's eyes narrowed suddenly. "Hell, there's a back door, too!"

Together they thundered up the steps and crashed into the stillness of the little church. And together they came to a screeching halt.

Sloane hadn't tried to escape at all. He and Hallie were standing at the front of the church, calm as you please. Slowly Shad and Jericho pulled their hats off and walked down the short narrow aisle to join them.

Preacher Osgood ran one bony finger around his too tight collar. His Adam's apple bobbed up and down uncertainly, and he cleared his throat for the third time. He glanced over at his wife, Temperance. The tall, spare woman with mousy brown hair and kind eyes nodded at her husband approvingly, silently urging him on about his business.

Zachariah Osgood returned her nod, then looked to the couple standing in front of him. The groom looked as though he'd been in a fight, and the bride was more pale than he'd ever seen her.

Strange. The whole thing was strange. Imagine being dragged out of a warm bed just after dawn to perform an "emergency" wedding! And just what *kind* of emergency was it? he wanted to know.

He'd tried to question Micah, but true to himself, that wild-eyed young man hadn't said one word more than he'd absolutely had to. And no amount of arguing from the preacher had swayed him from his mission in the slightest.

Micah wanted his sister married, and that was that. The preacher scowled at Micah one more time for good measure. Surely this "emergency" could have waited for a more civilized hour!

But the Benteen brothers were not cowed. They stood just behind the marriage couple, their shotguns cradled in their arms. The empty church stood silent testimony to the oddness of this wedding, but, the preacher sighed, better married than not. Zachariah Osgood was a firm believer that a good marriage was the making of most men.

He had no idea who the bridegroom was, but he knew Hallie Benteen. A fine girl, if a mite too spirited and a bit free-thinking in her ideas. The preacher nodded to himself, acknowledging that perhaps being a wife would be the best thing *for* Hallie. Slow her down just a little. Give her something else besides the stars to think about.

His tired eyes swept over her. Heaven knew, it was a step in the right direction, just getting her to wear a proper dress! A young woman her age wearing the britches she usually favored—well, it was downright indecent!

"Dearly beloved . . ." he began, filled with a sudden feeling of rightness.

Ritter's eyes followed the shaft of sunlight that poured in from a nearby window to spill over the parson's thinning gray hair and shiny head. Storm clouds must have split apart some, he told himself absently. He heard the droning voice repeating the familiar words of the ancient ceremony and felt Hallie's hand on his arm tremble. Instinctively he lifted his own hand to cover hers.

In truth, he understood the trembling. Here he was, becoming a husband—to a woman he didn't know—in front of men who'd just as soon shoot him, he was sure.

From the corner of his eye he glanced at Hallie and found himself admiring the proud lift of her chin and her smooth, rosy complexion. If he wasn't touching her hand, he would never guess that she was the slightest bit nervous about this wedding. She stood as straight and tall as if they'd been courting for years and she had a church full of friends to celebrate with her.

"I will."

He watched her lips move and heard her voice, clear and steady. In the back of his mind Ritter knew the preacher was addressing him now. The older man was running down the list of dos and don'ts, promises and vows. The gunfighter's mind raced. This was it. In a moment, unless he thought of something quickly, he would be a married man. Married to a woman he knew nothing about other than the fact that she was saddled with three crazy brothers.

He shook his head and smiled to himself. If it hadn't happened to him, he never would have believed it possible. Ritter Sloane. Gunfighter.

Husband.

A strained silence finally reached him. He came back to himself with a start and glanced down first at Hallie. She was glaring at him. He turned to look at the parson.

"Well, son?" the older man asked, apparently not for the first time. "Do you so promise?"

With his woolgathering, Ritter'd missed his cue. His

last chance to try to stop this nonsense was upon him. As he opened his mouth to speak, though, he heard something else from directly behind him. Sharp, distinctive, three separate *clicks* echoed in the tiny building. He didn't need to look behind him to know that all three Benteen brothers had just cocked their shotguns.

Ritter took a deep, ragged breath and answered firmly, "I will."

Preacher Osgood smiled. "You're man and wife." When the young couple didn't move, he prompted, "It's legal now, boy. Give 'er a kiss!"

Chapter

Four

HALLIE'S NEW husband turned her slowly to face him, and she looked up at him. For the first time she noticed the fine lines at the edges of his soft, pale blue eyes. And though she hadn't seen much sight of it, she knew then that her husband had done a lot of laughing once upon a time. Her gaze swept over the lock of blond hair that tumbled over his forehead and the purplish bruise on his jaw. His grip on her shoulders was gentle, yet firm as he pulled her closer.

Her heart thudded painfully, and her mouth went suddenly dry. She could hardly breathe with the expectation of a kiss.

Just thinkin' about it brought on a herd of butterflies dancin' and flyin' around her stomach.

Then he dipped his head and touched his lips to hers in a kiss as soft as a whisper. Disappointment welled up inside her, and it was all Hallie could do to keep from asking out loud, "Is that all?"

Well, for corn's sake! He'd done better than *that* when he was asleep!

"Well," Micah grunted, "that there wasn't much to see."

"No, sir," Jericho piped up. "It don't appear that he's puttin' his heart inta this a'tall."

"Mayhap he'll do better when there ain't a crowd watchin' him," Shadrack said, wanting to give his new brother-in-law the benefit of the doubt.

Hallie's eyebrows shot up. She'd had just about enough of her brothers for one morning. She frowned, disgusted, and looked from the preacher, to Temperance, to Ritter, then finally to the three men standing behind her. "Why don't y'all wait outside?"

Micah looked as if he might argue, and Hallie was all set to give him what for, but thankfully, Shad stepped in.

"C'mon, boys," he said softly, with a smile for his younger sister. "Let's us get the horses set."

As the three of them moved off, Micah grumbled and tossed a glare back at his new brother-in-law.

Ritter reached for Hallie's hand and pulled it through the crook of his elbow. Just before he led her out of the church, she looked toward Temperance to thank her for being their witness.

But the parson's wife didn't even see Hallie. The woman some folks considered plain was staring at Ritter, a dreamy expression on her face and stars in her eyes.

The day passed quickly. *Too* quickly, Hallie thought as twilight touched the cabin yard, lengthening shadows, and making it necessary for her to light the lamps in the great room.

She tossed the still-lit straw into the hearth fire and dusted her palms on the seat of her britches. Almost nervously she checked the long carved table for the fifth time to reassure herself that everything was ready for the men. The four of them would be coming inside any time now. She didn't know about her husband, but Hallie knew she could count on her brothers to eat everything in sight and then some.

Husband.

She pulled in a deep breath and fought to control the nervous flutter of excitement building in her stomach. She'd had all day to think on it, and she'd finally decided that maybe things had worked out for the best after all.

Oh, she'd never been in a great hurry to have a husband, true. She'd lived all her life with men, and Hallie'd always told herself that the *one* thing she didn't need was another man underfoot. But, she thought with a smile, there was one thing she *did* want.

A baby. And to get one she *had* to have the other.

Of course, she'd thought about this before now. In fact, she'd kept a wary eye out, watchin' for a likely-lookin' prospect to give her a baby. But in all her twenty-two years she hadn't come across a single man she was willin' to lie with. Until today.

Oh, true, she didn't know much about him. He was a gunfighter, but that didn't make no difference. Hell, everybody she knew carried a gun—and used it from time to time. He seemed like he was brought up real good. Prob'ly come from good folks, she told herself. He had nice manners and such, and Hallie was willin' to bet that he knew how to read and write, too.

Prob'ly a lot better than she could. Of course, she told herself silently, he prob'ly hadn't taught himself how to read with scraps of old newspapers like she had, either. Nope, as well spoke as he was, he no doubt went to a *real* school. With lots of books. And smart teachers.

Her eyes glazed over as she imagined what it would have been like to go to a proper school. Maybe she coulda learned somethin' about the stars firsthand from somebody who really studied over 'em. Maybe . . .

Abruptly she shook her head and tugged at the edge of the cloth she'd spread over the table and straightened the lie of a fork. No sense in wishin'. If wishes was horses, beggars would ride. 'Sides, she thought and lifted her chin, she was doin' just fine on her own. What with the professor's books and such.

Glancing out the front window toward the barn, her breath caught as she saw her husband, surrounded by her brothers, heading for the house.

Lordamighty, she thought with a sigh, that Ritter Sloane was a *real* pretty man.

"Where'd you learn to do such a thing?" Shadrack asked as he heaped another spoonful of potatoes onto his plate.

Ritter shrugged. He'd picked up so many little pieces of information over his years of wandering, he'd be hard put to remember them all.

"What'd he do?" Hallie asked as she poured everyone more coffee.

"Nothin'," Micah mumbled around a mouthful of venison.

"Nothin'?" Shadrack shook his fork at his brother. "You know durn well, Micah, you been tryin' to fix that ol' sore spot on Satan's back for close on a week now and ain't managed it yet."

"What happened?" Hallie demanded.

"What happened is"—Shad smiled at his younger sister—"your new husband there put some kinda salve on Satan that's got the ol' bastard damn near purrin'. *If* a horse could purr."

"It's true," Jericho added with a grin. "Made Micah mad enough to spit glass, too!"

Micah pushed away from the table and took a swipe at the closest brother, but Jericho ducked, still chuckling.

"You don't know if he fixed the damn horse or not. It'll be awhile 'fore we know for sure." Jericho's laughter only served to whet his anger.

No one said anything.

Micah tossed his fork onto his plate and wagged one finger at Ritter. "Mister, you may have *them* fooled, but not me! I got my eye on you, Sloane. And gunfighter or no, you try to run off or do anything else I don't like, and you'll answer to me."

Silence dropped over the table. Slowly Ritter laid down his knife and fork and raised his eyes to Micah's. The two men stared at each other, oblivious to the strained, unsettling quiet in the room. Finally, after a long minute, Micah looked away uneasily. Ritter said nothing. Instead, he picked up his fork and took another bite of venison.

In a fury Micah snatched his coat off a nearby peg, yanked open the door, and stomped out, slamming it behind him.

"Don't pay Micah no mind," Shad said quietly. "Ma always used to say that he got the temper meant for all three of us to share."

"True, true," Jericho put in and leaned back in his chair, his long legs stretched out in front of him, crossed at the ankles. "Micah's got more prickly spots than a porcupine.

Me and Shad here, though, is different. Ain't a helluva lot that bothers us." He cocked his head to look at the blond man across from him. "But I got to say, Sloane. On this I side with Micah. Don't you do nothin' to shame my sister. It would pain me to hunt you down."

Ritter watched as the tall man slowly unfolded himself and stood up. Grabbing his coat, Jericho added with a smile, "Think I'll go out and give Micah somebody to yell at for a spell. Always makes him feel better . . . gettin' it off his chest."

The three people left at the table looked at each other. Hallie pushed her untouched food around on her plate and wished that Shad would go on out, too. She'd never realized before how underfoot the boys were. There was some things she wanted to talk to Ritter about, and she wasn't gonna do it in front of her brother!

As if reading her mind, Shad stood up and smiled shyly at her. "I'll, uh . . . go out to the barn now. Why don't you just leave all this here on the table, Hallie? Me and the boys'll take care of it for ya tonight."

She nodded and noticed that Shad was avoiding her eyes. If she didn't know better, she'd swear he was blushing!

The last of the triplets moved toward the door, grabbing up his coat as he went. He didn't look at the couple behind him but said quietly, "We'll be outside a couple hours, I reckon. Maybe more." Quickly then, he pulled the door open, stepped outside, and shut it again behind him.

"Well, I never . . ." Hallie stared at the door in stunned surprise. Though she'd wanted to be alone with Ritter, she hadn't really expected it to happen so soon. And wasn't that just like Shad to let her know he'd keep her brothers away from the house for a couple of hours?

"Hallie," Ritter spoke quietly.

"Yes?" She turned to her new husband and smiled. Finally they would be able to talk. And maybe do some more of that kissin'.

"I can't stay," he said, and Hallie felt her plans begin to slip away.

Maybe he shouldn't have said it flat outright like that, Ritter told himself sternly. He reached for his coffee cup and stole a quick look at her. The sparkle had faded from her eyes, and surprisingly, he found he missed it. There was something about the woman . . .

"What do ya mean?" she countered quickly, the sparkle replaced with a flash of anger.

It seemed that Micah wasn't the only one in the Benteen family to be cursed with a quick temper.

"Exactly what I said." His voice even, he tried to explain. "I tried to tell you earlier, Hallie. There are people expecting me."

Her copper-colored eyebrows shot up.

"All right," he amended, his right hand raised slightly. "I *could* send wires to those people. But it's not just that. I'm a gunfighter, Hallie. That's all I know how to be. And a gunfighter is *not* good husband material."

"Reckon it's too late to worry about that."

"No, it's not." He frowned and pushed away from the table. Standing, he crossed the great room to the massive stone fireplace. Staring into the flames, he said softly, "Despite what your brothers think, *nothing* has happened between us. And if I leave now, nothing will." He leaned one hand on the mantel and propped his booted foot on the hearth. "We could arrange for an annulment."

"What's that?"

He turned and glanced at her. She was perched on the edge of her chair, elbows on her knees, chin cupped in her hands. Firelight danced off the silver loops in her ears, and her short, curly hair shone a deep red, like banked coals. Ritter took a deep breath and turned away again.

"It's a paper from a judge. It means that the marriage never happened."

"Like a divorce, y'mean."

"No." He shook his head. "A divorce ends a marriage. An annulment says there never *was* a marriage."

She laughed gently.

"What can you possibly find in all this to laugh at?"

Hallie wagged her head from side to side and stood up. "You really think some paper or other would be enough for the boys? No, sir. This weddin' *did* happen. You maybe don't want to think so, but it *did*, and ain't no paper gonna change that any."

"Hallie . . ."

"Now, if you want to hear somethin' from me"—she walked up beside him—"mayhap we could strike a bargain."

He raised his head and looked at her warily. "What sort of bargain?"

Hallie grinned and plopped down on the hearth. Glancing up at him, she patted the spot beside her. "Set down and I'll tell ya all about it."

Ritter sat down but carefully kept a few inches of empty space between him and his new wife. He had the distinct feeling that he wasn't going to like what she had to say. But, he acknowledged silently, he didn't have many other choices open to him but to listen.

"Now," she said, clenching her hands together tightly

in her lap. "I been thinkin' on this all day . . . ."

Ritter's brow furrowed and he strangled a sigh.

"The way I see it," Hallie continued, "is us two are married now, whether you like it or not . . . ."

"Yes, but—"

"Hold on, hold on." She frowned at him. "Give me a minute here. I'm gettin' to it."

He nodded.

"The boys're gonna be watchin' you almighty close for a while, so you ain't gonna be goin' anywhere right off."

He nodded again.

"So, I figured you and me could maybe work somethin' out between the two of us."

Ritter sighed heavily. "What's your idea, Hallie?"

She grinned, despite the soft blush creeping up her face. "Well, you're fixin' to get away, and if truth be told, I don't rightly *want* a husband. . . ."

He stared at her in stunned surprise. She didn't *want* a husband? Didn't most women want to be married? For the first time since this whole strange situation started, Ritter felt a tinge of disappointment mixed with an unexpected flash of anger. Was it that she didn't want *any* husband? Or was it simply that she didn't want *him*?

Somehow, he felt vaguely insulted.

Well, hell. What was wrong with *him*?

He gritted his teeth, forced all of his peculiar thoughts aside, and tried to concentrate on what she was saying.

"Like I told you before, in about six weeks the boys'll take off on their huntin' trip. Once they leave, you can, too."

He ignored the fact that she appeared as anxious to be

rid of him as he was to go. "What makes you think they'll leave me behind when they take off?"

She waved one hand at him. "Oh, I figure by then, they'll be trustin' ya well enough. 'Specially if they see ya actin' . . ."

"Yes? Acting what?" That blush on her cheeks had deepened to a rich, rosy red.

"Well, shoot." She lifted her chin and looked him square in the eye. "If they see ya actin' all sweet and lovin' on me, they won't figure ya to leave!"

"Uh-huh. And you'll tell them I died?"

"Yeah."

"And *bury* me?"

"That's right." He frowned at her and she hurried on. "Well, not *really*, for corn's sake! I'll just pile up some dirt and plant a cross on it. Hell, even the *boys* won't dig up a grave just to check!"

Ritter wasn't so sure about that himself, but that was beside the point for right now.

"You said a 'bargain.' You've told me what *I'll* get out of this. What about you? What is it *you* want, Hallie?"

"A baby."

His jaw dropped and he leapt to his feet.

Well, for pity's sake, Hallie thought disgustedly, it wasn't like she was askin' him to birth it for her! All she needed was his seed! She'd do the rest herself.

"A *baby?*"

She nodded, her face screwed up in confusion at his reaction.

"You don't want a husband, but you *do* want a baby?"

"Sure." Hallie stood up and crossed her arms over her chest. "Always did want a baby of my own." She looked up at him. "And why in blue blazes would I want a man of my own permanent? I got plenty enough menfolk about here already! But I can't get a baby by myself. And now that I got me a husband, all legal and proper, why not a baby?"

He pushed his hands through his hair and turned his back on her. She could tell by the set of his shoulders that he was some upset, but for the life of her, she couldn't figure out why. Didn't she come up with a way for him to go on about his business? Hadn't she thought of everything? What more did the man want?

Suddenly he spun around to face her. "I can't believe this! You want me to get you with child and then just sneak off, leaving you to care for it on your own?"

"On my *own*?" She cocked her head to one side and stared at him. "It ain't likely I'll *ever* be on my own! My brothers'll be here. Prob'ly forever. Can't imagine no woman wantin' to marry one of 'em. *They'd* help me."

"Your brothers." His right hand shot through his hair again, and Hallie could see he was giving it a good tug while he was at it. "Just what kind of man would that make me, do you think, Hallie Benteen?"

"Hallie Sloane," she corrected, raising her right hand.

His head dropped back on his neck, and she thought she heard a muffled snort of laughter. But she must have been wrong. When he looked at her again, there wasn't a trace of amusement on his face.

"I'll be pleased to tell you, *Mrs. Sloane*, that I am *not* the man to create a child, then turn my back on it!"

"Well, why the hell not? *You* don't want it. *I* do."

"And I would be double damned before I'd hand a child of mine over to those crazy brothers of yours!" His voice climbed with every word until he nearly shouted his last comment. "Those three together don't have the brain God gave a rock!"

Hallie jumped up and faced him, her face flushed with righteous anger. "You got no call to say that about 'em. They're good folks. Every last one of 'em! Hell, they didn't shoot ya when they could have, did they? No, by thunder, they didn't. Now," she said slowly as she pulled in a calming breath of air, "I reckon you got reason enough to be sore at 'em right now, but you'll see. You get to know 'em, Ritter, and I'm bettin' you'd even come to like 'em."

He groaned and inhaled sharply.

"You think on it and you'll see I'm right, Ritter." She stepped up to him and laid one hand on his arm. "In this here bargain, we both get what we want. You get to light out of here, and I get a baby with no husband underfoot."

He looked down at her hand on his arm and shook his head slowly. "It won't work, Hallie."

"Sure it will." She smiled up at him and took one of his hands in both of hers. "Now, we'd best get on to bed. The boys'll be comin' in sooner than you know." She started to walk, but he stood stock still.

"Nope." He jerked his head toward the hearth. "I'll sleep on the floor there."

Hallie dropped his hand and put both hands on her hips. "Now, you really think the boys're gonna start trustin' ya if ya don't even sleep in the same *room* with your own *wife*?"

Ritter stared at her, and she felt another blush climb her cheeks. For heaven's sake. He didn't have to make this any harder than it was. After all, it wasn't like they was *strangers*. Hell, she'd already slept with him!

"Ritter, ya already seen me in my altogether once. I ain't got nothin' different since then."

He laughed. Slowly at first, it started as a low rumble deep in his chest until it exploded and filled the room. "Lady, you are about the rarest thing I have ever come across."

She shifted uncomfortably. "Don't see what's so dang funny. Hell, my own ma and pa never even laid eyes on each other till the day they was wed. Mama used to say they went to bed strangers and woke up friends." She smiled at her new husband tentatively. "That wouldn't be so bad, would it?"

"No." Ritter shook his head and lifted one hand to cup her cheek gently. "I would be pleased to have you count me as a friend, Hallie Sloane."

"Good." She grinned again and rubbed her face against the palm of his hand. "Does that mean you'll think on the baby bargain?"

He sighed heavily. "I'll think on it."

She grabbed his hand and squeezed it. Then, tugging him along behind her, she headed for her bedroom.

Thankfully, there was a screen of sorts set in the corner of her room. Ritter wasn't a shy man by any means, but if he could, he wanted to avoid watching his new wife strip out of her clothes. There was only so much a man could take.

He stifled a groan as he looked down at the narrow bed, covered with a brightly flowered quilt. Not enough room for two there. Not if he intended to keep his distance. And he did.

Ritter pulled off his boots one after the other, then sat down on the floor, leaning back against the high-mattressed bed. It would probably take every ounce of strength he possessed, but he intended to keep his hands off his lovely new wife. Despite her idea, he had no intention of leaving her with child. If she became pregnant, he wouldn't be able to ride off at all. And he knew that riding away from her would be the best thing for all concerned.

Gunfighters didn't live long enough to make good family men.

He just had to make *them* understand.

"You in bed yet?"

Ritter glanced over his shoulder at the blanket-draped corner, then turned away again uncomfortably. "No, Hallie."

"Oh."

A long minute passed and Ritter shifted position slightly, hoping she would just finish what she was doing, turn out the light, and go to sleep.

"Ya got your back turned?"

His brow furrowed. Surprisingly enough, it seemed that *some* things made even Hallie shy. "Yes, ma'am."

"All right, then, I'm comin' out."

He heard her quick steps across the wood floor and felt the mattress behind his back sag when she climbed on. In spite of himself Ritter felt his breath quicken and was sure he could hear his heartbeat drumming in his ears.

"I'm in now, Ritter. You can come on to bed now."

He shook his head. "I'll, uh . . . be sleeping down here, Hallie. More room."

The feather mattress shifted as she moved. In seconds

he felt her breath on his cheek, heard her soft-pitched voice close in his ear.

"You mean you ain't gonna—"

"No. I ain't."

"But that ain't fittin', Ritter. This here's our weddin' night."

"Hallie . . ."

"Oh, all right." She moved again. Her right hand lay on his shoulder, and it was all he could do not to turn and grab it. Pull her over his shoulder into his lap and kiss her soundly. She patted his shoulder firmly. "I know we said you was gonna think on the baby idea . . . but couldn't you at least come up here and just *sleep* close by? It gets mighty darn cold in here at night, Ritter."

He groaned silently. Sleeping beside her without touching her? Maybe if he slept in his clothes. He had to admit that already the wood floor was chilly. He felt the draft of icy wind swirling over scrubbed planks. Besides, they *were* married, he told himself. Why should he sleep on a cold hard floor when his wife's bed was right there for the taking?

Because it would be a helluva lot safer, he warned himself, even as he moved to join her. Standing, he looked down at his new wife and his eyes widened. "*What* is that you're wearing?"

She glanced down at the faded pink long johns. The material was so threadbare in places, she thought you could prob'ly see as much pink skin as anything else . . . but still. It was warm. And clean.

"An old pair of Shad's drawers."

Ritter shook his head, waited for her to slide over a little, then stretched out *atop* the quilt, next to her.

"That how you're gonna sleep?"

"Yep."

"In your clothes?"

"Yep."

"Outside the covers?"

"Yep."

"You're a strange one, husband," she said quietly, then curled up to his side, wiggling her bottom until she found a comfortable spot.

Ritter rolled his eyes heavenward. *He* was strange?

"Oh, and Ritter?" she asked, stifling a yawn.

"What is it, Hallie?" Ritter tried to scoot away from her bottom as she moved in even closer.

"About the baby?"

"I *said* I'd think on it."

"I know." She yawned again. "But while you're thinkin' on it . . . could you maybe think on makin' it a *girl* baby?"

"What?"

"I'd surely admire to have a girl." She snuggled in closer. "Seen enough boys and men to last a lifetime."

Ritter stared, amazed, at the back of her head. Of all the . . . As he started to tell her that she couldn't very well just order up a girl baby like she would a new hat, he stopped. Her soft, steady breathing told him that she was asleep.

Slamming his arms behind his head, Ritter gazed at the beam ceiling overhead and tried to concentrate on the knotholes instead of the gently rounded woman cuddling into him for warmth.

Chapter

Five

"He did *what?*" Hamilton Butler leapt up from the oversize leather chair and stomped around the edge of his paper-strewn desk. Only five feet nine in his stocking feet, Butler weighed no less than two hundred pounds—not an ounce of it fat. Even men who stood taller than he backed up uneasily in the face of his temper, as did the young cowhand Butler shouted at now.

"Speak up, man!" The older man's too long gray hair fell on either side of his enraged features. "Ritter Sloane did *what?*"

"Uh . . . seems like he, uh . . . married Hallie, boss." A low, furious growl rumbled from deep inside Hamilton Butler's chest, and the cowhand inched backward a step. He reached up and tugged at his already opened collar nervously.

"Are you sure?"

"Yessir." His voice squeaked and he cleared his throat before continuing. "Dixie? Down to the Silver Spur?"

"Yes, yes . . ." Hamilton waved the explanation aside. He knew the woman well. In fact, it would surprise a lot of people if they knew *how* well he knew Dixie.

"Well, boss, seems like she saw the Benteens ridin'

into town real early this mornin', and she was some surprised, since Micah and Jericho about drunk the bar dry last night—"

Butler sighed his frustration with the length of the tale.

"Anyhow," the young man hurried on, "a blond fella was ridin' with 'em, and they went straight on to the church whilst Micah went to fetch the preacher."

Hamilton ground his teeth together, turned, and marched to the massive open hearth to star into the fire. When the younger man stopped talking, he urged quietly, "Go on . . ."

"Reckon that's about all, 'cept that Dixie done some askin' around later and found out that Hallie married that Sloane fella that quit on ya."

The beefy man leaned forward and curled his stubby fingers over the edge of the oak mantel.

"She figured you'd want to know, so she sent me on out here to tell ya." He looked around the big house warily, obviously wishing he were anywhere else but there.

A long, silent moment passed during which the only sound was the crackle and snap of the fire licking at a fresh log. The cowhand shifted from foot to foot, anxious to be off.

Dixie figured he'd want to know, Butler taunted himself silently. And he'd be willing to bet that right now the woman was buying a round of drinks to celebrate the Benteens' putting one over on him. Jaw clenched, he glared at the fire below. Damn the Benteens and damn Dixie, too! That infernal woman had taken pleasure in needling him ever since she'd won free and clear title to the Silver Spur in that durned poker game!

Privately Hamilton Butler was *still* sure that she'd cheated him somehow. Though he told himself, if she had . . . it had sure as hell been worth it—at the time

But that wasn't important right now. The only thing that mattered *now* was this damn fool business with the gunfighter, Sloane.

When Hamilton Butler at last turned to face the messenger, not a trace of emotion touched his features. Stiffly the older man dug into his pants pocket and pulled out a worn buckskin poke, closed with a rawhide string. He opened the bag, dug inside, then flipped a gold coin to the young man across the room from him. Deliberately, then, Butler closed the poke and stuffed it back into his pocket. He turned around to face the fire once more, ignoring the cowhand's stammered thanks and the sounds of bootheels and jingling spurs leaving the room.

Hamilton leaned into the mantel, his powerful hands clenching the solid oak as if he squeezed hard enough, he would have his questions answered.

What the hell was going on? Ritter Sloane *married* to Hallie Benteen? Is that the real reason Sloane had quit? Because he'd already formed a partnership with the Benteen family? But how had he had time? As far as Butler knew, Sloane had never been in this part of Wyoming before.

It didn't make any sense.

In one quick motion he shoved away from the hearth, crossed the gleaming plank floor, and dropped into the chair behind his desk once more. He leaned forward, elbows perched on sliding towers of papers, and shoved his hands through his hair.

He knew those Benteen boys. They watched over Hallie

as if she were the last gold strike on the face of the earth. Why, men from Stillwater hardly had the chance to say hello, let alone *marry* her. Why would they allow a marriage between their sister and a notorious gunfighter?

Hallie. Lord, he told himself, it was hard gettin' old. Even harder to imagine that Hallie was old enough to be *anybody's* wife.

Unbidden, memories of Caleb Benteen, Hallie's father, slithered into his mind. He and Caleb had had some high times together in the old days. Butler sighed, remembering the boys and a pigtailed Hallie following him and their father on their fishing trips. He remembered, too, just how many times he'd sat at the Benteen table enjoying one of Mariah's delicious meals with Hallie on his lap and the boys wrestling like Indians in the middle of the room. Unwillingly, Butler recalled the laughter, the warmth of those evenings spent with friends, and wondered for a moment how everything had gone so wrong.

Now sweet Hallie was *married* to the very gunfighter *he'd* hired to drive the Benteens off their land!

He shook his head. What about Trib Benteen? The oldest brother had been gone for six months. How would the boys explain this marriage to *him* when he returned?

Hell! Hamilton snorted and sat up abruptly, his quick movement scattering white sheets of paper over the floor like a sudden snowstorm. The marriage and how they explained it wasn't his problem, he reminded himself. The *problem* was that now the Benteen family had their own private gunfighter to settle their disputes.

Deliberately he shoved all his memories to the back of his brain and told himself to forget them. Those times were long past and not likely to come again.

Hamilton told himself that the only way to fight fire was *with* fire. He reached into the nearest drawer, lifted out a bottle and a glass, and poured himself a stiff drink. After he downed half the amber liquid in one gulp, he snatched up a pen and rifled through the mess on his desk for a clean sheet of paper.

If he got the letter out right away, he should hear back in a week or so.

Dawn poked hesitant fingers into the small bedroom, slipping between the folds of the yellow calico curtains to lie teasingly over Hallie's eyelids.

She stirred slightly and tried to stretch. Her legs were trapped, though, and for a moment she thought she was back in the snow under that damned tree limb. But she was far too warm. Slowly realization spread through her, and she half opened her eyes to shoot a look at her husband.

On his left side, Ritter slept with his right arm across her waist and his long, muscular legs covering hers. Hallie turned her head farther into the feather pillow and studied the man's face, only inches from hers. In the uncertain light, golden stubble shone on his jawline and his blond hair fell over his forehead. Though he looked more relaxed than he did when awake, there was nothing peaceful about his expression. His closed eyes scrunched tightly, and he mumbled something under his breath that she couldn't quite catch. She stifled a gasp when his right arm tightened around her, pulling her close, and he turned his head sharply as if reacting to a sudden noise.

Dreaming, she told herself. And she couldn't help wondering what sort of dreams made a man twist and turn so in his sleep. Did he relive the gun battles he'd survived? And in his dreams did he still survive them?

Instinctively Hallie reached for him. She ran the flat of her hand over his chest, murmuring to him in as soothing a tone as she could. He seemed to hear her, for his sharp movements stilled and his expression calmed. And still she went on touching him. Gently she stroked the length of his arm, up over his shoulders and let her fingers trace over his whiskered jaw until she could smooth back the hair from his forehead.

Something odd was happening inside her. That fluttery feeling was back, and she wasn't quite sure why. Oh, she'd come to expect it now, even looked forward to it, when he kissed her . . . but surely, just *lookin'* at the man wasn't enough to stir up the butterflies!

Maybe, she told herself, she should test it. After all, she was his wife . . . if she wanted to kiss him, why the hell shouldn't she? Besides, she liked kissin' just fine. And with him asleep, *he'd* never know.

Cautiously she inched closer until she could feel his warm breath on her face. Gently then, Hallie touched his mouth with hers and, to her delight, felt his lips move in response. Bolder now, her tongue darted out to daringly flick at his lips, and when his mouth opened to her, she answered his call. Slowly, languorously, his tongue stroked hers. His arm tightened even further around her, and his free hand reached up, wound through her hair, and cupped the back of her head.

Hallie's breath came fast and furious. That fluttery feeling was gone now, replaced by something that felt as wild and raging as a brush fire she'd seen once. Suddenly Ritter rolled over, pinning her beneath him while his mouth continued to play with hers. One of his hands slid out from behind her and slid over her ribs to the swell of her breast. His thumb and forefinger encircled her nipple and the worn out pink fabric that covered it was no protection from the lightning strikes of pleasure that shot through her.

Hallie gasped for air, and Ritter's mouth moved to taste the soft flesh of her throat. His lips and tongue touched her skin with the lightness of a feather, and yet she felt it more deeply than anything she'd ever known before.

"Oh, my," she breathed softly and arched her back, straining to fill his hand with her breast. She'd had no idea that kissin' could lead to so much more.

Abruptly he stopped. She opened her eyes to find him wide awake and staring down at her.

"Oh, no," he muttered softly and rolled away from her to the edge of the bed. He stood up, grabbed his holster from the nearby chair, and threw it around his narrow hips. As he buckled it, Hallie thought she heard him say, "That's how I got into all this in the first place. . . . "

"Bout ready to get up in there?" Micah pounded on the closed door to emphasize his words.

Ritter spun around and pulled his pistol out in one smooth, practiced motion.

Hallie could hardly believe how fast he'd moved. Now she stared at him, fascinated. Balanced on the balls of his feet, Ritter stood facing the door, pistol in hand, knees bent. On his face a look of concentration that she hadn't seen before. Quickly she pulled the quilt up to her neck and watched as her husband slowly, carefully relaxed his fighting position.

This was what he meant by a gunfighter not being good husband material. The slightest sound might mean death to

a man like him. He was constantly ready to kill or be killed
No wonder it seemed that he'd forgotten how to live.

Ritter watched his three new brothers-in-law in
exasperation. He had no idea who was who or which
was which. And he couldn't understand how Hallie could
tell the three apart. They were as alike as three peas in
a pod. Or, he told himself wryly, studying their ragtag
clothing and wild, untamed hair and beards—as three hogs
in a wallow.

It appeared the triplets were also alike in another way.
None of them wanted to listen to reason. But, he vowed
determinedly, he would keep right on trying.

"When Butler finds out you've married me off to your
sister, what do you think that old cougar is going to do?"
he asked quietly.

One of the men paused, set the tines of his pitchfork on
the ground, and leaned his forearm on the long wooden
handle. "Knowin' Butler, he's most likely to rant and rave
some, then think of somethin' else."

"Exactly!" Ritter pushed away from the corral fence
and took a step closer to the other man. Maybe, he told
himself, maybe *this* one would listen! "He'll simply hire
another gunfighter. And the next one might not be bothered
by going up against a family."

The bearded man shrugged. "If he thinks he can push
Benteens off land we been on for more'n twenty years—
hell, he's welcome to give 'er a try!"

"Jericho's right."

Ritter looked up to another brother in the hayloft above
him.

"We ain't about to move on, gunfighter. So Ham Butler

can go right ahead and do his damndest."

"You're willing to put Hallie—your own *sister*—in the middle of a range war?"

A snort of laughter came from the farthest stall. When Ritter looked, he saw an auburn head poke out from behind the plank wall.

"What's so damned funny?" he demanded.

"You." The triplet stepped into the light and came forward. "You think we could keep Hallie *out* of this, even if we wanted to? Mister, you got a lot to learn about that wife of yours."

The man in the loft spoke up again. "Hell, if we tried to keep Hallie out of family business, she'd most likely shoot *us* before she went after the trouble! One thing you best remember, gunfighter. Benteens stay together."

"Amen," Jericho whispered.

Ritter pulled in a deep gulp of air and tried desperately to rein in the sudden flash of anger sweeping through him. It'd been years since anyone had provoked his temper, and yet, in the space of two days, the Benteen family had managed to make it a habit.

"All right," he said slowly, his steady gaze moving from one brother to the next, "let me say this one more time. . . ."

"Sloane—"

"No." He held up one hand. "Wait one minute. You three dragged me into this and—"

"As I recall," Jericho said thoughtfully, "you *jumped* in."

Ritter frowned at him. "I want to go talk to Butler."

"What the hell good would that do?" Micah called down from the loft.

"I don't know. Maybe none. But I think it's worth trying. Maybe I could talk him out of this business of hiring gunfighters."

"Huh!" Micah snorted. "Seems almighty odd, a gunfighter tryin' to talk a fella out of hirin' gunfighters!"

"Couldn't hurt none," Shad said and glanced up at his brother.

"You sidin' with him now, Shadrack?"

"I ain't sidin' with anybody. But if we can stop this here war 'fore it gets started, what's the harm?"

"Y'know, Micah . . ." Jericho rubbed his chin whiskers. "Mayhap they're right. . . ."

"Shit—you, too?" Micah dropped his pitchfork, swung onto the ladder, and climbed down to the barn floor. "What's wrong with you boys? Takin' up for *him*"—he jerked his thumb at Ritter—"against your own kind?"

"He's family now, too, Micah," Shad reminded him quietly.

"Yeah." Micah's gaze moved over his new brother-in-law, then switched back to the others. "But for how long? You know as well as me, if we turn our backs on him, he'll hightail it outa here so damn fast, we wouldn't see his dust!"

Ritter swallowed back an angry retort. Losing his own temper wouldn't do the slightest bit of good. He *had* to win Shad and Jericho over to his side. If he could stop Butler from escalating his war, maybe he could think of a way to get out of the rest of this mess.

"How am I going to leave with the three of you riding herd all the time?" he asked quietly. "Besides, why would I *want* to leave?" He thought fast. Hallie was right about one thing, anyway. The boys would relax their guard a little if he seemed to be satisfied with her. "Your sister is a fine woman. Pretty. Intelligent."

Micah frowned at him suspiciously.

Jericho's eyebrows danced over wide eyes.

Shadrack smiled softly and looked down at his feet.

"Besides," Ritter tossed in, "one of you could go with me. To Butler's, I mean."

"I'll go," Shad offered.

"No." They all turned to look at Micah. "I'm the oldest. *I'll* go."

"*You* ain't the oldest!" Jericho countered swiftly. "Trib is."

"Yeah, well, Trib ain't here, is he?"

Lord, Ritter thought dismally. *Another* one?

"And of the three of us *I'm* the oldest."

"Five minutes older," Jericho reminded him.

"Don't matter. All right, gunfighter," Micah said, "we'll go see Ham Butler. But I warn ya right now . . . it'll do no good. That ol' bastard's got a head like a rock. Ya can't tell him a damned thing! Talkin' to him is like talkin' to a stone wall!"

"Well, then," Ritter said, a grim smile on his lips, "it's lucky for me I've had some recent practice talking to walls."

By the time all of the chores were done, most of the day was gone. One thing Ritter was willing to grant the Benteens. There wasn't a lazy bone in their bodies. Those three had more appetite for work than anyone he'd ever known. In fact, Ritter hadn't done so much physical labor in one day since he was a boy, working at his father's shipyard, too long ago.

He snorted a half chuckle. He hadn't even *thought* about those days in years. But somehow, being around this tight-knit family had brought up memories of his own family. Memories he'd just as soon would stay buried. Pushing away his fatigue, he gave a quick look around him.

The four of them stood in the yard, saddling their horses for the trip to Butler's ranch. Ritter glanced at the three other men warily as he yanked the saddle's cinch strap. He didn't know whether to be relieved or worried that all three brothers were riding with him.

Though Shad and Jericho might have a taming influence on Micah's too quick temper, Ritter didn't feel right about leaving Hallie behind alone. Apparently, though, her brothers didn't share his concern. He shook his head slowly as he remembered how the boys had laughed at his worries.

"Hell, Hallie can shoot as good as Shad," Jericho told him, "and almost as good as me!"

Micah barely glanced at him. "Hallie can take care of herself, gunfighter. We done fine around here before you come along."

Nothing he'd said had made the slightest impression on any of them. Including his new wife. In fact, the only thing Hallie was mad about was not being allowed to go call on Butler herself.

At least, he told himself, the boys had drawn the line there. They didn't want to take the chance that Butler's men might shoot first and talk later.

Ritter flipped the stirrup down, then patted his horse's neck. Naturally, Hallie didn't agree with them. He glanced up at the front window to see her standing there, hands on her hips, watching their preparations.

Unwillingly, his gaze moved over her from her short, curly hair to the britches clinging to her shapely legs. He forced himself to look away, then settled his hat down lower over his eyes. He'd never met a woman quite like her. Soft, sweet, and innocent one minute and the next, ready to ride into the middle of a range war.

"Sloane?"

He looked up.

"You ready?"

Ritter nodded at the man who'd spoken, unsure just which brother it was.

Before they could mount up, though, the sound of approaching riders reached them. As one, the four men turned to face them.

"Shit."

"What the hell's *he* doin' here?"

"Who are they?" Ritter kept his gaze locked on the two approaching men.

"Sheriff Tucker and his deputy."

Perfect, Ritter told himself and waited for the trouble to start. He'd never met a sheriff yet who didn't want to try to scare him off.

The men drew their horses to a stop a few feet away, and the one Ritter guessed to be the sheriff leaned his hands on the saddle pommel. Slowly the older man's shrewd blue eyes moved from one of the triplets to another before finally settling on Ritter.

"You must be Sloane."

"That's right," he answered softly. Behind him, he heard the front door open and knew that Hallie had stepped out onto the porch.

"I'm Tucker. Sheriff of Stillwater." He jerked his thumb at the younger man beside him. "This here's my deputy, Hank Trask."

Ritter spared the deputy only a passing glance but noticed he had nervous hands that fidgeted with his reins. A nervous man was one to watch. Then the sheriff spoke again, and Ritter turned back to him.

The older man's lips twisted into a wry grin, and he tipped his hat back farther. "You fellas goin' somewheres?"

"Just takin' us a ride, Sheriff," one of the boys answered.

"Uh-huh. And where you plannin' on goin', Micah?"

Ritter frowned slightly. How could the man tell them apart?

"That any of your business, Tucker?"

"It is if you make trouble." The sheriff looked away from Micah to one of the others and asked, "Shadrack, you want to tell me what's goin' on here?"

"Nothin', Sheriff. Like Micah says."

Tucker's gaze slipped to the porch. He nodded briefly. "Miss Hallie."

"Afternoon, Sheriff."

"Oh, but 'scuse me, Hallie. It ain't *Miss* no more, is it?" Tucker's cool blue gaze moved to Ritter and stayed there. "I hear you're Mrs. Sloane now. Mrs. Ritter Sloane?"

"That's right, Sheriff," Ritter answered for her. "You ride all the way out here to congratulate us?"

The sheriff grinned and leaned his forearms on the pommel. "You *could* say that. You could also say that I heard Butler's hired gun had up and married one of the enemy, so to speak. Thought I'd best come out and see what's what."

Ritter carefully kept his hands in plain sight. He wanted no trouble with the man. A quick glance at his brothers-in-law told him none of them knew quite what to say, so he answered softly, "You heard right, Sheriff. Hallie and I were married yesterday morning."

"Kinda *sudden*, wasn't it?"

"Yes, I suppose it was." He felt Hallie's gaze and knew she was worried about how much he was going to tell the sheriff. Ritter turned his head, smiled at her, then looked back at the man on horseback. "Why, Sheriff, I took one look at Hallie Benteen and decided then and there to marry her. I consider myself most fortunate that she felt the same way."

A long, silent moment passed before the sheriff straightened up in his saddle. His gaze flicked from Hallie back to Ritter.

"Well, son," he said, "can't say as I blame you any. Hallie always was the prettiest little thing around here."

Ritter waited, sure there was more.

"I don't think you should be expectin' a weddin' present from Ham Butler anytime soon," the sheriff continued. "In fact, I think it'd be a right good idea for you all to stick pretty close to home for a while."

"Why's that?" Ritter spoke quietly.

"Because, Mr. Sloane, Butler ain't a man to take his disappointments easy." He looked up at Hallie again. "And because I'd surely hate to have to lock up a new bridegroom."

"Now, hold on, Sheriff," one of the boys said quickly.

"You hush, Jericho," Tucker admonished. "Mr. Sloane knows what I mean, don't you, sir?"

"Yeah, Sheriff." Ritter's fingers laced together and

tightened perceptibly. "I know."

"'Nough said, then. Hallie"—he nodded—"boys . . ."
Tucker pulled his horse around, his deputy following him
reluctantly, and in seconds they'd left the ranchyard.

Chapter

Six

"WELL, WHAT the hell was *that* all about?"

Ritter glared at the man beside him. "It was about me."

Hallie hurried across the yard to join them.

"What d'ya mean?" one of the brothers asked.

"It's what I tried to tell you. Gunfighters don't mix with folks." He glanced down at his arm where Hallie's hand rested. Quickly he looked away again. "That sheriff isn't going to be happy until I'm gone. One way or the other."

"Don't see what he's got to say about it."

"Micah's right," one of the boys said and swung aboard his horse. "Tucker's the sheriff of Stillwater. This ain't Stillwater."

Ritter watched as the others mounted up and sat their horses staring at him. Either they still didn't understand or they just didn't care what kind of trouble they'd brought on themselves. Ritter wasn't sure anymore who was crazier. Him? Or them?

"Let's get goin', gunfighter. We ain't got all day."

He shook his head as the men turned their horses for the road. As he stepped into the stirrup, Hallie stopped him.

"Thank you."

"For what?" He looked at her, catching his breath at the shine in her eyes.

"For not tellin' the sheriff how we come to be married."

"Oh."

She looked down and let her hand fall from his arm to her side. "I s'pose if you'd a told him, he might have helped you leave."

He nodded slowly. "Maybe. . . ."

"Why didn't ya?"

Ritter stared at her bent head and felt a tumult of emotion race through him. He wasn't even sure himself why he hadn't. He'd only known that he wouldn't see her humiliated for anything he'd done. That proud tilt of her chin was something he enjoyed seeing too much. He pulled in a ragged breath and quickly mounted his horse.

She looked up and he met her gaze before saying, "Let's just say I don't much care for sheriffs."

Something like disappointment filled her eyes, and Ritter felt like biting off his own tongue.

"C'mon, gunfighter!"

He turned toward the shout. "I've got to go," he said as he swung back to look at Hallie again. But she'd already turned away and was walking across the yard to the house.

"Boss?"

Hamilton Butler looked up from his desk. One of the ranch hands stood in his office doorway, a battered hat clenched in his fists. "What is it?"

"Men ridin' in."

"How many?"

"Four. Danny come racin' in a minute ago. Said it looks like them Benteens and that Sloane fella."

Fear clutched momentarily at Butler's insides, and he desperately fought it down. Forcing his voice to work, he said, "All right. I'll be out in a minute." The man turned to leave, but Butler called him back. "You tell the men I said no shooting. Not yet."

"Yessir, boss!"

The man's jangling spurs echoed in the stillness, and Hamilton Butler sat back in his chair. The Benteens? And Sloane? Why were they coming? What were they planning?

That tiny spiral of fear coiled inside him again. But he knew there was no one to blame but himself. *He'd* been the one to bring in a gunfighter. *He* was the one building a war on the hurts of the past. But he'd come too far to back down now.

He rubbed one hand across his clean-shaven jaw and stared down blankly at his desktop. Silently he considered the situation. It wasn't so much that he was afraid of the Benteens. Or even Ritter Sloane, though he was in no hurry to face any of them over gun barrels. It was more that he feared the beginning of the war he'd set into motion.

Everything had seemed so simple a couple of months ago. Hire Sloane. Get rid of the Benteens. Now, though, he wasn't so sure. It was like being on a runaway horse. You had no say where you went . . . you just gritted your teeth and held on tight.

Trying to steady his breathing, Hamilton yanked open the top drawer and cautiously lifted out his gun and holster.

His fingers trembled, but he ignored it. Slowly he stood up, swung the holster around his waist, and buckled the belt. He knew he was no match for the Benteen boys, let alone Ritter Sloane in a gunfight. But he'd be damned before he'd go out to meet his enemies unarmed.

Enemies. The Benteens.

Unconsciously his gaze swept to the object at the edge of his desk. He walked slowly around until his fingers could glide over the smooth, satiny surface of the stone. Without warning, Butler's mind recalled the day Hallie'd given it to him.

She couldn't have been more than eight. And she'd ridden all the way to his ranch alone to bring him a present. He remembered it like it was yesterday.

Her long red braids swinging, she'd raced to his side and opened her cupped hands to reveal a stone, worn smooth from countless years of river water racing over it.

"What's this?" he asked gently.

"A piece of a star," the little girl breathed excitedly. "I found it in the river. It musta dropped right outa the sky. . . ." Her eyes wide, Hallie's small fingers touched the stone reverently.

"A star?" he asked as he swung her onto his lap. "How do you know it's a star?"

"The way it shines, Ham!" She grinned up at him and held her treasure to the light. Indeed, when the sunlight hit the stone, it sparkled and shone brightly. And still, it couldn't compare to Hallie's eyes.

"And what are you gonna do with your star, Miss Hallie?" he asked.

"It's a present," she announced and placed her stone in his huge palm. "For you!"

His fingers curled over her gift, and he cleared his throat. "For me?"

"Uh-huh," she answered and threw her small arms around his neck to hug him fiercely. " 'Cause next to Papa and the boys, I love you best."

Hamilton Butler sniffed noisily at the memory. The echo of Hallie's childish voice slipped into the past. Slowly his fingers left the treasured stone and moved to the butt of his gun. How had this all happened? he asked himself. How had he lost so much?

Then his gaze strayed to the portrait hanging over the fireplace. The young man in the painting, stiff and proud in his Union uniform, looked back at Butler solemnly. After a long minute of silent contemplation, Hamilton Butler nodded grimly, then walked outside to meet the enemy.

They rode into the yard quietly, cautiously. At least a dozen Butler men stood outside the two-story ranch house. Some on the wide porch, some leaning negligently against the hitching posts, some walking in from the nearby barn. Not one of them made a sound or a hasty movement, yet their eyes followed the four riders steadily, belying their seemingly casual poses.

Ritter rode beside Micah with the other two men on his left. He'd positioned himself deliberately, wanting to be as close to the hot-tempered brother as possible. If there was any way to end this war now, he wanted to take it.

He wasn't about to let Micah ruin their chances for peace.

The oversize oak door opened and Hamilton Butler stepped out onto his porch. Immediately three of his hands took up protective positions around him. Ritter didn't look at any of the working ranch hands. Instead, he kept his gaze locked on Butler.

Just a few feet from the porch, the four drew their horses to a stop.

"Howdy, Ham," one of the brothers said softly.

"Shadrack." Butler nodded, then looked from one to the other of them. "Jericho, Micah . . . Sloane."

A brief flash of disgust swept through Ritter. Was *he* the only one in Wyoming who couldn't tell the brothers apart?

"Didn't expect to see *you* back here, Sloane," the older man went on.

"You just never know what's going to happen next in this life, Butler."

He nodded and took a step closer to the edge of the porch. "What do you boys want here?"

"We come to tell you—" Micah started loudly.

"Thought maybe we could talk this over," Ritter cut him off. Giving orders was not the way to deal with a man like Butler.

"Talk about what?" Hamilton ignored Micah and addressed himself to his former employee.

"This whole business, Butler." Ritter waved one hand negligently, encompassing the armed men littering the yard. "We could end it now. Before the killing starts."

"How?"

"You back off, that's how," Micah stated flatly.

Ritter groaned silently. He could see the red flush of anger sweep up Butler's neck.

"*I* back off?" the older man shouted.

"Yeah." Micah jerked his head at the older man. "Call off your 'dogs,' Ham."

A couple of men took exception to that insult and took a step toward the man on horseback.

"Get back!" Butler shouted at his men and advanced on Micah himself. "Now, you listen to me and keep your damned mouth shut!"

"Why, you—"

Even though the damage was already done, Ritter reached over and grabbed Micah's elbow to silence him.

"None of this woulda happened if it hadn't been for you Benteens!" Butler snapped. "Stickin' your noses in . . . comin' in with your high-handed notions. . . . If your pa hadn't—"

"We ain't talkin' about Pa here, Ham," Shadrack threw in quietly. "That was a long time ago."

"Not to me!"

Ritter's mind raced. Something was going on here that no one was talking about. What was it that everyone but him knew about? Shad's quiet voice went on arguing with Butler's high-handed shouts, but Ritter paid them no mind. This was no ordinary range war. He should have noticed that right off. As yet, there'd been no bloodshed. No midnight raids on opposing ranches. No rustling.

Briefly he tried to work through the confusion to an answer. But for the life of him, he couldn't figure out what the hell old man Benteen had to do with anything. As far as Ritter knew, the man had been dead for years!

He shook himself mentally and came back to hear Shad saying quietly, "This here's about you hirin' gunfighters. And fencin' range."

Butler glared at him for a minute, then let his gaze sweep

to Ritter. "Yeah, well, looks like I ain't the only one with a tame gunfighter, now, am I?"

Ritter fixed his gaze on the older man.

"That's different," Jericho argued.

"Yeah, how?"

"We ain't payin' him. He's married to Hallie."

"So I heard. But that still puts him on your side, don't it?"

Before any of the boys could speak again, Ritter said, "None of that's important, Butler. We came here to get you to call off the war. Now, you ready to talk?"

"Hell, no, I ain't gonna talk!" The bull of a man came alongside Ritter's horse, grabbed hold of the bridle, and stared up at the gunfighter. "And you got no say in this, Sloane. You quit me. Fine. That's up to you. But then you go on and marry Hallie and expect me to curl up and quit, too?" He flung the horse loose and took a step back. "No, sir. Nothin's settled, far as I'm concerned." He looked over at Jericho. "And that range's my land. I'll fence it if I've got a mind to."

"You know as well as me that everybody's always used that range, Ham. You got no call to go fencin' it."

"Why don't you try to tear it down, Jericho? Or better yet, let your gunfighter do it for you."

Micah finally shook Ritter's restraining hand off his arm. "We do our own fightin', Ham. You know that. And if that's how you want to play it, well . . . so will we."

"Done." Butler's dark brown eyes swept over all four men contemptuously. "Now, get off my land." Then he turned his back on them, climbed the steps, walked across the porch, and disappeared inside the house.

As Butler's men straightened defensively, the four riders

slowly turned their animals and rode away.

No one spoke until they were clear of the place. Then Micah glared at his new brother-in-law. "Satisfied now, gunfighter? That ol' bastard ain't gonna change his mind for nobody. Not even *Ritter Sloane*."

Ritter ignored him. Instead, his mind whirled with possibilities. He'd have sworn that when Butler first stepped outside, the man was reluctant. But that fleeting emotion had faded quickly under a flare-up of temper. He flicked a quick glance at Micah's stubborn features. The man was as set on trouble as Butler.

Hell, Ritter snorted disgustedly, if it was up to the two hotheads, there'd be no stopping a full-blown range war.

There was something else, too. Butler *wasn't* worried about going against Ritter Sloane.

Why?

A cold chill of certainty settled on Ritter. There could be only one reason. Butler'd hired another gunman. But who? And more important, when would he arrive?

It was cold. Bone-deep, bitter cold. Hallie snuggled deeper into Shad's old coat and pulled the fleecy collar up around her ears. Jamming her hands into the slash pockets, she sat down on the old wooden bench, stretched her legs out in front of her, and leaned her head against the high, carved back.

No matter how uncomfortable she was outside, it was better than sitting in that house one more minute. The men had been going over their visit to Butler for what seemed like hours, and she just didn't want to listen to it any longer. Trouble was coming. She knew it and so did they. And talking about it forever wouldn't change a damn thing. In his own way Ham Butler was just as stubborn as Micah. There wasn't a spot of backup in either of them.

Hallie sighed and watched her own breath mist in the cold air. Things were a helluva lot simpler when she was a girl.

Pushing away all thoughts of the men and their arguments, she stared up at the night, a half smile on her lips.

The night sky was so clear and black, the stars shone out bright and pretty like diamonds in God's own jewelry box. She'd only seen one diamond in her life, close up. It hung on a gold chain around Dixie Weaver's neck, and though it was a pretty enough thing, to Hallie's mind, it didn't hold a candle to the stars.

"What are you doing out here?" Ritter asked quietly. "Trying to freeze again?"

Hallie jumped, glanced over her shoulder, and smiled at him. "Didn't hear you come up. You're a mighty quiet man."

He shrugged and eased himself onto the bench beside her. "Long years of practice, I guess." Ritter shivered slightly and asked again, "What are you doing?"

Hallie looked at him, smiled again, then pulled one hand out of her pocket and pointed at the sky. "Just lookin' at the stars for a while. *And* enjoyin' the quiet."

He chuckled softly in understanding. Hours spent with her brothers had sent him, too, searching for a little peace. And even with all the talk, he still hadn't found out what he'd wanted to know. The *real* reason behind the feud with Butler.

Deliberately he pushed those thoughts aside for the time being. Right now, he told himself, all he wanted was to enjoy the hush of the night. *And* Hallie's company.

He tilted his head back and stared up at the heavens. After a long moment of silent study, he nodded and said, "They *are* pretty, aren't they?"

"Oh, my, yes."

"You know," he added as he settled into the seat and rested his neck against the bench back, "I don't believe I've taken the time to simply *look* at the stars in years."

"I come out here all the time," Hallie told him, "winter and summer." She looked at him. "The boys even built me this bench 'cause I forever had a crick in my neck from leanin' back."

He glanced at her. Her profile in moonlight was lovely. Deep blue eyes wide open and staring, a soft smile on her face . . . Ritter felt a soothing restfulness creep into his soul, and for the first time in longer than he cared to think about, he truly relaxed his guard.

In the quiet night, memories filled him. He recalled staring up into the same sky with the same sense of wonder he read on Hallie's face now. All the years of reading navigational charts and listening to the skippers of his father's ships came rushing back. Maybe, he told himself, Hallie would like him to tell her the names of the stars she was so obviously interested in.

"Did you know," she asked in a hushed tone, "that you see different stars in the winter than you do in the summer?"

"Yes," he said, surprised at her knowledge. "I know."

"Isn't that somethin', Ritter?" she breathed excitedly. "Somewhere clean on the other side of the world, somebody's settin' out in the yard lookin' at a summer sky." She shook her head and laughed gently. "While we're freezin', they're most likely swattin' bugs!"

"Most likely," he agreed and smiled into the darkness.

"Oh!" she cried and pointed at the sky, "Lookit there! A shootin' star!" She screwed her eyes tightly shut. "Make a wish."

He couldn't seem to tear his gaze from her. After a moment, he asked, "What did you wish for?"

She shook her head. "Can't tell. Won't come true if ya do." Her eyes opened again and she stared straight up, a look of awe on her face. "The night's so clear and pretty you can see all of 'em!"

He squinted. "All of what?"

"Right up there." She leaned over closer to him and pointed. "See it? That bunch there is Ursa Major."

Ritter pulled back a bit and stared at her in open astonishment. Where the devil had she heard that? "How did—"

"Course," she continued with a shake of her head, "that really means 'Big Bear.' " She threw him a quick look. "Can you make out a bear in all that? I surely can't."

"No . . ."

"But I reckon the folks that named 'em that prob'ly never seen a bear up close." She grinned. "If they had, they wouldn't't've made *that* mistake!"

He smiled, fascinated.

"And that little one down under it? That's the Little Bear. That's kinda nice, don't ya think?"

"What?"

"Puttin' the mama and baby bear so close together."

"Uh, yeah. Yeah, I guess that was nice." Ritter continued to stare at the woman entranced by the stars. She had caught him completely off guard. He never would have guessed that she would know so much about astronomy. And how had she learned it?

"But mayhap they did it 'cause of ol' Draco there, yonder."

"Hmm? What?"

She pointed again and he found himself following the clean length of her arm to yet another cluster of stars.

"Can't really see it too good right now. Kinda far down. But see how they stretch out and wiggle around some?"

"Yes," her breath on his cheek distracted him slightly but he was so enjoying her delighted conversation, he fought to concentrate.

"That there is Draco. It means Dragon." She turned her face to his, and they were only inches apart. Nervously she licked her lips and said, "Some fool named it a dragon and set it right down next to a baby bear. Don't seem right, does it?"

"No." His gaze moved over her face slowly. "No, it doesn't seem right, Hallie."

"But I reckon most of them fellas that study the stars wouldn't think about that."

"No, probably not." Ritter reached up and pulled her collar higher up around her ears. The silver hoops sparkled in the moonlight, and for a moment he allowed his fingertips to trace the outline of her small, delicate ear. She shuddered, and he pulled back slightly.

Fighting down his urge to pull her into his arms, Ritter managed to grind out a question. "How did you learn so much about the stars?"

"From Professor Adams." She shivered and scooted a

little closer to his warmth. "He used to be a teacher way back East. Anyhow, he moved here a couple of years ago, and me and him hit it right off."

A professor? Unbidden, jealousy stabbed through him and grew as she continued describing the man.

"He's got lots of books and such. Lordy, Ritter," she whispered, "he's so smart it almost hurts to hear him talk. It's a pure shame how he loves the whiskey."

Brilliant? *And* a drunk? Has the man won Hallie's sympathy?

"He lets me look at his books all I want and even explains things I don't quite catch."

Unconsciously Ritter's hand reached out to her again. He smoothed back the fall of curls from her forehead then gently cupped her cheek. There were *many* things *he'd* like to explain to Hallie, he thought with a rush of hunger so strong it shook him to his bones.

Her voice came softer now, more breathless as she rubbed her cheek against his palm. "That night you found me? I was comin' home from the professor's when that durned tree fell on me."

His sudden burst of anger that this unknown professor hadn't bothered to see her home died when she added, "It's a good thing I wouldn't let him walk me back here. He's so old, that tree prob'ly woulda *killed* him."

Old. The professor was *old*. Funny how one little word like that could make all the difference in the world.

"Someday," she went on, her breathing ragged, her eyes fastened on his lips, "someday I'm gonna get me a tele . . ."

"A telescope?" he helped.

"Uh-huh." She raised one finger to trace his jawline.

"You can see almost straight to heaven with one of them things, y'know."

"Yes." He leaned closer and kissed her forehead, his fingers sliding through her soft hair.

"I, uh . . ." Her eyes closed and she sighed gently at the touch of his hand.

The fresh, clean scent of her surrounded him, and Ritter felt himself drawn to her as inevitably as a bear to honey. Slowly he pulled her into the circle of his arms and marveled at how well she fit up against him. Her head in the crook of his arm, he studied her pale, moonlit features for a long moment and felt himself falling into the depths of her wide blue eyes.

Finally he lowered his mouth to hers.

At the first meeting of their lips, a hunger long denied flared into life and burned through his soul. Overwhelmed with the rush of pleasure filling him, Ritter's arms tightened, and she melded her body to his.

Her lips parted for him, and his tongue thrust inside, sweeping the warmth of her as if he were seeking his last breath of air. She moved against him, trying to get closer still. Even through her bulky jacket, Ritter's hands felt the luscious curves of her body, and his fingers itched to touch the warmth of her flesh. Shudders of delight coursed through him at her inexperienced eagerness, and her obvious pleasure only served to feed his own.

A groan escaped his throat as he clung to her tightly, taking all she had to offer and giving what little he had.

The cold forgotten, a warmth grew and blossomed between them until breathing itself became difficult.

Finally, reluctantly, he pulled back from her but couldn't

resist touching his lips one last time to hers before enfolding her gently in his arms. Awed, Ritter rested his chin on top of her head and listened to the thundering of his own heart.

Chapter

Seven

RITTER SWUNG the heavy ax again and felt the solid, satisfying thump as its sharp blade sliced through yet another stump of wood. His shoulders ached, his head was pounding, and despite the chill in the air, sweat rolled down his naked back and chest.

He set the ax handle on the ground and rested the blade against the chopping block. Slowly he leaned back, hands on his hips, until his tired muscles stretched and pulled. Then he straightened up and shoved both hands through his sweat-soaked hair. His gaze raked the ranchyard, absently noting the work that had been accomplished in the last week. He clenched his fists and winced slightly at the tender flesh of still-raw blisters.

Ritter glanced down then at his hands and snorted. They hadn't done anything more physical than pull a trigger and saddle a horse in more years than he could count. It was almost shameful that a grown man would grow blisters from doing a day's work.

He sighed heavily and looked toward the house. *She* was in there. With her too short hair and silver rings in her ears and her ready smile and kissable mouth . . . Ritter shook his head and reached for the ax again. With his free hand he grabbed up another log and set it on the chopping block. Pulling in a deep breath, Ritter swung the axe in a wide arc and brought it down clean in the middle of the stump.

The split wood fell to either side of the block, and he bent to pick both pieces up. Tossing them to the growing pile behind him, he lifted the ax again and slammed the blade deep into the block to protect its edge. Tired, he turned to the pile of fresh wood and began to gather the pieces up to stack alongside the front door under the porch.

Feet dragging, he went back and forth time and again until all the wood had been cleared away. Only then did he take time enough to lean his hip against the side of the house. There was still too much daylight left. It was only early afternoon. He would have to find something else to do.

From inside the house, Ritter heard Hallie humming a tune that he couldn't quite identify. But it didn't matter. It was the sound of her voice that clutched at his chest. He forced himself to move away from the cabin and well into the clearing. His heart racing, his blood rushed through his veins, and all signs of fatigue dropped away. Deliberately, he kept his gaze away from the house as he marched toward the barn.

He could clean out the stalls, he told himself firmly. Surely *that* would make him tired enough that he'd be able to sleep tonight, Hallie beside him or not! Ritter rubbed his forearm across his eyes, then straightened up and headed for the pitchfork.

Almost a week gone and he'd hardly said two words to

her. Hallie frowned and pulled back on the reins slightly to slow the horse down. She wasn't in any big hurry to get to town. After all, the sooner she got there, the sooner she'd be back home.

And she could do without all the grumblin' for a while. Between her brothers and her husband, Hallie'd heard the name Hamilton Butler more in the last week than she had in the last twenty years. And she was heartily sick of it.

Oh, she knew something had to be done. But was it *gettin'* done by them four forever talkin' about it? Why, the only place she'd had the slightest bit of peace all week was sittin' outside at night watchin' the stars. And even *that* wasn't the same anymore.

No. Now, she'd sit there, half listening for the front door to open and her husband to come out and join her as he had before. But it hadn't happened again. If anything, Ritter Sloane seemed even more determined than ever to keep his distance.

And without him beside her, the night sky didn't hold the same fascination anymore.

Oh, he was sure enough polite. And she had to admit, the man was a worker. Even the boys couldn't slight him there. She'd even noticed that Shadrack and Jericho seemed to be warmin' up to him some. But not Micah. There just wasn't an inch of give to that man. Brother or not, Hallie told herself, Micah Benteen was about the most hardheaded man she'd ever come across.

Until she'd met her husband.

Shaking her head, Hallie pulled her hat brim low and let her mind ramble. Naturally, the first thing her memory pulled up was that night under the stars with Ritter.

Even now, a week later, Hallie squirmed in the saddle just thinkin' about it. That man could kiss good enough to curl a body's toes, she told herself. It was a pure shame he didn't want to do more of it.

She *still* found it hard to believe that all that kissin' and huggin' hadn't led to a proper weddin' night at long last. Why, when he'd stretched out on top of the covers that night, like he didn't mind at all, it was all she could do not to hit him with somethin'.

Not that she was a wanton or anything . . . but the kisses he gave her had stoked a fire in her blood that was purely *ragin'* to be either built up or put out altogether. He didn't seem in no hurry to add more kindlin' to the blaze, she told herself . . . yet at the same time, the hot, searchin' looks he'd been shootin' her all week hadn't exactly dampened her flame any, either.

And watchin' him today while he was choppin' wood had been about enough to drive her right pure out of her mind. The play of his back muscles, the strength of his shoulders, even the sight of his long-fingered hands on the ax handle was enough to make her throat dry. She'd finally had to sneak out of the cabin, grab a horse from the corral, and leave.

She frowned and patted her horse's neck when the big animal tossed his head.

How could she make her plan work, though, if Ritter wouldn't even *kiss* her again? Still, she told herself, it was early days yet to be givin' up. Though her new husband hadn't exactly agreed yet to givin' her a baby, he hadn't said *no*, either.

For just a moment she let herself imagine what a child

of Ritter's would look like. In her mind's eye, she saw herself holding a blond, blue-eyed baby to her breast. She'd be nestled in the big rocking chair, in front of the fire, Ritter alongside her.

She pulled her horse to a stop. Now, hold on, she told herself firmly, the plan was for you to have a baby and your husband to "die." Remember, she chided herself, you don't *want* a husband?

Well, no. She never really *had*. But she was willin' to admit that, sometimes, havin' a husband was a real pleasurable thing. Hallie smiled softly and, nickered to her horse to get him moving again. If she put her mind to it, she could bring back that feeling of his arms wrapped around her, his mouth on hers, the warm strength of him . . .

She shivered and shook her head. No doubt about it. She had to convince that husband of hers to find some more time for cuddlin'.

Maybe if she could get his mind off Hamilton Butler for a while . . . As soon as she got to town, she thought determinedly, she'd go see Dixie.

The Silver Spur was quiet. Too early for the piano player and most of the regular drinkers to be busy, there was instead only a handful of men sprinkled throughout the bar. And except for the huddled group of three men at one table in the far corner, the crowd so far seemed made up of solitary drinkers.

Hallie's gaze swept over the nearly empty saloon quickly. She spotted Dixie behind the bar and went to her side.

The older woman's still-black hair was dressed high on her head with a few curls and a drooping emerald green feather hanging down on the side. Her matching green satin dress was cut low with sheer black lace covering her chest and climbing to a high collar. Cinched in tight at the woman's narrow waist, the gown fell to the floor in graceful folds that rustled gently with her every movement.

Hallie knew Dixie to be at *least* fifty years old, and yet her wide brown eyes, high cheekbones, and ready smile, coupled with a near perfect figure, was enough to have even much younger men droppin' at her feet.

"Well, hello, darlin'," the older woman said, smiling in greeting. "Didn't expect to be seeing you in here again!"

"Why not?"

"Oh"—Dixie grinned and shrugged her lace-clad shoulders—"didn't think a 'proper' married woman would be *allowed* in a saloon."

Hallie shook her head slowly. If she didn't know Dixie was teasin' . . . She leaned her forearms on the bar top. "You ever know anybody to not *allow* me something I want to do?"

Laughing, the other woman patted Hallie's arm gently. "No, honey, I sure haven't. Not since your pa anyway. Since he passed on, I don't believe anybody's bothered to try. Except Trib, of course."

Trib. An image of her oldest brother flashed through Hallie's mind. Everything would be so much easier if only he'd come home. At least *he* could ride herd on Micah. And she had the oddest feeling that Trib and Ritter would like each other just fine. Besides, Trib might be able to talk Ham Butler out of all this nonsense.

She pushed those thoughts away when she realized

Dixie'd said something she missed. "What was that?"

"I said, I saw the Professor the other day. He says you haven't been by his place in more than a week." Dixie's eyebrows rose curiously. "He was also pretty surprised to hear you were married . . ."

Hallie flushed. "I shoulda gone to see him. Let him know, I guess . . . but we been stayin' pretty much to home lately."

"Yeah. You *and* your brothers. Do you know this is the first time in about five years I haven't had at least *one* broken window in over a week?"

Hallie smiled.

"At least," Dixie continued, "I think I can figure out why *you* haven't been in town much. I hear tell Ritter Sloane's a mighty good-lookin' man . . ."

"He is," Hallie said too quickly, then added, "but that's not . . . I mean . . ."

"Hell, honey, you don't have to tell me a damn thing."

Hallie gave a quick look over her shoulder to make sure no one was close enough to listen. "Can I talk to ya for a minute? Alone?"

"Sure." Nodding to her bartender, Dixie filled two cups with strong black coffee, then stepped out from behind the bar and walked to a corner table. After they were seated, Dixie said, "What's wrong?"

Hallie's fingers curled around her coffee cup. Now that she was there, she wasn't quite sure where to start. Taking a deep breath, she decided to just plunge on in and hope for the best.

Quickly, in a hushed tone, Hallie told her old friend exactly how her "wedding" had come about. With a flush of color climbing her cheeks, she even admitted that she still hadn't become a "wife."

A long, quiet minute passed before Dixie said thoughtfully, "Y'know, somehow I'm not surprised. I never knew any of you Benteens to do a thing the usual way."

"Dixie, I don't know what to do." Elbows on the table, Hallie pushed her hair out of her face and leaned her chin on her hands. "Everything's a mess. The boys are just waitin' for Ritter to do somethin' wrong . . . Ritter's chafin' at the bit to get shy of all of us . . . Ham's not backin' down from this fight . . ."

"And you, darlin'?" Dixie prodded. "What about you? What do you want?"

"Hell, I don't know anymore." Abruptly Hallie leaned back in the captain's chair and propped one booted foot on her knee. "Ritter's hardly talked to me for a week now. Ever since we . . . uh . . ."

"Looked at the stars?"

"Yeah."

"Well"—the older woman sighed—"I don't claim to understand men any. Lord knows, I've never met a woman who does. But I *have* known a few in my time." A soft smile crossed her face as she looked at the much younger woman. "And it appears to me that your new husband, gunfighter or no, is runnin' scared."

"Scared? Ritter?" Hallie shook her head and snorted indelicately. "Of what?"

"You."

Head cocked, Hallie eyed Dixie carefully. "Me? Why the hell would he be scared of me?"

"Who knows? Maybe you make him think. Maybe you make him feel things he doesn't want to feel." She laughed suddenly. "Hell, maybe he's afraid to touch you for fear of those damn brothers of yours!"

"No," Hallie murmured thoughtfully, "I don't think he even gives the boys a second thought."

"Then it must be you."

Was it possible? Was he as nervous around her as she was around him? Hallie would never have considered the possibility if not for Dixie. But now that she had, it made a strange kind of sense. It might explain why he pulled away from her anytime they got to kissin' . . . still, it was awfully hard to imagine Ritter Sloane afraid of his wife!

"Sometimes, Hallie," Dixie went on, her fingers toying with the handle of her cup, "when a man's too much alone, he forgets how to be with people. And who's more *alone* than a gunfighter? Must get to the point where they don't even *try* getting to know folks." She sighed. "How hard it must be, forever saying goodbye."

"Maybe . . ." Hallie'd have to give it more thought. But for right now, she changed the subject abruptly. "You heard anything from Ham lately?"

The other woman's plucked black eyebrows lowered, and all trace of a smile fled. "No. Not for quite a while. Why?"

"Ritter says if Ham hired *one* gunfighter, he'll likely hire another."

"Good figurin'."

"Do you know somethin'?"

"No." Dixie lifted her cup to rouged lips and took a sip. She shuddered slightly at the taste and set it back down.

"But it isn't like Ham to give up easy. Lord knows, he's been after *your* family for what, now . . . thirteen years?"

Hallie nodded.

"I'm only surprised it took him *this* long to get around to hiring guns." Dixie reached across the table and squeezed the other woman's hand. "Haven't seen any 'special' gunmen coming into town, but"—she leaned closer—"see those three in the corner over there?"

Hallie's gaze flicked to the little group, then back again. "Yeah, what?"

"New hands. Just signed on for Ham." Her lips quirked. "Don't much look like regular ranch hands, do they?"

"No. Guess they don't." She chanced another look. The three were fairly young and too well dressed to make their livings solely from the back of a horse. Most working cowhands didn't make more than thirty dollars a month, she well knew. And from the look of those three, they saw more than that, regularly.

"Are there more like them?"

Dixie shrugged. "That's the talk. Seems Ham is filling out his bunkhouse with fighters, not workers."

Hallie fell silent and tried to keep her gaze away from the three men.

"Oh, would you look at . . ." Dixie snorted a half laugh, then nodded her head toward the batwing doors. "Look at that."

Glancing over her shoulder, Hallie smothered a laugh. All she could see was the bottom half of a very large woman. Her tiny shoes scuttling back and forth, her blue-gray skirt swinging agitatedly with her jerky movements. Occasionally a flash of gray hair appeared at the top of the doors as the woman went up on her toes, trying to see either around, under, or over the doors to the saloon.

"For God's sake." Dixie stood up and shook her head. "I've known that woman for over twenty years. You'd think she'd just come inside if she wants to see you."

Hallie chuckled. "I've never known Elmira to set foot in the saloon."

"No one has." Dixie grinned. "But when no one else is around, Elmira's been known to come in for a cup of coffee with me."

"Really?"

"Yes." The older woman's lips straightened into a firm line. "And don't you tell a soul, either. I believe she enjoys the 'adventure.' "

Dixie crossed to the closed doors to have a chat with the other woman. Hallie stayed rooted in her chair and stared into the dregs of her coffee, as if seeking answers to the questions flying through her brain.

Vaguely she heard a chair scrape against the hardwood floor and the sound of bootheels coming closer. She paid no attention, though, until the man stopped directly beside her.

"Hey, darlin'," he said, reaching for her arm, "how 'bout you come on over and have a drink with me and my friends?"

Hallie looked up into the young feral face of one of the three men from the corner table. Thin lips held in a sly smile, his blue eyes narrowed as they watched her, and Hallie had only a moment to note the difference between this man's eyes and her husband's, a known gunfighter.

Ritter's eyes held life. Feeling. The eyes she stared into now were cold and empty.

"Uh, no," she said softly, tempering her refusal with a halfhearted smile. "I got to be gettin' on home now. But thanks for the offer." She pushed away from the table and stood up. But when she turned her back on the man, he grabbed her elbow and swung her back around.

"You ain't leavin' yet," he whispered. "Me and my friends're lonely. A fine-lookin' woman like you will surely liven up the afternoon."

Her fingers curled into a useless fist, and Hallie fought down the tendril of fear climbing her spine. Determinedly, she kept her voice even, steady. "I 'preciate it, mister. But I really *do* got to get on home. My, uh . . . *husband* will be waitin' on me."

"Husband?" His eyes narrowed and he grabbed at her left hand. "Don't see no ring . . ."

Hallie looked around uneasily. Dixie was just now pushing Elmira back out onto the porch and coming toward her.

"Here, now, cowboy," the older woman said, smiling, "what seems to be the problem?"

"No problem. Just buyin' the *lady* a drink is all."

Hallie stiffened at his tone but kept her mouth shut.

"Don't think she wants one, cowboy."

"Now, Dixie, is it?" He leaned toward her. "I don't much care *what* you think. *Or* what she wants." His gaze swept over Hallie's tight-fitting buckskin britches approvingly. "I figure any woman that'll wear a outfit like *that* wouldn't mind havin' a drink with us boys."

From the corner of her eye Hallie saw Dixie's bartender bend down and reach for the shotgun kept under the bar. Unfortunately, another one of the three men saw him, too.

"All right, barkeep," a voice from the corner said slowly, "you pull that gun of yours out real careful and set 'er down on the bar."

Hallie looked past the man holding her to see one of his friends, pistol in hand, aiming at John, the bartender.

"Now, darlin'," her captor said with a smile, "you gonna have a drink with us, or does Mac over there"— he jerked his head—"give that bartender a brand-new hole in his fat head?"

Hallie felt Dixie's fear as though it were a wavering cloud settling over her. From the corner of her eye, she saw John, sweat beading on his forehead, staring at the armed man. She really didn't have much choice.

"All right, mister, I'll have a drink."

"Well, good!" He grinned, let go of her elbow, and dropped his arm around her shoulders, pulling her tight against him. "I just knew if you thought about it some, you'd see the right of it." He looked up at his friend. "Mac, you go take that ol' gun from our bartender friend now. Wouldn't want him to have second thoughts, now, would we?"

Hallie's mind spun in twenty different directions. Absently she saw the other man do her captor's bidding, then return to the table with a glass for her. Somehow, most of the other customers in the bar had managed to slip outside during her little confrontation. Now, beyond one or two others, she and the three Butler men were the only people left in the saloon.

Excepting Dixie and John.

The man holding her squeezed her shoulder familiarly,

then let his hand slide down her spine to her waist. He leaned over and chuckled throatily. "Gunfire don't sound good during a party, y'know."

Hallie shivered slightly and tried not to pull away. She couldn't afford to make him angry.

After smoothing the flat of his palm over her behind, he let his hand rest on the curve of her hip. It was all she could do not to shove him from her and stomp on his damned hand until every bone in it was broken.

When they reached the table, her captor dropped into the closest chair, then pulled her down on his lap. Laughing, he buried his face in her neck and announced, "Y'know, I believe I like short hair on a female. Helluva lot easier to nuzzle on your throat this way."

She gritted her teeth and tried to think. Maybe one of the customers who'd left would go for Sheriff Tucker. Maybe.

"Y'know darlin'," the cowboy said, taking her chin between his fingers and turning her head to him, "ya never should've tried to tell me you was married. Ain't no way I was gonna believe *that*."

The other two men laughed loudly, and one of them slid a full glass of whiskey over to her. Her captor picked it up and brought it to her lips. He pressed the glass against her mouth, and when she wouldn't part her lips for him, he pulled down on her chin, forcing her mouth open. He managed to pour just some of the fiery liquid down her throat—the rest spilled down the front of her gray flannel shirt.

She jerked free, but his hand moved to the back of her head and forced her to look at him again.

"Ain't a man alive would let his woman wear a outfit

like this," he said and smoothed his other hand over her thigh. " 'Sides, what kind of fool would let a woman like *you* wander around with no brand on your finger?"

"I reckon that'd be me."

Ritter! Hallie looked toward her husband standing in the doorway and felt her fear melt away.

Chapter

Eight

"WHO'RE YOU, mister?"

Ritter took another step farther into the saloon. Behind him he heard the soft, moccasined footfalls of his three brothers-in-law. The batwing doors swished open as they entered the darkened building. He didn't bother to look at them as he heard them spread out just behind him.

Instead, Ritter kept his gaze locked on the younger man across the room. The one holding Hallie captive on his lap. The one whose hand still rested on her thigh.

He swallowed back a surge of anger.

"I believe," Ritter said in a remarkably quiet tone, "I just told you that. I'm the *lady's* husband."

Hallie grinned and looked from her husband's stern features to her captor's wary frown. She tried to get up then, but the man's hand clamped down on her thigh.

Ritter's eyes narrowed perceptibly.

"I don't know who the hell you think you are, mister," the foolish young man said, "but I don't see no ring on her finger. Do you?"

One of Hallie's brothers started forward, but Ritter held up one hand to stop him.

"Boy," Ritter ground out, still facing his opponent,

"don't you push me. I am making every effort to keep my temper in check."

"Jed," the man who'd pulled a gun on the bartender whispered into the silence. His eyes shot a nervous look at the quiet blond man. "Jed, shut up quick. Don't you know who that is?"

The man ignored his friend. Pushing Hallie off his lap, he stood and faced the intruder. Legs spread at a comfortable distance, he held his arms out at his sides, his hand within easy reach of the polished, black-handled pistol on his right hip. Chin lifted defiantly, his voice unconcerned, he said, "I don't care who the hell he is."

"You best care, Jed. That's *Ritter Sloane*."

A blanket of quiet dropped on the saloon. From somewhere to the right a clock ticked, the sound unusually loud. Late afternoon sun poured in through the front windows, sending bursts of color dancing off the stained-glass lampshades on the hanging chandeliers. Not a soul in the place moved.

Hallie felt as though she were in a dream. The kind of nightmare where everything but the dreamer is moving so fast it's impossible to stop it. The quick flash of relief that swamped her at first sight of her husband had slipped away, leaving in its place an overwhelming sense of uneasiness. Someone on her left fidgeted nervously in his chair, and the resulting creak of wood sounded out like a scream in the stillness.

She'd never seen that look on Ritter's face. His features carefully blank, all of his concentration was centered on the damn fool standing beside her. Hallie's gaze moved over her husband again. He had the look of a man that most people would step aside for.

His dust-colored hat was pulled down low over his eyes, and his long-sleeved white shirt was cuffed and buttoned tightly above his wrists. But her eyes kept returning to his hands. Tanned, long fingered, they seemed totally relaxed, unlike the man called Jed, whose hands trembled as they hovered over his holster.

Unless someone backed down, she was about to witness a gunfight. Hallie's stomach churned furiously with the force of a sudden, dreadful vision appearing in her mind. She saw it clearly. Her husband, lying on the floor of Dixie's saloon, a bright red stain on his shirtfront. She saw herself, kneeling over him, trying to stop the flow of blood. She saw his pale blue eyes widen in surprise, then slowly close forever. She felt the sharp sting of tears in her eyes and blinked them away furiously. The too real image shattered, and she was back in the saloon, waiting.

This is what he'd meant when he'd told her that gunfighters didn't make good husband material. This is what his life was. A never-ending set of challenges from men eager to prove themselves.

Her gaze lifted to Ritter's face. She had to stop this. She wouldn't let him die because some big-talking, drunken, loggerheaded half-wit was too foolish to back down.

Hallie took a tentative step toward her husband, but he ignored her.

It was as though she didn't exist for him.

From the corner of his eye Ritter saw Hallie move. But he couldn't acknowledge her. He couldn't afford to let her presence shake his focus. Every scrap of his concentration was set on the man called Jed. If Ritter looked into her eyes, he knew his opponent would snatch at the momentary distraction. And one moment was all that was needed.

Poised and ready, Ritter waited. It was a familiar scene to him, played out all too often over the years. He looked into the other man's eyes and saw the customary glimmer of panic overshadowed by an almost frantic desire for the courage to stay put and face the gunfighter.

An eternity-filled minute passed before Jed shifted uneasily under the blond man's unwavering, steely stare. "She didn't say nothin' about bein' married to *you.*"

One blond eyebrow lifted and the gunfighter answered, "You're blaming *your* mistake on my wife?"

"No." Jed swallowed convulsively. "No, I . . ." He glanced at his two friends' piteous expressions and seemed to draw up a surge of bravado. He swung his head back to look at the famous gunman. "I ain't sayin' a damn thing more." He widened his stance and lifted his chin. His still-trembling hand waited over his pistol grip for the signal that would mean a thunder of noise and, undoubtedly, death.

Why? Why were the young fools so intent on dying? In the last week or so, Ritter had begun to rediscover the joys of simply *living.* Of hard work, good food . . . *family.* Unwillingly, visions of Hallie moved through his brain. Her smile, her shining eyes, her kiss . . . and suddenly Ritter knew that he wanted to give the young pup across from him one more chance to back down. To live.

"Boy," he said softly, "this doesn't have to come down to a shooting. There's another way." Ritter felt everyone's surprise but kept talking. "You just apologize to my wife, there, then get on your horse and ride out. Simple as that."

"You tellin' me to leave town?" The younger man's brow wrinkled thoughtfully.

"I think that's best, yes." Ritter held his position and waited for the man's answer. He found himself hoping it would be the right one. He was so goddamned tired of death.

"Do it, Jed," one of his friends whispered urgently. "Don't be a fool!"

"Yeah," the other of the three agreed, tossing an uneasy glance at the gunfighter. "Remember who that is. Ain't nobody gone up against Ritter Sloane and lived to tell the tale."

"There ain't no shame in gettin' shut of a bad deal all around," the first one added.

"Listen to your friends, mister." Hallie spoke up quietly and waited for him to look at her before continuing. "No use in dyin' for no good reason, is there?"

Ritter watched the man weigh his chances. In the younger man's eyes flashed worry, fear, eagerness, and finally determination. Ritter sighed heavily. He'd seen that expression before and knew that the young man had made the wrong choice.

It was always the same. He'd hoped for a moment that *this* time it would be different. That *this* time the young fool wouldn't exchange his life for his pride.

Ritter felt the breathless expectation in the room. The charge of horrified excitement. Not for the first time, he asked himself why it was that so-called *normal* folks seemed to reap so much satisfaction from watching someone else's death. Was it a fascination for death itself? Or did they feel a sense of relief that it was someone else and not themselves?

He stared into the younger man's eyes and felt a swell of regret. Ritter's fingers moved fractionally, as if already holding his too familiar six-gun, and he dimly noted that the three men behind him were moving to stand on either side of him. Without looking away from his near panicked adversary, Ritter said quietly, "You three stand clear now. This is between him"—he jerked his head slightly—"and me. Hallie, you step aside."

"No."

Goddammit! Ritter silently cursed a blue streak. His teeth gritted, his gaze never leaving the man opposite him, he said again, more forcefully this time, "Hallie, do what I say. Get back. Now."

"I said no."

"Dammit, Hallie," one of the boys called out, "you stay the hell outa this!"

"Hush, Micah," she answered and stepped a little closer to the thunderstruck man waiting to draw on Ritter Sloane. "I ain't gonna be quiet, and I ain't gonna stay outa this."

"Hallie . . ."

She shook her head, and Ritter could only watch in mesmerized fascination as she snatched the younger man's gun right out of its holster.

"Hey!"

Hallie leapt nimbly back and away from the mortified tough.

"Give me back my gun, you hear?"

"No, I won't." She pointed the pistol at him and turned her gaze to her furious husband. "Now, I ain't about to stand here and watch the two of you shoot at each other from no more than ten feet away. Most likely, *both* of ya would be killed."

Ritter's left eyebrow quirked.

"Now, you go ahead on," she continued. "Do whatever

it is you think you got to do and get it done with."

"This how you won all them gunfights, Sloane?" Jed sneered at the famous man. "Get a man disarmed, then shoot him?"

Ritter said nothing for a long moment. In fact, he could hardly think, let alone speak. He stared at Hallie and could see that she was obviously *very* pleased with herself. His heart hammered erratically in his chest. She'd taken a helluva chance. That fool might've panicked at her sudden movement, turned, and fired on her before she could duck. *Anything* might have happened.

Anger rose up in him again, and he promised himself that he would deal with Hallie later. In private. As for now, slowly, Ritter bent over and untied the rawhide thong from around his right thigh. He glanced up and saw his opponent licking dry, nervous lips. When the thong was loose, he straightened and unbuckled his gunbelt. Turning slightly, Ritter handed his holster and gun to the nearest triplet, then swung back around to face the man who'd started all the trouble in the first place.

"You're not going to get shot . . . *Jed*, is it?" He took a couple of long, measured steps forward. A splotch of red fell on the younger man's forehead as he stepped back into a patch of sun-washed colors. Ritter kept advancing. Nimbly his fingers undid the buttons on his cuffs and rolled his sleeves back over his forearms. "But you *are* going to get the tar beat out of you, boy."

Jed looked from side to side, as if for help, but everyone else was as stunned as he was. A gunfight, they'd expected. A *fistfight* was something else.

He'd no sooner had the thought than Ritter's fist crashed into his cheek and he was sprawled out on the floor. Jed shook his head and moved his jaw experimentally. He looked up at the man standing over him, then grasped the hand the gunfighter offered. As he was pulled up from the floor, though, Jed swung his left fist in a wide arc that caught the blond man unawares.

Ritter staggered with the blow and backed into one of his opponent's friends. That man gave him a mighty shove that sent him crashing into Jed again. Both men fell to the floor in a flurry of blows.

Hallie tossed Jed's pistol to one of the crowd standing on the sidelines and launched herself at the man who'd attacked her husband from behind. Clinging to his broad back, Hallie locked one arm around the man's neck, wrapped her legs around his thick middle, and brought her fist down again and again on the back of his head. Her target started spinning wildly in an effort to shake her loose, and soon she was holding on just to stay put.

In seconds someone lifted her free, and she barely had time to look at Micah before he dropped her and drove his work-hardened fist into the freed man's face. The man dropped as if he'd been poleaxed, and Micah whirled around looking for a fresh fight. Before he was set, someone punched him in the face, and Micah's head snapped back with the impact. Hallie's eyes widened as she watched her brother sink to the floor, holding his jaw.

The private fight had grown. Even the onlookers had joined the fray, and now tables, chairs, and glassware lay shattered on the polished floor. Dixie ducked behind the bar as a chair flew in her direction. The six-foot mirror behind her splintered with the chair's impact, sending shards of glass tumbling down onto the wide counter below it, smashing glasses that had come all the way from St. Louis without a scratch.

Then, just as Jericho was tossed through the front windowpane onto the boardwalk, a gunshot rang out, and all fighting stopped.

Ritter looked up, and though his left eye was already swelling, he saw the sheriff standing amid the rubble, looking down at the combatants with disgust. Someone moved on his right, and Ritter glanced over in time to watch Hallie push herself out from under a smashed table. She grinned at him, and he was hard put to keep from smiling back.

Remembering how this had all started helped.

"What the blazes is going on in here?" Sheriff Tucker's voice thundered into the sudden quiet. His quick eyes scanned the fallen brawlers as he waited for an answer. Then his gaze fell on Ritter. "This *your* doin', Sloane?"

After pushing himself to his feet, Ritter leaned back down and lifted a semiconscious Jed from the floor. The younger man swayed, and the gunfighter righted a chair and dropped the man into it. "I suppose you could say it was my fault," he answered finally.

The sheriff frowned thoughtfully. "Might've guessed, I reckon. Though I'd expected better of you. Never heard a thing about you bein' a saloon brawler."

One pale hand slapped the bar top, and Dixie pulled herself to an upright position. Her gaze moved over the remains of her saloon, and she shook her head disgustedly. "Tucker," she said, "this wasn't Sloane's doing. At least not completely." She glared at the Benteen boys, one after the other. When Jericho climbed through the now empty space where her window used to be, she sent him an especially hard stare. "He had *help*." Turning back to the sheriff, she pointed at Jed, who was on a slow slide out of his chair. Ritter caught him by the shoulder and yanked him back up. "Besides, it was *that* one who started it!" she accused. "He was botherin' Hallie, and when her husband objected, the damned fool wanted to shoot it out."

The sheriff's eyebrows lifted.

"It was Sloane didn't want a shooting!" Dixie glanced at the gunfighter, then looked back at the sheriff. "Anyhow . . . they worked it out with their fists instead." She lifted her hands eloquently to encompass her ruined building. "As you can see."

"That true, Sloane?"

Ritter ran his forearm over his mouth and wasn't surprised in the least to see a trail of blood mixing with the sweat and dirt. Every bone in his body hurt, and yet, despite the bruises and the aches, he felt good. He hadn't had to kill anybody. "That's right, Sheriff."

"All right," Tucker said loudly, "that accounts for you two. What about the rest of these yahoos?" His gaze flew around the room, pausing every now and then on a particular face.

"Well, Sheriff . . ." Shad's voice was muffled. "Get off me, damn you!" He pushed the limp body of one of the brawlers off his chest and staggered to his feet. A purplish bruise was already staining his left eye, and his shirtfront was torn clear down to his belt buckle. "Sheriff," he said again, "you know us Benteens stick together. When our brand-new brother-in-law got himself in a mess, it was purely natural for us to jump on in and help 'im."

Ritter rolled his eyes toward heaven. *Help?* What would have been a simple two-man disagreement had turned into a free-for-all because of their *help*.

"That'th tho, Tucker." Micah's lips were a mass of bruised and puffy flesh. He must have bitten down on his tongue, too, because his words were coming out pretty strangled. "That thonofabitch there"—he jerked his head at the instigator of the fight—"thtarted all thith. It'th *hith* fault!"

Everyone in the place stopped and stared hard at Micah while trying to make sense of what he said. Sheriff Tucker's eyes narrowed, then he shook his head and went on.

"Yeah," the sheriff was saying, "I know you boys. And I know you'll be stayin' in town this evenin' puttin' this place back together for Dixie. Y'hear?"

"Sure, Sheriff." Jericho grinned and pulled a loose sliver of glass out of his jacket pocket. Dropping it to the floor, he crossed the room to stand beside his family. "Don't we always?" Then he ignored the sheriff and looked hard at Micah. "Say something."

"Thay what?"

Jericho laughed. "Nothin'."

Sheriff Tucker's hard gaze swept the room. When he came to Ritter Sloane again, he paused. His expression grim, he said softly, "This is only gonna get worse. You know that."

"Yeah. Yeah, I know."

Tucker nodded, hooked his thumbs in his belt buckle, took a deep breath, and exhaled it in a rush. "I don't want trouble with you, Sloane. Stillwater's a peaceful little town. I mean to see it stays that way."

Hallie stepped across a broken chair and stopped beside her husband. Looping her hand through the crook of his arm, she looked at the sheriff. "It wasn't us, Sheriff. We already told you that."

"Hallie"—the older man sighed—"when you've got *his* name, you don't *have* to start somethin'. People come from miles around just itchin' for the chance to make a reputation quick."

"That ain't Ritter's fault," she protested.

"Yeah, it is. And he knows it as well as me."

Ritter's lips pressed tight together, he met the sheriff's stare steadily. He couldn't deny any of it. It was true. It was also something he hated. But he had no idea how to stop it. These challenges had been going on for so many years, they'd become a part of his life. And there was no way out. As long as Ritter Sloane lived, there would be another man waiting for the chance to kill him and claim a reputation.

He'd tried to explain it all to the Benteens. But none of them would listen. Maybe *now* they would.

"All right!" Dixie shouted suddenly. "Fight's finished. Tucker, you get goin' now. But you can take that damn fool of Butler's with you! I got to get my place put back together."

"Yes, ma'am." Sheriff Tucker reached over, grabbed Jed's shirtfront, and hauled him out of his chair. With the younger man mumbling incoherently and stumbling over his own feet, Tucker led him through the doorway and down the street toward the jail.

"Micah, Jericho, Shad?"

All three turned to look at Dixie.

"You boys get busy. I want this place ready to go come nightfall." Then she sighed. "Well, at *least* by tomorrow." With a none-too-clean bar towel, she pushed broken shards of glass onto the littered floor. "I swear, I never *seen* so much trouble as when you three come to town! Of all the . . ." She kept muttering as she walked toward the storeroom door.

Jericho grinned, Shadrack pushed his rust-red hair out of his eyes, and Micah frowned. "What the hell'th *she'th* tho mad about? *We* got to clean thith meth up!"

Slapping his brother on the back, Jericho burst into laughter, stepped over one of the fallen combatants, and followed Dixie, Micah right behind him.

Shad paused for a moment and glanced at his sister. "You all right, Hallie?"

"Fine, Shad."

He nodded and joined his brothers.

She looked up at her husband, her eyes moving over his split lip, the swelling on his left jaw, and the spreading bruise over his left eye. His hat gone, Ritter's blond hair fell across his forehead, and his pale blue eyes were narrowed as he looked at the destruction around him.

"Ritter?" she said softly, tugging at his arm. "This wasn't your fault. Don't pay no mind to Tucker."

Slowly he turned his head and looked down at her. She hurried on. "I *mean* it. You done the right thing. Hell, if Tucker wants to blame this on somebody, he ought to go out and get Ham Butler! This whole mess is 'cause he's hirin' fightin' men!"

Ritter snorted and shook his head. "No, Hallie. This wasn't Butler's fault, or Jed's fault, or even *mine*!"

Her brow wrinkled.

"The fight had nothin' to do with Ritter Sloane, or the Benteens, or Ham Butler." His hand covered hers and squeezed. "This . . . *mess*, dear wife, was *your* fault."

Chapter

Nine

"*MY* FAULT?" Hallie gaped at him. Eyes wide, her index finger jabbing at her own breast, she said again, louder this time, *"My fault!"*

"That's right." Ritter looked around the room, his gaze moving over upturned tables and chairs, spilled beer, and shattered glass. Finally he spotted what he was looking for, crossed the room quickly, and snatched his crumpled hat off the floor.

"Hah!" Hallie clumsily made her way closer to him, despite all the obstacles. "If you hadn't showed up, all full of piss and vinegar, none a this woulda happened!"

One pale eyebrow rose over his good eye and Ritter nodded. *"Very* nicely put, Mrs. Sloane."

"Damn you anyway, Ritter! If it wasn't for me, you'd have been in a *gunfight*, for corn's sake!"

He cocked his head and stared at her. "I *am* a gunfighter, Hallie. It's what I do. Besides," he added, brushing at the dirt on the crown of his hat, "if you hadn't come to town, *alone*, none of this would have happened."

"Yeah, well if you hadn't been nuzzlin' and cozyin' up to me in the first place, you wouldn't have to worry over me at all, would ya?"

"True. And if you hadn't gone out in a snowstorm, *alone*, and let a tree fall on you, I wouldn't have had to save you, would I?"

She chewed her lip for a moment, then countered, "If you hadn't hired on with Butler, though, you wouldn't have been nowhere *near* our place that night." Hallie jerked her head in a sharp nod, crossed her arms over her chest, and stared at him, proud that she'd brought the whole situation home to roost with him. As it should.

Slowly Ritter put his hat on, wincing as he settled it over the bruises and lumps. Then he met her gaze squarely and pointed out, "If I *hadn't* been at your place that night—you'd be dead."

"Oh."

"That's right, 'oh.' You'd be frozen solid under that damn tree. Hell, your idiot brothers probably wouldn't even have found you until spring thaw!"

"Don't you take in on the boys, now, Ritter Sloane! Wasn't they just right alongside you, *helpin'* you?"

"You call that *helping*?"

Jericho's laughter boomed out from behind the storeroom door and both of them turned sharply in that direction. But the door didn't open.

Finally Hallie sighed tiredly. "Ritter, how 'bout we just call this here a draw and go on home? I am purely tuckered out."

He turned his head to look at her. She saw the suddenly determined glitter in his eyes and wondered what he was plannin' on. Before she could ask, though, Ritter pulled a deep breath into his lungs, grabbed Hallie's hand, and started for the door.

"Where we goin'?" She tried to slow him down, leaning

back against the pull of his hand, but it was impossible. He simply tugged harder, and she found herself running to keep up. "Ritter, what in the name of creation are you up to?"

He flicked a glance back at her and frowned. "Something I *should* have done before this!"

Hallie's mind raced with the possibilities *that* statement created. But she didn't have much time to think about it. He was already crossing the street, heading for Elmira Huggins's store.

The bell over the front door jumped and clanged when they entered, and Elmira had to leap back out of the way. Hallie knew the older woman had been standing just inside the door, trying desperately to keep an eye on what was happening at the saloon. No doubt she'd be getting all the details from Dixie by nightfall.

"Hallie dear," the round, friendly woman cooed. "Is everything all right? You weren't hurt in that melee, were you? Good heavens, the noise was absolutely *frightful*. Sounded as though a buffalo herd was stampeding through Dixie's place." Her sharp brown eyes moved quickly from Hallie to Ritter and back again. "I hope no one was hurt."

"No, Miz Huggins," Hallie said, knowing full well that the woman wanted to hear *everything*. "Nobody got hurt any."

"Oh, well." The woman's face fell into disappointed lines. "That's good." She darted a quick look up at the purpling bruise over Ritter's left eye. Her own eyes narrowed, and she chewed at her lip thoughtfully.

"Madam."

"Hmmm?" Elmira Huggins shook her head sharply and silently cursed herself for wandering off. The man had been speaking to her, and she might have missed something important already! "Yes?"

Ritter sighed and avoided looking into those too sharp eyes. "Do you happen to carry a selection of *rings*?"

"Rings?"

"Rings. Specifically, wedding rings."

The woman's lips pursed, and she fairly twinkled with delight as her gaze fell on Hallie. "Why, yes. Of *course* I do!" She grabbed Hallie and tugged her toward the counter. "It just so happens I have a *lovely* little ring right over here that would look *wonderful* on you, my dear."

Hallie stared up at her husband and desperately tried to read his features. But there was no indication of what he was thinking. He simply stood there while Elmira dragged out a single wooden tray holding all manner of rings. In fact, he didn't speak at all until the woman held up a particularly gaudy ring with a "ruby" so big it'd take two hands just to wear it.

"This is a lovely piece," Elmira murmured softly, her index finger caressing the huge chunk of red glass.

"Yes, yes, it is. . . ."

Hallie turned on him. "If you think I'm gonna *wear* that thing, mister . . . well, you best forget that notion, here and now."

Elmira frowned at her.

Ritter ignored her.

"Actually, Mrs. Huggins," he was saying, "*this* was more what I had in mind. . . ." He took a wide gold band from the tray and inspected it closely, turning it this way and that in the waning light.

"Now, just hold on a durn minute here, Ritter," Hallie warned.

"This will do fine," Ritter said to Elmira. "How much do I owe you?"

"Oh, my," the woman said, her hand to one rounded cheek. "Let me think, now . . ." She began rummaging through one of the drawers behind the counter, flipping through page after page of figures. "Ah, yes, here we are!" Then she turned to face him, a question in her eyes. "That one there is five dollars, Mr. Sloane."

"Five dollars!" Hallie's voice cracked.

"It's one of my best, Hallie."

"And worth every penny, I'm sure," Ritter soothed her. He reached into one of his pockets and pulled out a gold piece. Sliding it across the counter, he said, "Would you just apply the change to the Benteens' bill? They *do* have one, don't they?"

"Lord love you, yes! Yes, indeed!"

"We've been payin' on it regular, Elmira." Hallie's eyes flashed dangerously as she glared at her husband. "Us Benteens can take care of it our ownselves, Ritter. We don't need you to do it for us!"

"Now, now, Hallie," Elmira cooed as she slipped the gold coin into the cashbox, "you should learn right off not to argue with your husband, dear."

"Wise advice, indeed, ma'am." Ritter bowed his head and grabbed Hallie's hand. As they went outside, he heard Elmira shout, "Be sure to come back, now!"

On the boardwalk Hallie pulled up short, snatching her hand free of Ritter's grasp. "What do you think you're doin', mister? Buyin' me rings, payin' our bills . . . The boys ain't gonna like that much, y'know . . ."

"Hallie," he ground out through clenched teeth, "I don't much care *what* your brothers like." Then he grabbed her left hand and forcibly uncurled her fingers from the fist she'd made. Holding her ring finger straight up, he slid the wide band on with a satisfied nod. "*That* should do it! Even that fool Jed wouldn't be able to miss this ring."

"I reckon not!" Hallie pulled her hand back and immediately tried to tug it off. "It's so damn big it's weighin' my hand down!"

He reached out and pushed her other hand away. "Leave the ring be, Hallie. If you'd been wearing one of these today, that scene in the bar might not have happened." In the space of a heartbeat his expression changed, softened. "That's my fault. I should have thought of it before, but—"

"Oh, hell, Ritter"—she smiled and shrugged—"don't worry about it any." Looking down at the ring again, she sighed. "Well, I don't suppose it'd hurt me any to wear it till you leave, now, will it?"

She watched his smile fade and his eyes darken and couldn't figure out what she'd said to make him mad all over again. But once again she had no time to think as he began dragging her down the boardwalk toward the center of town.

As the afternoon light faded into dusk, they moved from store to store in a steady progression. Nothing she said slowed him down, much less stopped him. Unwillingly, Hallie visited the dressmaker, the milliner, the gunsmith—where her husband bought her a beautiful two-shot derringer—then finally back to Elmira's for a pair of ladies' shoes.

Everywhere they went, it was the same story. The

townsfolk's initial fear of Ritter was washed away in the face of his charming manner and his seemingly unending supply of gold coins.

Hallie had been prodded, poked, pinned, tugged, and altogether disgruntled for what seemed forever before Ritter was finally ready to call a halt and head for the cabin. At the livery stable she stood beside the rig Ritter'd rented to carry all their packages home.

Her gaze moved over the mountain of brown-paper-wrapped parcels, and an odd twinge of hurt battled with the excitement she felt over her new things.

Leaning back against the wagon, Hallie bit at her thumbnail and remembered the dressmaker's face as she'd brought out gown after gown for Ritter's approval. *Ritter's approval.* Hallie'd known the woman her whole life, and yet Cora'd hardly *looked* at her the entire time they'd been in the shop. No, it had been "Yes, Mr. Sloane. . . . Of course, Mr. Sloane. . . ." It was enough to make a body sick. Grown women fawnin' all over a man just 'cause he was pretty and rich to boot.

All she had to do was close her eyes, and she could see the whole embarrassing scene all over again. While Ritter sat himself in a chair by the front window, Cora'd had Hallie in the back room, trying on more dresses than Hallie'd ever seen before. And each time she got one just so, she'd trot Hallie out so Ritter could take a look at her and decide if it was "acceptable."

And the men weren't any different, she told herself hotly. Why, Gus the gunsmith fairly crawled all over himself to talk weapons with the famous gunfighter. He hadn't even bothered to ask Hallie after the boys.

She couldn't understand what was happening to everybody. Hell, she didn't even understand what was happening to *her*. She should have been pleased with the dresses and whatnots her husband had bought her. Hadn't she always wanted a *real* set of girl's underdrawers? All that lace and the soft material felt real good against her skin.

But, Hallie thought as she glanced down at her worn buckskins, him buyin' all that stuff, didn't it just mean he didn't think much of the *real* her? She stiffened when she heard his bootsteps approaching. Well, no matter the fine feathers . . . Hallie knew that, deep down, she'd always be wearin' buckskin. And nothin' Ritter Sloane could do would change that. Whether he liked it or not.

"Hallie?"

She turned around to face him and ignored the stable owner's beaming face.

"Are you ready to go?"

She bit her tongue to keep from shouting, I've been ready to go for two hours! Instead, she nodded and climbed up onto the seat before he could come around to help her up. Keeping her eyes straight ahead, Hallie felt the wagon sway when Ritter got in. From the corner of her eye, she saw him reach forward for the reins and heard him tell the hostler, "I'll get your rig back to you tomorrow."

She didn't say anything. But when the stable man called out after them, "Be sure to come back now!" Hallie growled, low in her throat.

Without lanterns on the buggy, the trip to the ranch was a slow, cautious one. Quiet, too. Ritter glanced at his wife from the corner of his eye and saw that she hadn't changed position in the slightest. Back ramrod stiff, eyes straight ahead, and chin lifted stubbornly, Hallie was determined to ignore him.

He gripped the reins tightly and the horse reared its head back angrily in response. Relaxing his hold again, Ritter pulled in a deep breath and tried to think.

Reluctantly he thought about the mad shopping trip he'd dragged Hallie through. He'd never come across a woman so thoroughly hardheaded. Why, the women he'd known over the years would have *loved* having him spend his money on them. They'd have cooed and smiled their way through hundreds of dollars. But not Hallie.

All right, maybe he hadn't gone about it the right way. Maybe he should have been polite and patient. But his patience had met the end of its rope when he'd walked into the saloon and seen that bastard running his hand up Hallie's thigh. Even now a swell of anger rose in him at the memory.

It was those damned tight-fitting buckskins of hers, he knew. Every day his own eyes followed every move she made. Her curved backside and shapely legs drove him to the edge of madness . . . Was it any wonder they had the same effect on others?

Hell, couldn't she *see* what she did to a man just by walking past him? Couldn't she see that it had taken every ounce of his hard-won self-discipline to keep from holding her, touching her?

Suddenly she shifted on the seat beside him. Scooting down farther on the seat, she propped her right foot up on the edge of the rig and rested her hand on her upraised knee.

Ritter tore his gaze away from the enticing line of her leg and swore silently. No. She didn't know.

But dammit, her *brothers* had to know! Being men, they should have realized years ago that their sister had no business parading around in public in clothes that invited trouble.

The buggy hit a hole in the road, and the two people were slammed together for a moment. Hallie pushed away quickly, and Ritter said, "Why don't you just spit it out, Hallie?"

"What?"

"I said, spit it out." He glanced at her in the moonlit darkness, then turned his gaze back to the road ahead of him. "You've had something to say ever since we left Stillwater, and I'd just as soon hear it as watch you trying to keep quiet."

"Wouldn't do me no good to say it."

"Well, now, how do you know that if you don't try?"

"Hmmph!" She snorted inelegantly and glared at him. "I know 'cause I just spent the best part of two hours *tryin'* to tell you while you hauled me all over town like some child!"

His fingers tightened on the reins, but he kept his voice calm. "Fine. Tell me now."

She turned toward him, and even in the chill of the night, Ritter felt the heat of her fury.

"All right, I will." She pulled in a deep gulp of air and started talking in a rush. "Just who the *hell* do you think you are, Sloane? Who gives3 you the right to drag me in and out of stores, buyin' me things I don't want and ain't gonna wear? Nobody, not my brothers, nor my pa when he was alive, *ever* did to me what you did today."

"What did I do that was so terrible?" His own anger was surging again despite his efforts to contain it.

"What did you do?" Hallie's voice rose and seemed to echo off the dark shadows of the trees lining the road. "Hell, you made me look like a damn fool! Draggin' me into Cora's place, then sittin' there like a damn king or somethin', tellin' that woman what I'd wear and what I wouldn't." She leaned in close, and he felt her breath on his cheek. "Well, I'll tell you somethin', *Mr. Sloane*, I ain't gonna wear a *one* of them dresses."

"You will if you plan on going into town again."

"Hah!" She sat back hard. "Not on your life, gunfighter. And there's not a damn thing you can do to make me."

"Don't you push me, Hallie."

"Like I said, mister. You ain't my brother *or* my pa. You got no say in anything."

He jerked back on the reins suddenly, and the horse reared to a stop. Ritter slammed the brake handle home, wrapped the leather reins around it, then turned to face the infuriating woman beside him.

In the vague half light of moonlit shadows, Ritter stared at her, anger battling with the desire he'd been denying for too long. His gaze moved over the stubborn set of her jaw to her lips, clamped together mutinously, to the moonlight winking off the silver hoops in her ears. Almost before he realized it himself, he was pulling her to him, wrapping his arms around her, and lowering his mouth to claim hers.

There was nothing gentle in his kiss. Nothing soft or seductive. Only a furious need to touch, to quench a thirst that seemed to have been with him a lifetime. He groaned when her lips parted under his, and he felt her last token resistance melt away. Eagerly his tongue explored her warmth, tasting her, reveling in the overwhelming sensation of coming home.

Hallie's arms snaked up around his neck, and she pressed herself against him. Shifting slightly, Ritter drew her onto his lap and his hands moved frantically over her trembling body. It was as if he couldn't move quickly enough. Couldn't touch her enough. His right hand slid over her back, around her small waist, and up to her breast. Only then did he slow his movements. Gently, reverently, he cupped her breast, and his thumb moved over her peaked nipple with a touch as soft as a sigh.

Hallie moaned and he swallowed the sound, unwilling to break a kiss that filled him with more contentment than he'd ever known.

Finally he pulled back and looked down into her eyes. She reached up and laid her palm against his cheek, and Ritter was shaken to the core by her touch.

Suddenly, though, the buggy rocked violently as the horse pulled against its restraints. He snatched at the reins and, at the same time, shifted Hallie back to the seat beside him. Once the horse was under control again, Ritter spoke softly to the woman next to him.

"I'm not your brother, Hallie. Nor your father." He glanced at her. "I'm your husband."

She met his gaze steadily. Even in the darkness Ritter saw that her breathing was still ragged. Desperately he looked away from the rise and fall of her breasts and stared into her eyes instead.

"No, you're not," she argued quietly.

"What?"

"I said, you're not my husband. Not rightly. A few kisses and a gold ring don't make you a husband." She straightened up and drew in a shaky breath. "No husband

I ever heard tell of slept on top of the covers away from his wife."

"Hallie . . ."

"No, sir." She turned away and looked off down the road. "We had us a bargain, and you ain't lived up to your end of it."

"I told you I'd think about that."

Hallie shook her head slowly. "You're out of time, gunfighter." She cocked her head and looked at him. "See, I don't know a whole lot about this husband and wife stuff, but I ain't ashamed to admit that I purely enjoy it when you kiss me and . . ." Her gaze dropped.

Ritter lifted her chin and waited for her to look at him before answering, "I . . . enjoy that, too, Hallie."

"Then what's wrong? Why do ya have to go on thinkin'? Why can't we just . . . *you* know! Is it 'cause I ain't a lady? Is that it?"

"No!" he shouted at her, and the horse jumped, startled. How the hell had all this happened to him? he wondered. "It's nothing like that, Hallie. And you *are* a lady. A *true* lady. You have courage, strength, and a gentle heart."

"Then what the hell's keepin' you, man? I ain't never done this kind of thing before, but even *I* can tell ya like to touch me! Your breathin' goes all funny, and I hear your heart poundin' every bit as hard as mine!"

He groaned.

"We're married. Legal. I don't see why you don't want to give me a baby! Appears to me that the gettin' is most of the fun!"

"Hallie . . ." He shook his head. It was impossible to argue with that kind of logic.

"No, sir." She laid her left hand on his arm, and they

both looked down at the wide gold band on her finger.
"I'll let you think on it till we get back to the ranch. Then
you decide, Ritter. Are you my husband or ain't ya?" She
reached over to touch his cheek with her right hand, and
he felt the warmth of her down to his soul. "And if you
are fixin' to be my husband . . . well, then, you and me
can get started on that baby girl right off."

Chapter

Ten

HALLIE MOVED through the dark ranch house confidently. Pausing only for a moment, she struck a match taken from the sideboard, then held the tiny flame to the wick of an oil lamp. She turned the wick down a bit, replaced the glass chimney, and tossed the spent match into the cold fireplace.

Taking a deep breath, she crossed the floor to her bedroom and went inside. Ritter'd already dropped the packages they'd brought home on the floor by the closet, and her eyes went unerringly to one of the smaller parcels. Slowly she bent down to pick it up. The brown paper rustled as she gripped the soft bundle tightly. Turning her head slightly, Hallie looked over at her bed and just managed to control the shivering that began at the base of her spine.

There was no backing out now, she told herself. Not after all her brave talk. She would have Ritter's decision soon, and whatever it was, she'd have to live with it. And even though she wanted him to choose her, she couldn't quite squelch the butterflies flyin' in her stomach.

What if she did somethin' wrong? What if she wasn't any good at this?

Hallie looked in the small mirror on the wall and saw her own wide eyes staring back at her. Her teeth worried her bottom lip, and she wondered frantically if there was somethin' she was supposed to know.

She heard him moving around the great room and then the familiar sound of a fire being laid in the hearth. Determinedly she set the package down and began to unbutton her shirt. One way or another, things between them would be settled soon.

Ritter glanced at the partially closed door to Hallie's room and saw her shadow move across the wall. He looked away and stared down into the flames just beginning to lick at the fresh logs he'd laid on the grate.

Outside, the wind had picked up, and the first teasing drops of rain began to pelt the windows.

Ritter pushed himself to his feet and jammed his hands in his pockets. Frowning down into the fire, he tried to make his mind work rationally. But no matter how many times his brain reminded him of who and what he was, a small voice urged him to forget all that. To be Hallie's husband in reality, as well as name. That same voice whispered that he didn't *have* to leave. That somehow, he would find a way to stay with her. To finally find a home. A family.

He cursed quietly, pulled his hands free, and shoved them through his hair as if he could quiet the voices in his mind. But there was no end to them. Just as there was no end to his need for Hallie. He'd tried. Lord, how he'd tried. But simply being around her was enough to drive him to the end of his endurance. Her voice, her laugh, her smile. The way her short hair curled around her ears, and the way those silver hoops danced when she moved. The curve of her hip, the touch of her hand, the way she sighed into his mouth when he kissed her . . .

An all too familiar tightening gripped his body, and he groaned softly with his need for her.

The floorboards in the other room creaked as his wife moved about quietly. His wife. His brows drew together and he squinted into the growing fire. She was right. They *were* married. Legally. There was no reason for them to continue to stay apart.

No reason except the one he could never forget. A man who made his living from death was hardly the kind of man *anyone* should want for a husband!

And yet . . . he leaned forward and curled his fingers over the mantel. One boot propped up on the hearth, his head fell forward, his chin on his chest. Would it be so wrong? Hell, even her *family* thought they were truly man and wife!

And what about the baby she wants? his mind questioned. Could he really leave her, knowing that she carried his child? God knew, it would be hard enough just turning his back on Hallie . . . though he knew that it would be the best possible thing for her. Marriage to a gunfighter was not the life he'd wish for her. She deserved better.

Besides, he reminded himself with a sudden surge of hope, there were ways to prevent conceiving a child. He would just have to be careful. Controlled.

Abruptly he straightened. That was that, then. He'd made up his mind. For what little time they had together, Ritter wanted at least the *pretense* of a real marriage. He wanted to know the feeling of belonging . . . for however long it lasted.

He heard nothing, and yet somehow, he knew she was there. Waiting. Slowly he turned to look at her. His breath rushed out and his heartbeat staggered. She stood in the open doorway of her bedroom with only the palest glimmer of lamplight behind her.

His gaze moved over her slowly, lovingly. The nightgown he'd bought her to replace those threadbare long johns she slept in was not accomplishing what he'd thought it would. Somehow, he'd thought that a long-sleeved, high-necked white gown would be much easier on his strained nerves than the clinging drawers that showed far too much of her body for his comfort. But he was wrong.

The supposedly chaste gown only served to whet his curiosity for what lay beneath it. Her breasts, defined by the lay of the soft material, rose and fell quickly with her nervous breathing, and her bare toes peeked out from beneath the hem of the gown. Suddenly all he wanted to do was to lift the nightdress off completely and run his palms over her body until he lost himself in the warmth of her.

Her eyes sparkled in the reflected firelight, and he swallowed heavily. Rain pounded against the roof, and Ritter felt his heartbeat quicken to match it.

He pushed away from the mantel and crossed the room to her. When he was just a step away, he stopped. She looked up at him, and the nervous hunger in her green eyes swamped him. But still, he thought to give her one last chance to change her mind.

"Hallie," he whispered, one hand reaching for an auburn

curl lying against her neck, "are you sure?"

"I ain't the one who wasn't sure, Ritter. It was you holdin' back. . . ."

His fingers moved over the flesh of her throat, and he felt her tremble.

"So," Hallie breathed, her tongue moving over suddenly dry lips, "did ya make up your mind?"

He nodded and his fingers slid over the curve of her ear.

"Well, then"—she turned her head into his touch and managed to say—"what's it gonna be, Ritter? Husband . . . or not?"

He moved in closer to her, cupped the back of her head with one hand, and covered her mouth with his. His breath was warm on her cheek, and Hallie jumped a bit when his other hand curved around her waist and pulled her tight against him. Finally, though, he broke the kiss and whispered, "I'll be your husband, Hallie . . ." She looked up into his eyes and read sadness there. "For as long as I can."

Before she could answer, he swept her up into his arms and cradled her against his chest. He stepped into her bedroom and kicked the door shut behind him. After quickly walking to the bed, he tossed the old quilt back with one hand, then gently laid her down in the center of the mattress.

The butterflies in her stomach began to swarm, and she heard her own blood rushing through her veins. She couldn't tear her eyes from him as he stood beside the bed and slowly took off his shirt. As each button pulled free, Hallie's gaze dropped with the loose fabric. The hard, muscled expanse of his chest drew her touch as surely as a magnet. When she reached for him and her fingers gently slid over his skin, he inhaled sharply.

Quickly then, he undid his gunbelt and slipped out of his boots and pants. For the space of a heartbeat he stood quietly under her steady gaze, then lay down beside her, drawing her into the circle of his arms.

And then Hallie was swept into a tornado of feelings, each more exciting than the last. His mouth on her neck, his tongue teasing the soft flesh of her throat. His breath hot against her skin, Hallie closed her mind to everything but him. Eyes closed, head tilted back into the pillow, she heard the rain and the wind beating against the house, and never had she felt so safe.

Ritter's right hand reached down and lifted the hem of her new nightdress. As he drew it up the length of her body, his fingers caressed her skin, bringing gooseflesh that had nothing to do with the cold. She shuddered slightly when his hand slid over the inside of her thigh, but parted her legs for him so that she might experience more of his touch.

He smiled and moved his fingers instead to the tiny pearl buttons at the neck of her gown. One by one, he pushed them free and dipped his head to kiss the line of flesh exposed to him. When the buttons were finally finished, Ritter slipped the gown off over her head and sighed his satisfaction.

For one crazy moment Hallie wanted to pull the blanket up over herself but then Ritter bent his head to her breast and took her nipple into his mouth. All nervousness fled as a surge of pleasure filled her, and she arched her back, trying to get even closer. His tongue flicked damp heat against the sensitive bud, and she reached for him blindly, needing to touch him in return. Hallie ran her hands over his broad back and smiled at the sigh that shook him. As her fingertips slid down his sides, Ritter shifted position slightly and levered his body just over hers.

Then he began to move slowly, brushing their naked chests together even while his right hand slid down over the curve of her hip, across her abdomen, and down to the center of the heat engulfing her.

Hallie jumped when his hand cupped her damp, tingling flesh. But he soothed her with a whispered caress. And as his fingers slipped inside her body for the first time, Ritter captured her moan with his mouth. She opened for him eagerly, wantonly. His tongue moved over hers in a slow dance of promise while his touch drove her to the edge of madness.

Hallie couldn't seem to be still. It was as though her body had been awakened all at once, and if she didn't move, she would shatter. Her hands moved over Ritter's chest and back. Her nails dragged along his skin, and she raised her hips against his hand, searching for something she couldn't quite name. His thumb moved lazily over the bud of her sex, and Hallie tore her mouth from his, gasping for the air that wouldn't come fast enough. Her head tilted back on her neck, knees bent, she silently willed him to do more. To touch more of her, to create more of the almost unbearable sensations coursing through her body.

Every inch of her flesh was on fire. It was as though she were climbing some unseen hill. With every step she came closer to the top. To completion. And each step racked her already trembling body with new shudders. Dimly she heard his voice, whispering to her, caressing her ears with the soft sound even as his hands tormented her flesh with almost agonizing tenderness.

She licked her lips and opened her eyes slightly to see Ritter, his pale eyes smoky, watching her. Hallie groaned and turned her head aside. She couldn't bear to have him see how little control he'd left her with. But Ritter wouldn't be ignored.

He pulled his hand from her warmth and quickly positioned himself between her thighs. When he didn't touch her again, Hallie opened her eyes to slits and looked at him. In the lamplight his muscled chest shone with perspiration, and when he ran his hands up over her chest to cup both breasts, Hallie smiled at the sight of his sun-browned skin against her pale, milky flesh. Then she raised her gaze to his, and her breath caught in her throat.

In his eyes was more hunger, more passion than she'd ever hoped to see, and instinctively her hips moved in invitation before she could stop herself. As if he could read her mind, Ritter let his hands slide over her heated body while he held her gaze with his own.

His thumb grazed the edge of her erect nipple, and she bit down on her lip and stifled the moan that threatened to escape. Deliberately then, Ritter leaned over her and caught her lips with his own teeth in a brief, nibbling kiss. When he pulled back, he waited for her to open her eyes and look at him.

"Don't hide your pleasure from me, Hallie," he whispered and lowered his mouth to the line of her throat. Her pulse beat madly beneath his lips, and she barely heard him add, "Give me your sighs," before his lips moved to close over her nipple once more. This time, though, he began to suckle her, and Hallie gasped aloud, all fear of embarrassment gone. Lightning like shots of pleasure stabbed her, and she felt the power of his mouth down to her bones. All she could think of was getting closer to him.

She held his head to her breast with one hand and wiggled her hips in a silent appeal. He pulled back almost regretfully, giving the tiny pink bud one last kiss before straightening before her. His hands slipped under her hips to cup her behind, and when he lifted her for his entry, Hallie held her breath, eyes closed.

As she felt his body moving into hers, though, she smiled and reached for him. Her fingers clutched at his thighs, drawing him in farther. He filled her with himself, and Hallie groaned only slightly as she adjusted herself to his presence. Then he began to move, slowly at first, giving her time to learn the dance, and when she began to race with him to the conclusion, Ritter's fingers moved to stroke the core of her. Gasping for breath, Hallie shuddered under the avalanche of feelings until she felt her soul splinter. His cry echoed her own, and Hallie rocked him in her arms as he joined her.

The saloon was still a mess. Dixie pursed her lips and stared at the broken tables and chairs littering the floor. Her eyes swept to the bar, and she frowned into what was left of her elegant mirror. Several jagged images of herself stared back and glared at the men behind her.

Abruptly she spun around, hands on hips and one foot tapping impatiently against the floor.

The Benteen brothers were actually more hindrance than help, she knew, but by heaven . . . when they wrecked the place, they could damn well put it back together. Even if it took them all night! Watching Jericho and Shad laugh at Micah's attempts to talk, she sighed and told herself that it no doubt would.

Shad leaned on his broom handle and smiled down at Micah. "Say somethin' else," he urged.

Micah glared at him.

"C'mon, Micah," Jericho added, "you ain't usually so shy."

"Are you three going to work or not?" Dixie called from across the room.

"Sure, Dix." Jericho looked up and smiled. "Got about all the glass cleaned up. We're gonna need some hammers and such to fix the tables up, though."

She shook her head. "They're in the back room where you left them the last time."

Shad dropped the broom. "I'll get 'em."

A blast of cold wind rushed through the broken front window, sending a sheet of rain over Dixie. She yelped and jumped back. "Shad, bring some canvas out of the storeroom, too."

"Reckon so. It's turnin' into a helluva blow, huh?"

"Yes." She turned flashing eyes on him. "In fact, it's raining so hard . . . you boys might as well stay right here tonight and finish up the job."

Jericho groaned and dropped into one of the few chairs still standing.

Dixie wasn't moved.

"Thay, Dikthie," Micah started but was drowned out by Jericho's laughter.

Micah kicked at his brother and went on. "Ya mind bringin' uth thome beerth? Thith ith thirthty work here."

Shad leaned against the wall and tried to cover his grin with one hand while holding his middle with the other.

Jericho didn't even try. He laughed so hard he nearly fell out of his chair.

Dixie ignored both of the laughing fools and brushed aside Micah's furious expression.

"What in heaven's name is wrong, Micah? I've seen you in any number of fights—you've never talked like that before."

"Aw, I bit my tongue, and now ith all thwole up."

Her eyes rolled and she turned to get the beers. It would be a long night.

Ritter settled back against the pillows and drew Hallie in closer. Her head on his shoulder, he stared across the room at the flickering lamplight and tried to understand what had just happened to him.

Never in his life had he experienced anything like making love to Hallie Benteen. No, not Benteen, he silently corrected. Hallie Sloane. His wife. Idly his fingers moved through her short curls and toyed with one of the silver hoops lying against her throat. His heart still pounded in his chest, and his breath was still uneven, ragged.

He ran his hand down over her shoulder and stroked her soft skin. She sighed and snuggled in closer to him, her breath warm on his flesh. Lightly then, Hallie's hand slid over his smooth chest until her fingers settled on one hard nipple. He shuddered and caught her hand in his.

Her head tilted back against his shoulder, she whispered, "Somethin' wrong, Ritter?"

He snorted. "No. No, Hallie, nothing's wrong." He lifted her hand and studied the gleam of the gold band in the lamplight.

As if reading his thoughts, she wiggled her fingers and

said, "Reckon I really *am* your wife now, ain't I?"

His hand curled over hers, and he pressed it to his chest. "Yes. I reckon."

She kissed the pulse beat in his throat and chuckled softly.

"What's so funny?"

"Oh, nothin'," she answered, "it's only that . . ." Hallie pulled back to look at him, her eyes sparkling and her cheeks flushed. "Well, it's a pure wonder there ain't children runnin' all over everywhere, is all."

"What?"

She leaned in and moved her mouth over his for a brief kiss. "Children. Babies." Deliberately she boldly brushed her breasts over his chest and smiled at the rough feel of his skin beneath hers. "Why, if makin' babies is *this* much fun, I'm surprised we all ain't hip deep in youngsters!"

Babies. Ritter stifled the groan threatening to choke him. Dear God, he'd forgotten all of his high-minded ideas about control. About preventing a child. His eyelids squeezed shut as he admitted silently that he'd forgotten everything except the wonder of Hallie. He slanted a look at her. Even now it might be too late. Even now his child could be quickening in her.

For one instant he allowed himself to feel the swell of pride and pleasure that rushed through him at the thought. How he would have enjoyed seeing her small body grow with his baby. How he would have loved it.

She moved her leg up over his thighs, and he pulled in another strangled breath. His brief, fanciful notion disappeared in the face of the truth. It wouldn't happen. He wasn't destined to experience that kind of life. That kind of happiness. It would be better for both of them if they remembered that.

How could he have been so stupid? Never before had he lost the upper hand in *any* situation. She moved again, and he felt her lips trailing over his chest. His hand slipped to her back, and he *tried* to make her stop. But she refused to be halted by his strong grip, and then her mouth closed over his nipple, her teeth and tongue doing to him what he'd done to her such a short time before.

"Hallie . . ." Words caught in his suddenly too dry throat. Despite his best intentions, his body was already responding eagerly to her caresses.

"Hmmm?" Still she didn't stop.

"Hallie, we shouldn't, uh . . ." Ritter groaned and pulled back from her. "It's too soon. You're going to be sore enough as it is." He pulled in a shaky breath and tried not to look at her small, perfect breasts, nipples hardened in anticipation.

She smiled softly, shook her head, and moved in closer again. "I feel *fine*, husband." Her fingers teased one of his nipples while she bent her head to the other. In between kisses, she told him, "I been ridin' horses every day for years, Ritter." She slowly rubbed her breasts against him. "I don't think ridin' my man for one night is gonna hurt me any . . ."

"Oh, Lord . . ." He groaned once more and let his head drop onto the pillow. How could he argue with a woman like that? How could he find control when in truth he really didn't *want* it?

She moved again and lay full length atop him. His hands slid up and down over her flesh until he felt as though he were on fire. Her lips came down on his, and when her tongue entered his mouth, all thoughts of resistance ended. Ritter couldn't think anymore. All he knew was that he had to have her. He had to hold her and be held.

His arms closed around her, and when she planted her thighs on either side of his hips, he knew he was lost. She pulled back from him just slightly and rose up on her knees.

Her gaze locked with his, Hallie's fingers moved with a feather touch over his abdomen and then slipped lower until she found what she sought. With gentle, caressing motions, her touch took him higher and farther than he'd thought possible. His hands gripped her thighs, and when she slowly, languidly lowered her body onto his, Ritter groaned at the exquisite torture she dealt him.

Head thrown back on her neck, Hallie sat atop him and ground her hips in a slow circle. She smiled as she rocked her body on his, and then gradually she raised up on her knees only to impale herself again inch by tantalizing inch. He watched her every movement. Every soft, secretive smile that curved her lips, every breath that shook her. Her actions fed his hunger, and he couldn't have looked away if it had meant his life.

Her undisguised pleasure in lovemaking was an aphrodisiac more powerful than any magic potion, and suddenly his need for her was overpowering.

Ritter reached out and took her distended nipples between his fingers. She moaned from deep in her throat and leaned toward him slightly, giving her body into his touch while at the same time moving her hips in a ceaseless motion that drove them both higher than the time before.

Then Ritter's fingers slid down her rib cage, over her flat belly, to the neat triangle of curls that rested where their bodies met. Tenderly his fingers stroked the center of her, bringing Hallie to the brink of ecstasy. He watched spasms of delight cross her features until he reached the end of his patience.

And when neither of them could stand the wait a moment longer, Ritter clasped her hips tightly and began to move her body in the ancient rhythm already so familiar to them.

This time they reached their quest together, and locked together, they rushed eagerly into the flames consuming them.

Chapter

※

Eleven

Cheyenne, Wyoming

THE TALL, dark-haired man leaned back in the captain's chair, his long legs stretched out and crossed at the ankles. Idly he crumpled the letter in his right hand and tossed it to the table. Ignoring the fascinated stares of the other men in the saloon, he lifted the shot glass of whiskey and tossed the contents down his throat. He grimaced slightly at the raw, burning liquid, then set the glass back down carefully.

The letter had taken more than a week to find him. But, he told himself, it was worth the wait.

Ritter Sloane. The dark man smiled softly as memories drifted through his mind. It had been too many years since they'd last met. He frowned suddenly, thinking. It was in Tucson, four years ago. That little matter over rustled cattle. Too bad, he thought, that because of the interference of the local cattlemen's association, he and Sloane had lost their chance to face each other.

Abruptly the man straightened up and reached for the whiskey bottle in front of him. He poured himself another drink. It was his second. He never allowed himself more

155

than two, though at times like this, he wished he did. As if taking prescribed medicine, the man swallowed the second shot of whiskey as he had the first. Quickly, so he could enjoy the warmth of the alcohol without having to taste it.

"Mr. Pine?" A nervous, skinny man with a too long face hovered near the table.

"Yes," he answered, his voice a low rumble carrying over the whispered comments filling the room.

"Livery man says your horse is ready, Mr. Pine."

The skinny man looked about ready to jump out of his own boots.

"Fine," the dark man said. "Tell him I'll be along directly." He didn't even smile when the messenger turned and scurried out of the saloon.

Slowly he pushed himself out of the chair, dipped one hand into his pocket, and flipped a coin onto the table. Nodding at the bartender on the way out, the lean man heard only a few of the whispers that started as he left.

"Know who that is?"

"Yeah, I know."

"Who?"

"Nathan Pine, that's who."

"Nathan Pine? The *gunfighter?"*

"Yep."

"Wonder where he's headed?"

"Don't know. You just be glad you ain't there."

The morning came covered in low-hanging clouds that clung to the tall trees surrounding the cabin with a soft, cold grip.

Hallie moved in closer to Ritter's warmth and tugged

the quilt up over them both. Nose to nose on the pillows, she opened her eyes to find him watching her steadily. She reached up and pushed a stray lock of blond hair off his forehead, then ran her fingers lightly down the line of his jaw.

She stretched her legs a bit and winced at the soreness accompanying the movement. He'd been right about that after all. Prob'ly shouldn't have tried it a third time. But, she told herself, the night she'd spent had been more than worth a little discomfort. Staring back into the pale blue eyes she felt she knew so well, Hallie asked quietly, "What are you thinkin' about?"

"Nothing really." His arms tightened around her and he smiled.

"Come on," Hallie urged with a laugh. "It's somethin'. What?"

"All right, but it's going to sound a little foolish."

She waited and smiled again as he kissed her forehead gently.

"I was lying here watching you sleep and trying to figure out how you came to be called Hallie."

"What?" She grinned at him.

"Told you it was foolish." He leaned his forehead on hers. "But those three brothers of yours all have Bible names. I was wondering why it was you and your oldest brother . . ."

"Trib," she helped.

". . . don't." When he finished speaking, he tugged the quilt even higher around her shoulders and pulled her into his warmth.

"Well, that's easy enough explained," Hallie started. "Trib, he's the firstborn?" She felt him nod and went on. "Well, Mama said that it took her near three days to birth him. So when he finally come out, she named him Tribulation, for being such a tryin' child."

Ritter chuckled softly and urged her on. "And you? How did you get named Hallie?"

She tilted her head back and smiled at him. "Well, I was last born, y'see. Mama said after four boys, she took one look at me and shouted out 'Hallelujah!' Papa wrote it down in the Bible and that was that!"

Grinning, Ritter raised up slightly and ran one hand down the length of her body. As he bent his head to kiss her, he whispered, "You were named just right. *Hallelujah!*"

Hallie laughed and pulled him even closer.

"Hey, Hallie! How come you ain't got breakfast ready?" Jericho's voice shattered the morning as surely as a gunshot.

Ritter cursed and his head dropped to his chest. He rolled to one side of his wife and glared at the closed bedroom door.

"Don't pay 'em no mind," Hallie whispered and slid her fingertips over his chest. "Maybe they'll go on about their business."

But fierce pounding on the door belied that hope quickly.

"Hallie! You in there?"

She muttered something under her breath, propped herself up on one elbow and shouted, "Yes. I'm in here!"

"What's goin' on?"

Shad's voice had joined Jericho's. She rolled her eyes and felt the bed shift as Ritter moved to get up.

"Are you sick or somethin'?" Jericho called.

"No, I ain't sick, Jericho!"

"Well, how come you're still abed then?" Mumbled voices sounded as the brothers talked quietly to each other, then Jericho asked, "Sloane in there with ya?"

She flicked a glance at her husband in time to see him pull his pants up over his long legs. Hallie sighed regretfully before answering her loggerheaded brother. "Hell, yes, he's in here with me! We're married, ain't we?"

"Well, sure, Hallie. It's only that Micah thought maybe Sloane would . . ."

Ritter grumbled and jammed his arms through the sleeves of his shirt. Hallie agreed with whatever it was he was saying. Right now she'd cheerfully wish *all* of her brothers to the other side of the country! She scooted out of bed, wrapped the sheet around her, and marched clumsily to the door. When she pulled it open, the boys had the decency to look embarrassed, at least.

She watched as they looked from her to Ritter and back again before turning their gazes to the floor. But before she could say a word, Micah entered the room, walked up to his brothers, looked hard at her, and shouted, "What the Tham Hill'th goin' on here?"

Hamilton Butler stood uneasily on the boardwalk outside the Silver Spur Saloon. He shook his head as he stared at the old brown canvas stretched across Dixie's front window. *That* must've made her madder'n all get-out, he knew. He was suddenly thankful that he'd been nowhere near town during that fight.

Shifting from one foot to the other, he rubbed the toes of his boots on the backs of his pant legs. When that was done, he yanked off his hat and smoothed his hair back, then straightened the string tie around his too-tight collar.

He breathed in deeply, then blew it out in a rush. No point in putting it off any longer, he told himself. It sure as hell wouldn't get any easier. Quickly he glanced one way, then the other, and sighed his satisfaction. At least no one else was out and about this early. He purely hated the thought of other folks knowing his business.

Butler took two long steps, pushed the half door open, and went inside. His sharp gaze swept the interior, and he winced at the still-evident signs of the brawl the night before. Bits of broken glass lay in the corners, and the chairs that were beyond mending were stacked against the far wall. The whole place reeked of whiskey, and Butler guessed that a lot of Dixie's stock had been broken as well.

"What do you think, Ham?"

He spun around.

Dixie stepped out of the shadows and up to the bar. She picked up a match, struck it, and lit a lamp. After she slid the chimney back into place, she turned the wick up and looked at him. "Like it?" She waved one arm in the direction of the rubble. "You should've been here. You'd be surprised how little time it takes to break everything to pieces."

"I, uh . . . heard about the fight," Butler said and took a step closer to the bar.

She turned her back on him and went back to the table she'd been sitting at when he came in. Lifting the coffeepot off the nearby stove, she asked, "You want some coffee, Ham?"

"Yeah, Dixie. Sure." He gripped his hat tightly in both hands and walked to the table. When she'd poured them both a cup of the strong, hot brew, she sat down opposite him.

Covertly he studied her for a moment. Her long black hair was dressed as he liked it best, pulled away from her face and hanging loose down her back. She wore a dark red dressing gown with a plunging neckline and long sleeves. The same kind of ruffles that lay against her well-defined cleavage fell limply over her wrists and almost covered her small hands.

A handsome woman, Butler told himself. He'd missed her.

"Seen enough, Ham?"

His gaze snapped up to her chocolate eyes and saw the amusement there. Grudgingly he said softly, "Not near enough." He looked down at his coffee cup. Somehow it was easier to talk when he didn't have to meet her eyes. "It's been too long, Dix."

"That was your choice, Ham."

Her voice was soft, silky. Just the way he remembered it. And she was just as stubborn, too. Slowly he raised his gaze, allowing himself the time to enjoy the sight of her freckle-dusted chest. Suddenly his eyes narrowed. Cocking his head, he asked, "What happened to the necklace, Dixie?"

She reached up and lay one hand at the base of her throat. "I don't wear it anymore, Ham. If you'd come around, you would have known that."

Despite his best efforts, he found himself getting angry. He made a deliberate attempt to control his voice, though. "Why aren't you wearing that diamond, Dix? Hell, I went all the way to *Denver* for that damned thing!"

Her eyebrows shot up, and her lips quirked slightly. "I know. I was with you."

He placed his palms flat on the table and pulled in several deep breaths. Yelling wouldn't get him anywhere. He sure as hell ought to know that by now. If anything, Dixie only got *more* stubborn when she was yelled at. Butler tried again. More quietly this time. "I remember the trip, Dixie. What I want to know is, where is the diamond? You said you'd never take it off. Do you remember *that*?"

"Yes, Ham. I remember." She sat up straighter, chin up, chest out. "I also remember you saying something about letting the past bury the past? About finally lettin' go of the old hurts and gettin' on with the years you got left?"

He gritted his teeth and fought down the rush of temper swelling through him. If anyone but Dixie had talked to him like that . . .

"I took the necklace off the night you first sent for Ritter Sloane."

"Goddammit, Dixie!"

"Don't you take that 'Lord of all Wyoming' tone with *me!* This is *my* place, Hamilton Butler. You watch how you talk to me in it."

"Dixie, you don't understand." His breathing ragged, he tried desperately to rein in his anger.

"I understand plenty, Ham." She leaned across the table and stared directly into his eyes. "I understand that you've started something around here that can only end in disaster."

He didn't say anything, and she went on.

"Take a look at my place here." She swept one hand out, then slapped it down onto the table. "One of those gun-happy saddle tramps you hired started all this."

"I know." He looked up at her. "That's why I came in today. I heard about Jed and Sloane gettin' into it and—"

"Jed and Sloane? It may have started out like that, but it ended up a brawl—Devil take the hindmost!"

"I'll pay for the damages—"

"The hell with your money, Hamilton Butler!" She reached across the table and grabbed one of his powerful hands in hers. Squeezing it tightly, she added, "It's your damned money that started all this in the first place!"

"How the hell do you figure that?"

"You're payin' warrior wages to those new 'ranch hands' of yours, aren't you?" He looked away and her head jerked a nod. "Just as I thought. Well, those damned fools have more gun sense than common sense! Do you know *why* that fight started last night?" He opened his mouth but she rushed on, not giving him a chance to answer. "I'll *tell* you why! Because that good-for-nothing Jed grabbed Hallie and started to . . . well, he had no business touchin' her like that."

"He did *what* to Hallie?" No one had told him anything at all about Hallie being involved. In fact, the man who'd brought Ham the news about Jed being in jail had said precious little about *anything*.

"He was runnin' his hands all over her!"

Ham jumped to his feet and glared down at Dixie. "No one told me that! If they had I'd a gone straight to the jailhouse and shot the son of a bitch myself!"

"Lotta good that would've done."

"Is Hallie all right?" His teeth ground together in a fury of repressed anger.

"Yes."

Shoulders slumped with relief, Hamilton took another moment to collect himself before thundering, "Hell, why didn't *Sloane* shoot him?"

"Hallie stopped him. But that isn't the point here, Ham."

"What the hell *is* the point, woman?" This wasn't going at all as he'd hoped it would.

"You. You and your stubborn hatred for a man long dead is going to get people killed."

"Don't talk to me about Caleb Benteen, Dixie. I won't listen. Not even from you." He turned for the door, but she jumped up, raced around the table, and caught him before he went more than a few steps.

"I will talk about him. Thirteen years, Ham. Thirteen years you carried that damned grudge against Caleb. You already know I think that was wrong in the first place. . . ."

His jaw tight, he glared down at her, refusing to listen.

"All right. I won't talk about Caleb," she conceded. "At least, not today. But by heaven we *will* talk about this other you've started! What I want to know is why *now*? Why did you wait till now to send for a gunfighter? Why are you goin' against Hallie and the boys when you've always treated them like your own?"

Butler looked over her head at the door. He stared blankly at the only means of escape and tried not to hear her insistent voice prodding at him.

"Tell me, Ham."

Her hands smoothed over his forearms, and for a brief, glorious moment Butler allowed himself to remember the softness of her touch. To recall the nights they'd spent together over the years. All the times Dixie'd been his only friend. The times they'd lain together and listened to the silence of the night.

"Tell me. Why now?"

Her voice scattered the memories into the darkest corners of his mind. He pulled in a deep, shuddering breath, and slowly his anger dissolved. Her questions were too much like the ones he'd been asking himself. And though he knew the answers, it shamed him to admit it. Even to Dixie. He looked into her eyes and felt himself being drawn into them as he had so many times before. And suddenly the need to talk overwhelmed him.

"It was Trib," he finally said softly and looked down at her hands, still gripping his forearms.

"Trib? Why . . . ?"

"He came by the ranch house before he left six months ago."

"And?"

"*And . . .*" Butler's head fell back on his neck, and he squeezed his eyes tightly shut. "He was so full of vinegar. So pleased to be goin' off on his own. Said he wanted to see some new country. Said he was tired of listening to the boys argue and wanted to meet some new folks." Butler snorted a laugh. "Hell, I hadn't seen him look that pleased with himself since before the war."

"Then what . . . ?"

He straightened suddenly and met Dixie's eyes pleadingly. "Don't you see, Dix? The last time he was headed off to see 'new things' was when him and Devlin rode off to war together."

Dixie's brow furrowed and she bit at her bottom lip to keep from interrupting him.

"Then, after the war . . . only Trib came home." His voice broke. "Shit, I don't even know where Dev is buried!"

Dixie threw her arms around Hamilton Butler's broad shoulders and held him tightly. When he bent his head and burrowed his face into the curve of her neck, she sighed and looked heavenward. She might have known it would come down to Devlin. It always had.

And as hard as she tried, Dixie knew she could never understand the pain of losing one's only child.

After a few long minutes Butler straightened up again and sniffed loudly. He kept his arms around the woman pressed so close to him and said softly, "I guess seein' Trib doing the things I imagined Dev doin' was what done it. Something inside me just burst open, and all the mad and the pain came pouring out. Suddenly all I could think was that I had to get the Benteens out of there. I just didn't think I could stand seein' 'em every day anymore. It just hurt too much." He inhaled sharply and blew it out again. "So I sent for Ritter Sloane."

Dixie sighed softly. At least she understood now. Tenderly she reached up and stroked his clean-shaven jaw. Ham always *had* been the kind to act first and think later. She smiled to herself knowingly. If he hadn't been, perhaps the two of them would never have come together. After all, would a well-thought-of man *really* take up with a woman who owned a saloon? Especially one who'd *won* it from him in a poker game?

Shaking her head slightly, Dixie looked into his eyes and saw what so few people knew existed. The gentle heart behind all the loudmouthed arrogance. At least, she told herself, she could make him feel a little better about the Ritter Sloane situation.

She pulled away slightly and smiled at him. "Well, in a way, that could be the best thing you ever did."

"How?"

"I think Hallie's . . . *fond* of him." Dixie smoothed her thumb over his cheekbone. "And it worked out all right. You don't have a gunfighter goin' up against the Benteens, and I don't think Ritter Sloane's plannin' on acting against you. . . ."

Hamilton stiffened and stepped back from her, running one meaty hand over his face. His face tightened, his eyes dropped, but not before Dixie saw the telltale flash of guilt. She sighed deeply. There was something else going on. Something she didn't know yet.

"Ham?" she asked cautiously, watching his features uneasily. "What is it? What else have you done?"

He turned and walked to the bar. Reaching behind it, he pulled out a bottle of whiskey and a glass. After pouring himself a quick shot, he gulped it down, then looked back at her.

Dixie braced herself. Somehow, she didn't think she was going to like what he was about to say.

"When Sloane quit me, I figured he'd be workin' for the Benteens. So, I . . ."

She took a half step toward him. In the strained silence, the ticking from the old clock behind the bar sounded out like a heartbeat. She only wished hers was as steady a rhythm. Forcing herself to take in a great gulp of air, Dixie took another step closer to him. Reluctantly she asked, "You did what?"

His gaze dropped. He stared down at the water ring on

the bar top and spun his empty glass in his fingertips. After what seemed an eternity of time had passed, he said softly, "I sent for Nathan Pine."

"What?"

Chapter

✳

Twelve

THE DAY had turned surprisingly warm. Hallie stretched her arms high above her head, then arched her aching back first to one side, then the other. She yawned and clapped one hand quickly over her mouth to stifle it.

Shaking her head, she blinked her eyes furiously, trying to wake herself up. But it was no use, she knew. What she needed was a long nap. Sighing, she glanced around the yard almost guiltily. Everyone was off doing chores. Running a ranch this size took a lot of work, and here she was, practically asleep on her feet.

Hallie idly picked up her washing stick and gave the pot of soaking clothes a few good stirs. Steam from the water floated up around her face, and suddenly the damp warmth reminded her all too well of the night before. She closed her eyes, and her lips curved in a half smile. Running one hand under the open collar of her shirt, Hallie leaned into the hot mist and let the memories come.

She sighed softly, recalling the sweet pleasure of Ritter's hands on her body. The clouds of steam became his warm breath against her neck. The tiny droplets of water forming on her throat and running down the front of her shirt were

169

beads of perspiration as Ritter plunged into her body again and again.

She licked suddenly dry lips and tried to steady her ragged breathing. A curl of desire formed in the pit of her belly and spread through her body quickly until her limbs shook with the force of it.

"Hallie!"

Startled, she jumped and splashed some of the hot water onto her worn buckskins. Spinning around, she glared at Shad. "What are you tryin' to do? Scare me to death?"

Her brother's eyebrows shot up, and he looked at her as if she was losing her mind. "Better scared than scalded," he said. "Another minute and you'd a been facedown in that washpot. You fallin' asleep or somethin'?"

She glanced down into the kettle filled with boiling water and dirty clothes. Maybe she would have fallen in. She wasn't sure. The only thing she *was* sure of was that she hadn't had her mind on anything but Ritter Sloane all day.

"Hallie? You feelin' all right?"

"Yes, Shad." Her voice was more snappish than she'd intended.

"If you say so. . . ."

She heard him walk away and didn't look after him. Instead, she forced herself to get back to business. Standing there daydreamin' and wishin' it was nighttime wouldn't get her work done.

Deliberately she lifted out a set of long johns with her stick and dropped them into the nearby pot of cool water. Grabbing the scrub board, Hallie began the unending chore of trying to keep clothes clean.

*   *   *

From across the yard Ritter watched her covertly. He leaned on the pitchfork's handle, his hands gripping the old wood unnecessarily tight. Ritter'd been on the verge of racing across the yard himself to keep her from tumbling into the kettle of hot water. Thankfully, Shad had spoken up when he did.

It wasn't hard for Ritter to imagine what she'd been thinking about that so distracted her, either. The same images of the previous night had been haunting him all day, too. Of course, having the triplets sending him suspicious looks all day hadn't helped any.

Ever since the brothers arrived home to find him and Hallie still in bed, the three of them had walked a wide path around him. Ritter couldn't decide whether it was embarrassment at having caught their sister in the act of being a woman or just plain anger that had kept them out of his way. But certainly their attitude toward him had changed.

Maybe Hallie was right. Maybe if they were convinced that he was completely smitten with his wife, they would relax their guard enough to go off and leave him and Hallie alone. Then he could "die" and leave Hallie and her three crazy brothers behind him for good.

He watched his wife bend over the scrub board and let his gaze wander over her now familiar form. Ritter inhaled sharply as she stood and stretched her muscles again. No matter the dresses and other things he'd bought for her the day before. There was a lot to be said for buckskin.

"Nathan Pine?" Dixie mumbled again. "What the devil were you thinking of?"

Hamilton Butler slammed his glass down onto the bar

top. His shoulders hunched up around his ears, he muttered defensively, "I don't know, Dixie. . . ."

She stared at his bowed head and heard her own heartbeat thundering in her ears. This changed everything. If Nathan Pine was indeed headed for Stillwater, there would be no safe end to this trouble.

Frantically she tried to think. There had to be a way to head him off. To keep him from reaching Stillwater. Good God, she thought dismally, there was no telling what would happen should Sloane and Pine come face to face.

A saloon in the West wasn't simply a place to have a drink and to help yourself to a free bar lunch. It was a meeting place. A stopover for travelers who would share what news they had and take away still more information to pass along somewhere else. And as the owner of a saloon, Dixie'd heard more than her fair share of information. True *and* false.

Now all the gossip she'd heard over the years came rushing back to her in a raging flood of information. Gunfighters, like everything else in the world, came and went. Except for a select few. Those few seemed to lead charmed lives and, for whatever reason, managed to survive long enough to become near legends.

Dixie couldn't even count all the times she'd heard her customers talking about the rivalry between Sloane and Pine. In the last few years especially. There'd been any number of situations where the two men had been on opposite sides, and yet somehow, a confrontation had always been avoided. Having met Ritter Sloane, Dixie was of the opinion that *he* lay behind the restraint. For all his name of gunfighter, Sloane seemed a quiet, thoughtful man in no hurry to further his own reputation—or to kill needlessly.

There was a certain admiration in men's voices when they spoke about Ritter Sloane.

Nathan Pine was another matter. She'd never met the man, but she heard the fear when her customers discussed him.

And now he was headed for Stillwater.

Determined, Dixie crossed the room and stood beside Ham at the bar. Struggling to keep her tone even, she said, "You've got to stop him, Ham. You've got to call him off."

He looked at her from under bushy eyebrows and shook his head. "Can't. It's too late."

"It's not too late! If you can't send a wire, wait till he gets here, then send him packing!"

A long moment passed, and Dixie held her breath. waiting. Finally Hamilton Butler straightened up and lifted his chin defiantly.

"I won't, Dix. I won't be made to look the fool."

"Fool?"

"Yes, dammit! A fool!" He pushed away from the bar and took two angry steps toward the door before turning back and shouting, "What do you think the folks around here are saying right now, huh? I'll tell ya! They're *laughin'*. At me."

"What are you talkin' about?"

"I'm talkin' about hirin' a gunfighter who quits and marries into the family he was *supposed* to be fightin' against!" His face flushed, Butler raged on. "You know good and well that's what they're sayin'. . . . Well, I won't have it! I won't be laughed at. And by God, if I knuckle

under to Sloane and the Benteens now . . . if I fire Nathan
Pine . . . I'd never be able to hold my head up around these
parts again."

"Think about what you're sayin', Ham. Do you really
want Pine to *kill* the Benteen boys? And Hallie?"

He waved her words aside. "It won't come to that.
They'll leave." He gave her a firm nod. "They will."

"You're only foolin' yourself, Ham. The Benteens won't
quit. And they won't go away." She held his gaze steadily
and tried to make him see what he'd started. "Death is
riding in here with Nathan Pine. And *you* called it down
on all of us."

"It's not gonna—"

"Go home, Ham." She turned her back on him. "I don't
want to see you here again." Her voice dropped. "Not until
you come to your senses."

"Dixie . . ."

She crossed her arms over her chest and tried to still the
tremors rocking her. It seemed a lifetime before she heard
Hamilton Butler's heavy bootsteps as he walked out of the
saloon.

The sun on his back felt good. He reached up and
pulled the brim of his hat down low over his eyes and
squinted toward the livery stable at the end of the street.
Absently he nodded and stepped aside for a visibly pregnant
woman with a toddler clinging to her dust-brown skirt. The
woman smiled her thanks, and he enjoyed the little start
of pleasure it gave him. It was very seldom that *anyone*
smiled at him.

He was much more accustomed to averted eyes and
scurrying feet at his approach. Men went out of their way

to avoid him, and women gave him furtive glances, almost as if they expected him to attack them at any moment. And some appeared half-disappointed when he didn't.

His bootheels tapped against the boardwalk, setting the small silver spurs to tinkling. After retrieving his horse from the livery, he'd go by Overland House and pack up. With any luck, he should be on the road in an hour or so.

He walked past a dry-goods store and caught a glimpse of himself in the big front window. A tall man, he was an imposing figure, he knew, and dressed to emphasize it. From his flat-crowned hat to his well-tailored coat and pants to the tips of his highly polished boots, he dressed totally in black, save for the pristine white shirt and gray vest. Sometimes, reputation had as much to do with appearance as performance.

Turning forward again, he walked on, enjoying the sounds of a lively city, yet anxious to be out and away from people again. He stepped off the boardwalk and crossed the wide street. Casually he walked into the darkened interior of the livery stable. He stepped quickly to his right, into the shadows, to avoid outlining himself against the bright square of afternoon light. Then he stopped, to let his eyes adjust to the darkness after being outside.

The familiar odors surrounded him. Hay, horses, leather, even a faint trace of the livery man's cigar lingered in the still air. The hostler called out from the rear of the building, "Be right there, mister."

Nathan Pine smiled softly. His always taut nerves relaxed just a bit, and he took one step farther into the stables.

An unidentifiable noise from the nearby corner caught

his ear and he tensed, waiting. It could be anything. Some varmint holed up in the warm straw . . . anything. Most likely, it was the hostler's helper.

Steady, plodding steps began heading his way from the back of the big barn, and Nathan told himself that he was making too much of nothing. Instead, he focused his attention on the wiry old man just stepping into the faded patch of light.

But then that noise came again, and with it came recognition. The sliding motion of a foot moved gently across wooden planks. He wondered briefly if the old man had set him up for a trap, but discounted that notion. There was no bounty on his head. The only reason most men tried to face down Nathan Pine was to build a reputation. And an old man wasn't exactly the kind to go lookin' for that. Besides—Nathan glanced at the whistling man headed his way—he didn't look worried.

Appearing unconcerned, Nathan Pine let his gaze wander over the stalls until he'd half turned toward the occupied corner. Every inch of his body screamed with a familiar tension. It was always like this. The waiting. Not knowing if *this* would be the day his luck ran out.

Deliberately he ignored the coming hostler and focused his attention on the unknown threat. Vaguely he heard the old man ask, "What'cha lookin' at there? Somethin' wrong?"

Nathan drew in a long, deep breath and continued the slow turn he'd begun a lifetime ago. At the same time a figure leapt from the corner, lifting a pistol toward Pine.

In less than a heartbeat Nathan had his own gun drawn and aimed at the shadowy presence. He saw the flash of his opponent's gun and heard the sharp report as the bullet went wide of its mark. Crouched down, Nathan took his time and coolly fired just as the other man's second shot echoed through the building.

A grunt of pain followed by a loud thump as his unknown attacker fell to the floor assured Nathan that *his* shot had gone exactly where he'd planned it to.

"What the hell . . . ?" The old man hurried forward, stopping beside Nathan to stare down at the dead man in the blood-soaked straw.

Voices shouting and the scuffling, hurried sound of running feet reached the two men just an instant before the stable was crowded with people, each straining to see.

Nathan Pine ignored them all. He looked down at the man who'd just tried to kill him: shaggy brown hair, lifeless blue eyes, and a sparse attempt at a mustache on his upper lip. The dead man couldn't have been much more than twenty or so. And he'd never get any older.

"Damn fool kid," the old man muttered.

"You know him?"

He looked up at the gunfighter through ancient, watery gray eyes. "Yeah. Yeah, I know him. Name's Johnny Deal. Figured himself a fast hand with a gun."

"They all do," Nathan commented dryly and glanced over his shoulder toward the tall man pushing his way through the crowd. His shock of blond hair only half covered by a beat-up hat, the man looked from Nathan to the dead man and back again. Nathan's eyes lowered briefly to the star on the blond's shirtfront, then flicked back up to meet his gaze squarely.

"What happened here?" the deputy asked of no one in particular.

"Who're you?" Pine countered.

"Travis Quinn." Careful blue eyes moved over the gunfighter. "I'm the deputy here."

The old man spoke up. "It was Johnny there, Travis." He jerked his head toward the body. "He jumped out at this fella, gun blazin'. He come up short."

"That what happened?" The deputy's eyes raked over Nathan.

"Yes. You can check the man's gun. He fired two shots and missed. I fired one and didn't."

Whispers shot through the crowd like free booze on the Fourth of July, and the deputy turned an angry stare on the crowd. "You all get out now. Show's over." There was a general shifting of feet and a few grumbles, yet no one actually made a move to leave. "Go on . . . *git!*"

Nathan pulled his pistol from its holster, opened the chamber, and pulled the spent cartridge free. Taking one from his belt loop, he silently replaced the fired bullet. When he finished, he found himself alone in the stable with the old man and the young deputy. The latter asked, "You're Nathan Pine, aren't ya?"

"I am."

"Thought so. Been in town long?"

"A day or two." From the corner of his eye, Nathan watched the old hostler's head moving from one man to the other, following the conversation.

"You figurin' on leavin' any time soon?" The younger man cradled his rifle in his arms and met the gunfighter's stare without a trace of fear.

Nathan studied him for a moment and felt a small swell of admiration. There was no backup in the deputy, and if he lived long enough, he just might make a helluva lawman. "Matter of fact, Deputy Quinn, that's why I'm here. Just came to collect my horse. I have a job waiting for me. I'll be leaving as soon as I pack up my things."

The blond nodded slowly. "That'd be best, Mr. Pine. I've got no cause to hold you for this shooting." He nodded toward the hostler. "Old Tom's word is good enough for me. 'Sides"—he spared one last glance at the dead man—"Johnny never did have much sense." He hitched his rifle higher in his arms and stared at Nathan again. "Still and all, it'd be best for you to move on quick, Mr. Pine. We don't want any more trouble here."

Nathan stiffened instinctively. No matter how often it occurred, being ordered out of town still rankled. He lifted his chin slightly and tugged at his lapels, straightening the fall of his coat. The old man beside him turned and headed off to one of the stalls, undoubtedly to retrieve the gunfighter's horse. The deputy watched him go, then said softly, "Tell Tom I'll have the undertaker come by for Johnny."

Nathan nodded.

Stepping toward the doorway, the blond added, "Goodbye, Mr. Pine. I don't expect we'll be seein' you in Cheyenne again for quite a spell."

Nathan let him go, knowing that he'd just been given another command. Still, he hadn't planned on coming back this way in any case. He glanced into the street and wasn't surprised to find that most of the curious crowd had found some excuse or other to hang about in front of the stable. No doubt hoping to *see* the next shootout firsthand.

He shook his head. Maybe he was getting too old for all this. Gawkers never used to bother him. Now he felt only disgust for those not brave enough to face him themselves, but more than willing to watch another man bleed and die.

Deliberately he turned his back on the crowd and walked to join the old man. The sooner he left Cheyenne behind him, the better off everyone would be.

Everyone, that is, but Ritter Sloane.

Ritter followed the boys outside and glanced immediately to the sky. A couple good hours of daylight left. He looked at his brothers-in-law as they shambled slowly toward the barn and shook his head. He'd never seen them as quiet as they'd been over the dinner table. They'd spent the entire time either staring at their never-empty plates or at Hallie and himself.

He couldn't blame Hallie for finally losing all patience and tossing the lot of them outside. He'd been about ready to bust, himself.

Micah turned around just then and looked at him. Probably checking to make sure he wasn't staying behind with Hallie. Disgusted, Ritter started walking after the three men. He couldn't figure out what the three of them wanted. It was *their* idea to marry him off to their sister. And now that they'd gotten what they wanted, it obviously wasn't making them happy.

Ritter smiled. Good. It was *his* pleasure to do anything he could to make those three just as uncomfortable as possible. Especially if all he had to do to accomplish that was to make love to his wife!

He was almost to the barn when a horse and rider careened into the ranchyard. Watching the stranger, he heard the boys come up behind him.

The towheaded youngster on board the rearing pinto

brought the horse under control quickly, then jumped down. Holding on to the reins, the boy hurried to Ritter, dug into his shirt pocket for a piece of paper, then handed it over.

"Hey, Davey," Shad said, "what's goin' on? Ain't that Dixie's horse?"

"Shore is," the boy said, glaring at the huge animal behind him. "He about shook my insides loose on the ride here, too! Don't know how Miss Dixie can stand 'im."

Ritter looked from the folded paper in his hands to the kid in front of him. "What's this all about, boy?"

He shrugged. "Miss Dixie give me a dollar to bring it on out to ya. She tol' me to wait and see if you wanted to tell her anything."

"Open it up, Thloane."

Ritter frowned at Micah and walked away from the tight group. Reluctantly he unfolded the small paper and read the brief message.

> *Ham has sent for Nathan Pine. Don't know when he'll be here. Can I do anything?*
>
> *Dixie*

A cold knot formed in the pit of his stomach. He lifted his gaze from the note and stared off into the trees at the edge of the yard. He could smell the wood smoke from the chimney. He heard the burst of birdsong and the quiet laughter of the boy behind him as he listened to Micah's strangled speech. The horses in the corral called to one another, and on the horizon, black thunderheads were massing for an assault.

Everything was the same as it had been a moment

before—and yet, everything had changed, too. Nathan Pine was on his way. And that one fact altered the whole situation.

Crumpling the paper in his fist, Ritter turned back to the kid. Forcing a smile, he said, "Tell Dixie thanks, boy. I appreciate it."

"Yessir." He squinted up at him. "That all you want me to say?"

"Yeah. Yeah, that's all." There wasn't a damned thing Dixie could do, and he knew it. It was enough that she'd offered. Ritter couldn't remember the last time someone had volunteered to come to his aid.

As the messenger mounted his horse, Ritter's gaze strayed to the house. Inside, Hallie was cleaning up after the afternoon meal. Soon the day would be over, and they would be together again in the darkness. They could close her bedroom door and pretend, for a while, that the rest of the world didn't exist.

His heartbeat lurched and his fingers itched to hold her again. He found himself wishing that the pretense could have gone on longer. That they could have fooled each other into believing that their marriage was a *real* one. That their future would actually be more than a few weeks.

Then he cursed himself for a fool. He'd known from the first it would come to this. If not now, then sometime. Sooner or later a gunman would turn up at the Benteen ranch and shatter everyone's illusions. Maybe it was just as well that it happened now.

Before Hallie began to care for him.

Before he began to believe in dreams.

The boy's horse raced out of the ranch yard, and as soon

as the kid was gone, the triplets surrounded Ritter. Slowly he looked from one to the other of them. His curled fingers tightened over the piece of paper.

"What is it?" Shad asked.

"Let'th thee it, Thloane," Micah demanded.

"What'd Dixie have to say?" Jericho tossed in.

Ritter's gaze never left the house. He stared hard at the closed door as if he could see Hallie, just beyond. He pulled in a deep breath and said quietly, "Nathan Pine's on his way."

Chapter

※

Thirteen

SHAD PULLED the wadded-up paper from Ritter's hand and straightened it out again. Silently he stared down at the writing as if the words would change if he concentrated hard enough.

Micah muttered a vicious curse and spat into the dirt.

"Pine?" Jericho said softly. "Nathan Pine. Isn't he that New Mexico gunman made such a name for himself down to Las Vegas a couple years back?"

"That's him," Ritter answered, his gaze still locked onto the ranch house.

"Why the hell's he comin' here?"

Micah glared at Jericho and gave him a shove. "Why do ya think? Butler thent for him." His eyes flicked to his brother-in-law. "Becauth of *him*."

Ritter's gaze shot to Micah, then in turn to each of the others. He saw the accusation on their faces. And he really couldn't blame them. If he hadn't shown up in this damned valley . . . if he hadn't found Hallie . . . if he hadn't been forced to marry her . . .

Hell. He shook his head and told himself that none of that mattered anymore. The only thing that mattered now was keeping Nathan Pine away from the Benteens.

Especially Hallie. And there was only one chance to do that.

"I have to go talk to Butler again," he said.

"We already tried that," Jericho argued. "Didn't do a damned bit of good."

"Seems like we made it worse," Shad said softly, his thumbs moving over the paper he held. "I'll bet Butler sent for Pine *after* we talked to him."

"How do ya figure?"

"Hell, Jericho," Shad countered, "if he'd sent for him before, he'd a been here by now."

"Don't matter." Both brothers turned to look at Micah. "We ain't talkin' to that ol' bathtard again. He wanth war, he can damn well *have* it!"

"I didn't say a thing about *we* going to Butler." Ritter turned and looked at the oldest triplet. "*I'm* going."

"No, thir. Either we *all* go or nobody goeth."

"This is between Butler and me, Micah. Nobody else." His features tight, Ritter looked at the other man through narrowed eyes. "Maybe I can get him to call Pine off— maybe not. But it's worth a try. And he's not about to listen if you three are there eggin' him on and makin' him even madder."

"What'd *we* do?" Jericho's astonished voice asked.

"I don't think you have to *do* anything. For some reason," Ritter went on, his gaze moving over the three of them, "you boys make him mad just *being* here."

"I don't like it," Micah muttered.

"I don't much care what you like," Ritter countered quickly. "We've been doing things your way. Now it's *my* turn. Besides, we don't know when Pine is set to get here. We can't leave Hallie on the ranch here alone. What if he just decides to show up here and open the ball?"

All of them nodded solemnly in agreement to at least *that* point. Then Shad pointed out: "Fine. Hallie shouldn't be left here alone to defend the place on her lonesome. But two of us here with her is enough. One of us can go with you."

Ritter inhaled deeply, slowly, and let the air out in a rush. "No. I'm not going to be riding right up to his front door this time. I want to get past his men so's we can talk quietly. Just the two of us. And it's a helluva lot easier for *one* man to sneak up on a place than it is for *three*. Besides, I don't want to have to worry about anyone's hide but my own when I go in there."

A long, silent moment passed and Ritter waited. He could almost *see* the three men thinking over what he'd said. He only hoped that they'd look at it from his side. Because come hell or high water, he was going to Butler's alone. Even if he had to hog-tie the whole damned Benteen family!

"What's the matter?" he prodded. "Still don't trust me? Still think I'm going to take off first chance I get?"

Nobody said a word to that, but Ritter saw a flicker of assent in Micah's eyes before he disguised it.

"You know, don't ya," Jericho remarked, "that whether we say yes or not . . . Hallie ain't about to go for this!"

Ritter's gaze shot to the man instantly. "I don't want Hallie knowing about this. Not till it's over."

"I don't know . . ." Shad shook his head worriedly. "For God's sake . . . you really want her ridin' into a nest of hired guns at Butler's place? *Anything* could go wrong! All it would take is *one* man cuttin' loose. That'd set the others off like skyrockets. Bullets would be flyin' all over the place, and *none* of us could protect her!" He paused a moment to get his anger under control again. It wouldn't do him the slightest piece of good to get into a fight with the three knot-heads. Finally he tried again, calmer now. "For once in your lives, why don't you three try thinkin' of your sister as a *woman*—not just another brother!"

Shad smiled self-consciously and lowered his gaze. "I reckon we already *seen* she's a woman, Ritter."

"Yeah." Micah cleared his throat. "All right. We won't thay nothin'."

"Unless," Jericho added, "she *asks*."

Ritter sighed. That was the best he could hope for, and he knew it. But if they could keep this away from Hallie until after his visit with Butler, he'd be willing to face her anger. Because, knowing Hallie, if she got wind of what he was planning, she'd trot right along after him. And just the thought of her bein' at Butler's if shooting started gave him a chill that went down to his bones.

"Ya know," Shad said thoughtfully as he fingered the note, "we *could* be jumpin' the gun, here. Maybe Pine won't come."

"He'll come."

All three brothers stared at Ritter. The quiet assurance in his tone was somehow more alarming than his previous anger.

"Why you tho thure?"

Ritter's lips quirked in a mockery of a smile. "Like you said, Micah, because of *me*."

"What'd you do to him?"

"Nothin', Jericho. Didn't have to *do* anything." Ritter pulled in a deep breath and blew it out again on a frustrated sigh. "I guess you could call what he's got against me—professional jealousy."

"Huh?"

Turning to Micah, he went on. "It bothers the hell out of Nathan that some folks consider me a faster man with a gun than him. I never *tried* to get the name of a gunman. It just . . . happened. But Nathan . . ." He shook his head slowly. "It's all Nathan Pine thinks or cares about. He's proud of his skills. And he *is* good. *Very* good. But that's not enough for him."

"I've known for years that sooner or later he'd find a way to push the issue between us, though I've avoided it as best I could."

"Why avoid it?" Jericho shrugged. "Wouldn't it be easier just to have done with it?"

Ritter looked at Jericho and tried to make him understand. "Nathan Pine wants to be the top man in his . . . 'profession.' He's tired of hearing about Ritter Sloane. He wants to be the only one folks talk about. If we meet, the only way things can be settled is for one of us to die. Now, I'm not ready to go just yet—and believe it or not, boys, I don't enjoy killing."

"That don't make any sense a'tall," Shad interrupted quickly. "Why should *you* bother him so dang much? There's plenty of other gunmen out there. Not just you."

Ritter snorted a half laugh. "There's not so many as you might think. Longley's dead. Hanged. Hardin's in jail. The Youngers are locked up—"

"But the James boys . . ." Shad argued. "And I hear tell of some youngster down in New Mexico . . . Billy somethin'."

"Billy Bonney." Ritter nodded. "Yeah. I know him. But

he won't last long, either. That temper of his'll do him in. And yeah, the James boys are still loose. There are some others, too, but it doesn't matter to Nathan. He takes it real personal that I'm still around taking what he sees as *his* jobs."

He turned back to stare at the house. "Pine will come. He'll come because I'm here. And he won't quit."

The brothers exchanged glances and reached a silent agreement. Deliberately Shad crumpled the piece of paper in his hand into a ball.

Finally, after a nod from each of his brothers, Micah said, "All right, then. *You* go. Talk to Butler. We'll thtay here."

"Good. It's settled." He kept his gaze on the house and saw through the front window that Hallie had lighted the lamps against the dusk. "I'll go at first dark tomorrow night."

"Tomorrow?" Micah pulled his hat off and threw it at the dirt. "Why tomorrow? Why not tonight?"

"I want Butler to have some time to think about all this he's set into motion. I want him to worry. To wonder if Dixie's told us about Pine and what we're planning on doing about it." And, he told himself silently, he wanted just one more night with Hallie. One more night to wrap himself in her arms before his new world got shot all to hell.

Hallie watched her husband for a long minute. With no lamp lit, the small room was aglow with moonlight. Ritter stood just to the side of the window, holding the curtains back with his fingertips and staring out at the night.

Quietly, on the balls of her feet, Hallie crossed the

room to stand behind him and snaked her arms around his
narrow waist. Laying her head against the smooth warmth
of his shoulder blade, she whispered, "What ya lookin' at,
Ritter?"

"Nothing, really—just the dark."

She moved one hand over his flat abdomen and smiled.
"I thought it'd *never* get dark!"

He chuckled softly and the sound rumbled through
his chest. Hallie smiled and let her fingers splay wide
against him. The fastenings of his jeans hung open, and
she deliberately dipped her hands under the waistband,
sliding across his belly and hips in anticipation.

Her touch sent small stabs of desire coursing through
him, and when her fingers moved over his already swollen
flesh Ritter's breath caught in his throat. Reaching back,
he grabbed her, pulled her around in front of him, and
wrapped his arms around her. He, too, had waited out the
last hours before nightfall. Even with Butler and Nathan
Pine never far from his mind, Ritter hadn't been able to
stop thinking about Hallie.

Resting his chin on the top of her head, he inhaled the
fresh, clean scent of her and ran one hand up the line
of her back. He smiled as the white cotton nightgown
bunched beneath his fingers. As eager a bed partner as
she was, Hallie was *not* the woman to stroll around her
bedroom stark naked. She nestled against his chest, and
her warm sigh brushed over his skin with the softest of
touches. His arms tightened around her, and somewhere in
the back of his mind a warning bell rang out. *Don't get too
close—Don't let her mean too much—Don't forget . . .
you can't stay.*

But why not? he argued with himself silently. If he

could manage to get rid of Nathan Pine . . . why *couldn't* he stay?

She shifted slightly and left a kiss in the center of his chest, and Ritter silenced the warning bells. It was far too late for those pitiful precautions. It had been too late for a while now. He already cared for Hallie. And it frightened him a little to think how much she had come to mean to him.

If he was destined to leave her behind, he would have to deal with that when the time came. But for now, whatever price he paid in misery later on would be worth the time spent in her arms.

Slowly he bent his head to hers and covered her mouth with his in a kiss that began gently, tenderly, and ended in an almost desperate longing. When he finally broke away and began trailing his tongue down the length of her throat, Ritter sensed that her need, her urgency matched his own.

She leaned into him, tilting her head to the side, silently telling him that she wanted more of him. That she wanted his touch to cover her like the morning fog on the mountain. She wanted to be swallowed up in him, to be so close that there would be no separating them.

His right hand swept down and dragged the hem of her nightgown up over her hip and then higher still until her breasts were cupped in his hands. His thumbs moved over her already erect nipples, and Hallie's head fell back on her neck at the delicious sensations he caused. She smiled and held tightly to his shoulders, his flesh strong and warm under her hands.

Abruptly he stepped back, letting the nightgown fall to her feet. She swayed a bit and opened her eyes when he scooped her up in his arms and carried her to the bed. Tossing the flowered quilt aside with one hand, Ritter held Hallie tightly and lowered them both to the feather mattress.

Slowly, carefully, he undid the tiny pearl buttons at the throat of her gown while her fingertips smoothed over his back. Her breath ragged with desire, Hallie pulled his head down and slanted her mouth over his. Her tongue moved across his lips teasingly until he parted them for her, and she groaned softly as his tongue met hers in a silent celebration.

Hallie closed her eyes and gave herself over to the incredible feel of his hands on her body—his mouth—his whispers in the soft moonlight. Slowly she realized that he'd managed to pull her nightgown off without her even noticing. All that she cared about was that now *nothing* lay between them. She arched her hips against him and smiled. He'd slipped out of his jeans, too. Her left hand swept down over his muscled chest, across his abdomen until her fingers encircled the hard warmth of him.

He sucked in a deep gasp of air, levered himself up on one elbow, and looked down into her eyes. "Lord, Hallie, what you do to me . . ."

Her fingers moved again, stroking his sensitive flesh, and she smiled when his pale blue eyes closed with the pleasure. She raised up slightly and kissed his chest, then let her lips and tongue trail across his skin until she found his flat, hard nipples. Daintily, delicately, she nipped at him with her teeth. When he couldn't stand it any longer, he groaned and breathlessly pushed her back down onto the mattress.

As her fingers continued to stroke him, Ritter bent over

her and took one of her nipples into his mouth. With each tender touch she gave him, he suckled at her. He began gently, caressingly, but as her passion grew and her touch became more demanding, so too did the pressure of his mouth.

Hallie arched her back. Each time his lips drew at her breast, she wanted to scream for more. While one hand stroked Ritter's swollen flesh, Hallie moved her other hand to touch his face. She opened her eyes wide and watched his mouth tease and grab at her nipple, and she let her fingers trail alongside his lips, silently begging him not to stop. He turned his head and left her breast. Slowly he drew the tips of her fingers into his mouth, one by one, and gave them the loving attention he'd shown her now aching nipples.

Hallie raised up, wanting to kiss him, to taste him, but he shook his head and pulled back. Reaching down, he lifted her hand from his body and kissed the palm before setting it free. Bereft, Hallie could only stare at him in dazed disappointment.

"It's all right, Hallie," he whispered, "we're just beginning. We have all night."

She smiled and reached for him again, but he shook his head and bent over her. With a feather-light touch, Ritter began moving his lips over her heated flesh. He followed every line, every curve of her body with his mouth, his tongue leaving a damp trail of kisses after him.

Slowly he inched downward, over the curve of her hip and around to the inside of her thigh. Hallie, eyes squeezed tightly shut, pushed her head back into the pillow and moved restlessly on the sheet. She felt his hands, sliding over her abdomen, over her breasts, and back down again to slip beneath her and cup her behind. She didn't know what he was doing . . . what he was planning . . . she only knew that it felt wonderful, and she wanted him to keep doing it.

And then she felt herself being lifted off the bed. His strong hands held her hips high and his fingers kneaded the soft flesh beneath them. Slowly Hallie opened her eyes to look at him. She felt almost drugged with passion. Beyond anything but *feeling*. She watched his smoky eyes darken with desire just before he lowered his mouth to cover the hot center of her.

She jumped, startled at the overpowering sensation. But somehow, she forced herself to keep her eyes open. And any sense of embarrassment vanished in the thrill of his mouth against the most sensitive part of her.

Body twisting helplessly, she threaded her fingers in his hair and held him to her. His lips, his tongue began to build a need deep inside her that Hallie was afraid could never be answered. Breath coming in short gasps, she climbed the familiar peak toward the release she knew waited just out of her reach. And when she came so near the end of her quest that she was shaking, Ritter stopped and set her gently down on the mattress.

"Holy saints, Ritter," she cried quietly, a catch in her voice, "you ain't gonna leave me like this, are ya?"

"No, Hallie," he whispered as his body covered hers, "never."

Then he plunged deeply inside her, and Hallie locked her legs around him. Eagerly, feverishly, she met each of his thrusts and urged him to give her more, to come into her deeper. Harder.

His lips came down on hers and Hallie opened her

mouth to him. His tongue and his body invaded her soul, and when she finally reached the shattering release awaiting her, she held tightly to her husband and took him with her.

"Oh, my," she breathed and lay her head against his shoulder. She was shaking so badly, it almost hurt to move.

"Yeah," Ritter agreed on a sigh. "Oh, my!" Every square inch of his body felt drained. Exhausted. He'd never guessed that such . . . *completion* existed. It was more than a physical release. So much more. It was more a joining of body, mind, and soul. He'd never felt such . . . *peace*.

She dragged her fingertips across his chest, and he snatched at her hand, holding it still. He didn't think he could stand much more. At least, not right away.

"Ritter?"

"Hmmm?" His eyes closed.

"Where'd you learn how to do that?"

His eyes flew open again. "What?"

She shrugged against him. "*You* know . . ."

"Uh . . ."

Her voice came again. Smaller this time. "Reckon I'm not the first you done it to, huh?"

His heart still pounding ferociously, Ritter's mouth flattened into a hard line. The hurt and disappointment in her voice was more than he could bear. None of the women he'd known over the years could hold a candle to this tiny firebrand with short, curly hair.

In fact, if it had meant his life, Ritter would have been unable to dredge up a mental picture of any other woman but her. He had to find a way to tell her that.

He reached down and cupped her cheek. Tilting her face up to his, Ritter looked deeply into her soft green eyes and told her the truth.

"In all the ways that matter a damn, Hallie . . . you *are* the first."

A slow smile curved her lips, and she rubbed her cheek against his hand.

"Good. I'd not like to think of sharin' you with some other woman."

He grinned and dropped his head back onto the pillow. "Right now, Hallie . . . I'm too done up for *you*, let alone anybody else."

"Aw . . ." She shifted slightly, moving in closer to him, and ran one hand over the soft, golden hairs sprinkled over his chest.

He sucked in a breath but didn't stop her.

"I'm sure sorry to hear ya say that, husband." She leaned over him and kissed one of his nipples.

"Hallie . . ."

She ignored him and reached across him for the other one. "Yessir," she said as she planted gentle kisses all over his chest, "I do believe I heard you say somethin' about 'all night'?"

"Now, Hallie . . ." He groaned and tried to force his mind away from what she was doing. It wasn't working.

"Yep. I'm *sure* that's what you said." She slid one leg over his and lay atop him, her toes moving against his shins.

He chuckled and shook his head. "You don't want to let a man rest a minute, do you?"

She planted her elbows on his chest and propped her chin in her hands. Cocking her head, she asked, "Now, why would you want to rest? Hell, you can *sleep* any ol' time!"

She wiggled her hips, and his hands came down on her buttocks, holding her still. "Apparently," he said with a crooked grin, "not now, though."

"Nah . . ." Hallie inched forward and kissed his lips lightly. "You know, husband, I think I'm gettin' to *like* bein' married a *whole* lot!"

"Yeah." He nodded, one hand moving up to her ear to toy with one silver hoop. "I'm gettin' kinda *fond* of it, myself!" Funny, he told himself, he wasn't as tired as he'd thought he was!

"Good." She rolled off him to the side and rose up on her knees. Hands on hips, she looked down at him.

While she stared at his naked body, Ritter fought down the ridiculous notion of covering himself with the sheet. The way she was watching . . . no, *appraising* him, he'd have given *anything* to know what she was thinking.

"Hallie," he started, "why don't you come on down here by me?"

"Nope."

"Why not?" What the hell was she up to?

"Well"—she grinned and wiggled her eyebrows at him—"since you're so blamed tired, I figured to let you just lay there awhile. Rest up."

He shook his head. "I don't believe I'm that tired anymore, Hallie."

"Rest'll do you good, husband," she countered and drew one hand across his abdomen. His body jerked in response. She looked down at his obvious arousal, then turned to meet his questioning gaze. "You just lay back, Ritter. I'm fixin' to show you just how it feels."

His heart staggered. "How *what* feels?"

She smiled again and bent over him. "*You* know."

"Hallie," he murmured quickly, "you don't have to—"
Her mouth closed around him, and he whispered, "Dear
heaven, Hallie!"

Chapter

Fourteen

"ARE YOU *sure*, Dixie?" Ritter asked again. "Maybe Butler said something about when he's expecting Pine and you forgot. Think."

"What the hell do y'suppose I've *been* doin'?" The older woman pushed her hair out of her eyes and reached for the nearby coffeepot. Filling her cup for the third time, she muttered, "I'm tellin' you, he didn't say."

Ritter set his cup down on the scratched surface of the table. "All right. I guess I'll just have to ask him myself."

She snorted indelicately. "Don't bother. *I* tried talkin' him out of this. He won't listen."

"I'll have to try anyway."

"He's too worried about lookin' like the damned fool he is. He'll never back down. Not on this."

Ritter watched the woman's face and saw the worry in her eyes. He recognized it easily because he shared it. From what he'd seen and heard of Hamilton Butler, Ritter was fairly certain what kind of man the rancher was. The kind of man Ritter knew all too well.

Abruptly he shook his head, shoving old memories back where they belonged. In the past. Pushing himself to his feet, he looked down at the woman and gave her a half smile. "Thanks for your help, Dixie."

"Wasn't much."

"Yeah, it was. At least I *know* that Pine's headed here. That gives me some time to prepare for him."

"Prepare what?"

He sighed and shrugged. "Don't know yet." Turning, he walked toward the door, but Dixie's voice stopped him.

"Not that it's any of my business," she said, "but how the devil did you manage to come into town without Hallie? Or the boys?"

"Hallie's takin' a nap"—Ritter grinned suddenly—"and maybe the boys are starting to trust me a little."

She snorted. "Yeah. And the Queen of England's comin' to tea this afternoon!"

Ritter chuckled, and over the sound of his laughter. Dixie added, "I don't know what you're up to, Sloane, but whatever it is . . . you go careful. I got a feeling Hallie'd be real upset if you went and got yourself killed."

The smile on his face died, and he stared at the woman for a long time before saying, "Don't you worry, Dixie. I'm *always* careful!"

He spun around and pushed through the batwing doors. Stepping out onto the boardwalk, he let his gaze move over the still-quiet street. Slowly he thought about everything Dixie'd told him. He hated to admit it, but she was right. He hadn't found out much. Still, knowing Pine was coming was at least an advantage.

Ritter pulled the brim of his hat down lower over his eyes and squinted into the morning sun. For the first time in nearly three weeks, there wasn't a hint of clouds in the deep, vivid blue sky. Idly he wondered if that in itself was some kind of omen. A sign of change.

He laughed at himself and started walking. If he wasn't careful, he'd be knockin' on wood and going out of his way to avoid black cats. Besides, any fool knew that the one thing you could count on in Wyoming was how fast the weather changed.

Ritter walked slowly down the wooden boardwalk. The sound of his bootheels echoed loudly in the quiet morning. He grinned. It was the first time in almost three weeks that he was alone. And for a man used to solitude, three weeks with folks was quite a stretch.

And yet, he didn't remember solitude as being so . . . quiet. Uneasily he glanced over his shoulder. Somehow it didn't feel right with no one alongside him talking or arguing or laughing. Ritter frowned, disgusted with himself. The first chance he'd had in far too long to be on his own and think . . . and what does he do? Wish for someone to talk to.

Deliberately he hurried his steps to the telegraph office. There were a couple of things he wanted to take care of, and the sooner he got them done, the sooner he could get back to the ranch. He refused to think about *why* he was so anxious to get back to the Benteen place.

"Hellooo! Mr. Slo-oane!"

He stopped dead and turned around slowly. Elmira Huggins was headed his way, her round shining face wreathed in smiles. Privately Ritter told himself that the storekeeper had sure gotten a lot friendlier ever since he'd paid the Benteens' bill.

"Mr. Sloane!" She laid one hand on her massive bosom and tried desperately to catch her breath. "Is, uh . . . Hallie with you?" She looked behind him as if expecting the woman to be hiding somewhere nearby.

"No, ma'am. She's at the ranch, I'm afraid."

"Tsk, tsk, tsk." She threw her head back and smiled. "*Such* a shame. And you two just married. You should have come to town together to do your shopping!" A playful pat on the gunfighter's arm followed that statement.

Ah, he thought with a slight smile. That's what's behind all this. She figured to make a few more dollars out of the newlyweds. Well, he couldn't hardly blame her. "We'll do that real soon, ma'am. Now, if you'll excuse me?"

"Business?" Her head cocked, she waited anxiously for him to speak. Elmira considered it her duty to know exactly what was going on.

Ritter shook his head. "Just a telegram, I'm afraid." He tipped his hat to her and started walking.

"Why don't you stop by the store for a cup of coffee before you leave?" she called out.

He waved one hand in acknowledgment and kept walking. All he needed was the town gossip following him around.

Nathan Pine reached for the coffeepot, set on a flat rock close to the campfire. After tapping the handle with his fingers first, he picked it up and poured himself another cup.

He'd only made a few miles yesterday, but he wasn't going to rush this trip. He'd waited too long for the chance to match himself against Sloane. And now, with their conflict finally coming to pass, he wanted to savor the anticipation of it.

In his mind's eye he saw it all so clearly. He and Sloane, facing each other. The long drawn-out moment when they would look into each other's eyes and know that finally, all would be settled between them. Then a thunder of guns . . . and Ritter Sloane lying dead in the street.

Leaning back against the trunk of an old lightning-struck tree, Nathan stretched his long legs out in front of him. Smiling, he lifted the tin cup to his lips and took another drink of coffee. Strips of bacon sizzled in a pan, and his horse, tethered nearby, cropped at a few of the first shoots of grass.

He looked up at the wide sky and sighed contentedly. No reason to hurry, he told himself. Ritter Sloane wasn't going anywhere.

Except hell.

At the telegraph office Ritter ignored the thin, bald telegrapher. More than used to curious stares, he kept his eyes down and finished writing out the wire he wanted sent at once. He handed it to the man and waited.

"Mighty long message, mister." The man's voice was as thin as he was. He squinted up at the gunfighter. "It'll cost dear."

Digging into his pants pocket, Ritter pulled out two gold coins and slapped them down on the counter. The little man's jaw dropped, and his long-fingered hand snatched at the double eagles as if they would disappear if left there.

One blond eyebrow rose slightly, and Ritter said, "Just send the wire right away. Keep what's left for yourself."

"Thanks, Mr. Sloane, sir." The scrawny man all but crawled over the counter in his excessive display of gratitude.

Trying not to show his contempt, the gunfighter only nodded. He'd seen the same reaction too many times over the years. People who wouldn't ordinarily *glance* at a gunman fell all over themselves being respectful and friendly as soon as *gold* entered the conversation.

Ritter turned and left the tiny building at the end of the boardwalk. Standing just outside the door, he sighed in satisfaction as he heard the man's fingers tapping out the wire.

Now no matter what else happened, he'd taken care of what needed doing.

The only thing left to do was try to talk some sense into Hamilton Butler. And silently he acknowledged there wasn't much chance of that.

A cold wind shot down the street and tugged at his hat. Ritter pulled his coat collar up around his neck and threw a quick look at the sky. Roiling black clouds were hurtling up from the horizon, and he told himself that if he was a man who put a lot of stock in omens, he'd hop on his horse and make tracks.

Instead, he walked back down the boardwalk toward Dixie's, where he'd left his horse.

He hadn't gone more than a few feet when a door suddenly slammed. Ritter spun about toward the noise and saw a little boy, no more than three or four, run down the front steps of a small house, headed for the street. Chuckling, Ritter watched the stark naked, soaking-wet child laughingly race through his front gate.

Then the door behind the boy opened again. A harried looking woman with flyaway brown hair, wearing a water-splashed apron, stepped out of the house yelling, "Jonathan!"

The boy didn't even glance at his mother. Laughing to himself, Ritter could see the kid was having the time of his life, even though he *had* to be freezing!

The child was almost across the street when a cowboy on a charging horse rounded the corner. Ritter looked from the boy to the horseman and felt something cold tighten in his chest. Shouting and firing his pistol into the air, the rider didn't see the boy. And he wouldn't. Until it was too late.

Ritter glanced back at the child. Still running and laughing, pleased as punch with himself for having escaped a bath. He had no more sense of danger than the horseman.

As if from far away, Ritter heard the woman scream at the same instant that he leapt from the boardwalk onto the dusty street.

In the space of an instant Ritter saw it all as though he wasn't a part of the scene. The laughing boy, his cheeks red from the cold, drops of water rolling down his plump body. The mother, still too far away to help, her face frozen in shock and fear. The rider, still bearing down on the boy, grinning like a drunken idiot as his gunshots shattered the morning quiet.

Ritter felt as though he couldn't move fast enough. His heart in his throat, he *willed* his long legs to cover the distance between him and the child in time. Everything but the boy vanished from his thoughts. The cowboy, the mother, the charging animal were all gone. He didn't even hear anything beyond the roaring in his own ears.

And then Ritter's arms wrapped around the child. As he snatched the boy up, they hit the ground and rolled, Ritter's big hand protecting the boy's head. Over and over they went until they were clear, and even then Ritter would have sworn he felt the horse's hooves brush his face.

Just as suddenly as it had begun, it ended. He lay perfectly still, the frightened little boy's shrieks ringing in his ears. Heart pounding, Ritter relaxed his hold, and the boy pushed free and on shaky legs ran for his mother.

Ritter didn't move. He knew he should get off the damned road, but he told himself he'd probably just fall over anyway. His legs were shaking so badly, he doubted they'd hold him up. He pulled in a deep, ragged breath, and eyes wide, he stared up at the ominous-looking sky and grinned.

"Pleased with yourself, are ya?"

Turning his head a bit, Ritter looked up into the sheriff's stern features.

"As a matter of fact, Sheriff . . . yeah. I am."

Slowly, like the beginning of a rockslide, the older man's lined, weathered face crumpled into a grin. "As well you should be, Sloane." He thrust one hand toward the gunfighter.

Without hesitation, Ritter grabbed it, and the sheriff effortlessly pulled him off the street. Immediately Ritter began to brush at his clothes. He was completely covered with fine, pale dust, and even when most of it was beaten out, his clothes looked more gray than black.

Sheriff Tucker bent down, retrieved Ritter's hat, and handed it to him. A hoofprint in the center of the crown made it clear to both of them just how close the man and boy had come to disaster.

"Looks like you could use a new hat, son," the sheriff said softly.

Ritter's long fingers worked the dent out of the crown, then plucked at the tear from the horse's sharp hoof. His gaze shot up to the man opposite him and he smiled. "Hell of a lot easier to buy a new hat than a new *head*!"

Sheriff Tucker opened his mouth to speak, but the boy's mother, still clutching her crying child to her breast, pushed him out of the way.

Standing in front of the man covered with dirt, her chin quivering, eyes awash with tears, the woman stared up at the gunfighter for a long breath-stopping moment. Then slowly she reached up and lay one arm around Ritter's neck. She raised up on her toes and kissed his cheek. Squeezing him tightly, she then laid her forehead on his shoulder and whispered, "Thank you. Oh, God, thank you a hundred times."

Ritter looked over the woman's head and saw the sheriff watching him like a proud father. He looked away quickly and patted the woman's shoulder. Slowly he drew back and looked down at the tear-streaked dirty face of the boy who'd caused all the trouble. Ritter grinned.

The kid's whimpering had stopped, and now, despite the snuffling, ragged breathing. the little boy was smiling up at the adults watching him.

"You got a handful there, ma'am," Ritter finally said.

"He is that," his mother acknowledged.

"Maybe it's time you started lockin' that door at bathtime, Rose." The sheriff chuckled and winked at the boy. "Or maybe I'll just have to come handcuff him for ya!"

Jonathan's laughter showed them all what he thought of the sheriff's threat. And as the tired woman carried her son home, everyone who heard the boy giggling knew that if given half a chance, the kid would be off and running again.

"Sloane . . ."

Ritter looked at the sheriff, a half smile still on his face.

"I think it's about time I bought you a drink. What d'ya say?"

"Sheriff"—Ritter shoved his battered hat down on his head—"I think I could use one."

The two men walked side by side to Dixie's place and only had to stop every few feet for yet another of Stillwater's residents to shake Ritter Sloane's hand.

"I don't see why you have to go back into town tonight," Hallie said for the tenth time in as many minutes.

Ritter pulled on his fleece-lined coat and slowly did up the buttons. For the first time in too many years, there was someone *worried* about him. He liked it. But he didn't much care for lying to her. Yet there was nothing else he could do.

"I told you, Hallie. The sheriff wants to ask me a couple of questions."

"It don't make sense. After what you did today for Jonathan, a body would think the sheriff'd ease up on you."

Ritter shook his head slightly. He still didn't quite understand how word about what had happened in town that morning had beaten him back to the ranch. But ever since Hallie'd found out about it, she'd fussed over him so much, he was glad it had. To his own surprise, he found he liked the fussing, too.

Even the boys were looking at him a little differently.

It shouldn't surprise him, he supposed, considering how the folks in town had reacted to his saving the little boy. Why, he'd been lucky to get out of town sober, with all the men wanting to buy him a drink!

"You ain't done a damned thing around here to get Tucker in a uproar!" Hallie continued and glared at her brothers, who were clustered around the long table.

Unusually quiet, all three of them immediately dropped their gazes back to the rifles they were cleaning.

"You'd think at least one of *you*"—she nodded at them—"would ride in with him!"

"Got to get things ready for huntin', Hallie," Shad countered, unable to meet her eyes. " 'Sides, your husband's a big boy now. He don't need no help." Shad's gaze slid to his brother-in-law, then away again.

"Let it go, Hallie." Ritter took his hat from the peg by the front door. "I won't be gone long." Quickly he opened the door and stepped through. He hadn't gone more than a couple of steps when he heard the door open again behind him.

Hallie ran up to him and threw her arms around his neck. Planting her mouth against his, she gave him a long, lingering kiss that made him uncomfortably warm despite the night air.

"You best ride careful, husband," she said when she finally pulled back. "You don't want to be runnin' into any of Butler's men when you're out there on your lonesome."

Since he was headed for Butler's home ranch, the chance of running into some of his gunhands was a lot higher than she thought. He stared down into her face and wished there was a moon out tonight so that he could see her more clearly. But in the next instant he cursed himself for a fool. If there *was* a moon, Butler's men wouldn't have any trouble seeing *him*, either.

"I'll be careful," he promised, then gave himself one more minute of holding her close before he set her aside. "Now, get inside before you freeze to death."

"All right," she said with a smile, her hands rubbing up and down her arms. "But don't you be gone long, y'hear? I'll be waitin' on ya." Then she turned on her heel and ran for the house.

Lemon-yellow lamplight spilled out into the yard, then disappeared when she slipped inside. The night was black again, and Ritter heard her last words echo through his mind.

She'd be waiting for him.

He knew she couldn't realize that those simple words conjured up the reality he'd been trying to ignore the last few weeks. Waiting. His eyes narrowed as he stared blankly at the closed door. Hallie waiting for him. Without warning, ghostly images rose up before him. In his mind's eye he saw Hallie, nervous, frightened, peering out windows, looking for him. Waiting for him. Not knowing if he'd be coming home again. Not knowing if he was alive or dead.

Why couldn't they all see that *that* was what he'd been talking about when he'd said gunfighters don't make good husbands?

A stab of cold that had nothing to do with the wind sliced through him, and Ritter had to force himself to turn and walk to the barn. His steps heavy, he told himself that he was a damned fool for letting himself believe that this time with Hallie could be anything but temporary. If he made it back from Butler's alive, there was still Nathan Pine to deal with. And if not Nathan, there would surely be someone else further down the line waiting to take on Ritter Sloane.

No. No matter *what* happened in the next few weeks, he had no future with Hallie. He stepped into the barn and glanced back at the well-lit cabin. Smoke came from the chimney, and behind the homemade curtains he saw the shadows of the people who belonged there.

Hallie deserved a normal life. The kids she wanted so badly. A husband she didn't have to worry would be shot at any moment. A husband who'd be around to love her for the rest of her life. She deserved far more than he could give her.

The best he could do for her now was to clear up this Butler mess and then get out of her life. His jaw clenched, he found himself almost hoping that she *was* carrying his baby. Oh, he'd been against it at first, but now . . . maybe if she had his child, she wouldn't forget him. He swallowed heavily. Just the thought of riding away from her was enough to kill him.

He tore his gaze away from the cabin and walked into the dark barn.

Ritter stepped down from his horse and tied the reins to a fallen branch near the base of a giant cottonwood. Cupping his hands, he brought them to his mouth and blew into them, trying to take the stiffness from his fingers, just in case. He'd never been much on gloves. Couldn't feel the gun or the trigger cleanly enough. Now he was sorry he'd never bothered to get used to them.

Resolutely he checked his pistol one more time, then pulled his Winchester from the saddle scabbard. His shallow, quick breathing sent white puffs of air into the night as he stood completely still and listened. The only sound was the cottonwood leaves brushing against each other in the wind.

Satisfied, he crouched down low and began to creep up on the ranch house a couple of hundred yards away.

Ears pricked, mouth dry, every few steps he paused to listen. But there was nothing. Silence lay over everything like a thick wool blanket. It was hard to breathe, and his legs ached from the effort to move soundlessly over the twig-scattered ground. When it seemed he'd walked forever, he saw a single lamp burning through the window of the long, low bunkhouse across from the main house. Cautiously Ritter moved closer, hoping to get some idea of just how many men he had to worry about.

The nearer he got, the more curious he became. There didn't seem to be any guards posted. And for the amount of men he'd seen the last time he was at the Butler ranch, it was almighty quiet.

Flattening himself against the plank wall, Ritter turned his head and peered through the dirty window. In the middle of the room four men sat around a lopsided table playing poker. An oil lamp stood on one corner of the table, and there was one more lamp burning in a wall bracket by the door.

He ducked down beneath the edge of the window and moved to the other side. From his new vantage point, Ritter could see that at least a dozen or more of the bunks were clearly empty. Thin husk mattresses were rolled up and stowed at the head of each cot. Only five beds were set up for cowhands.

Slowly Ritter pulled back into the shadows. Frowning, he tried to puzzle out what had happened. Where were all the gunhands who'd been there when he and the boys came to see Butler?

Were they even now moving on the Benteen ranch?

No. He dismissed that idea entirely. If it were true, he'd have heard *something* on his ride over. Glancing at the main house, he noticed that there was only one light burning that he could see. He hoped that meant Butler, at least, was there.

With a last look in the bunkhouse window, Ritter told himself that wherever the missing men were, they'd made it easier for him to reach Hamilton Butler. Carefully he inched away from the wooden structure and slipped from shadow to shadow as he crossed the yard.

When he reached the huge oaken doorway, he paused a moment, then quietly grasped the brass knob and turned.

Chapter

*

Fifteen

A BURNING log cracked and split, falling to the hearth floor in a shower of sparks. In the half light of a dying fire and one oil lamp on the far wall, Hamilton Butler stared at the portrait over the mantel. He lifted the cut crystal glass to his lips and tipped it, spilling the raw whiskey down his throat in a rush of liquid heat.

Shuddering slightly, he reached for the liquor bottle in front of him and poured another drink. His gaze locked on the stiff young man in the painting, Hamilton leaned his elbows on the desk and asked, "Why the hell did you go off to that goddamned war, Devlin?" A heartbeat's pause later he shouted, "Jesus! Why didn't you *listen* to me?"

The still figure stared back at him, but now it seemed to Hamilton that the young man was *frowning* at him. *Accusing* him of something.

"Don't look at me like that!" He blinked furiously, trying to clear his vision. "None of this was *my* doing! If you hadn't listened to Caleb Benteen and his tales of glory—*Glory*!" He took another sip of the fiery whiskey and clenched his teeth at the bitter taste. "Where's the damned *glory* in dyin' on some miserable piece of land thousands of miles from home? Huh?" He nodded

217

victoriously, knowing the boy in the portrait couldn't deny *that* statement. "All alone . . . dammit, Dev, you were *alone*. When you could've been here! With *me*!"

He sagged back against the oversize leather chair and tried to tell himself that his son's eyes *weren't* . . . disappointed. Stirring uneasily, Hamilton's gaze shifted away from his son's. Instead, he stared into the glowing red embers of the burned-out fire. Running one hand through his bushy gray hair, he muttered defensively, "You don't understand. How could you?"

Hamilton looked into the painted blue of his son's eyes again and said brokenly, "You don't know what it's been like. You gone. Then Trib comes by, off on some adventure or other. And the *rest* of 'em. Them damn Benteen boys—every time I turn around I run into one of 'em." He slammed his balled-up fist onto the desktop. "Don't you see? They're alive and you're *dead*. Dammit! This ranch was for you! All for you! Why'd you go, Dev?" He propped his head in one hand and muttered, "Why the hell did you leave me?"

"He *had* to."

Hamilton Butler jumped to his feet and stared at the man in the open doorway. He swayed slightly, grabbed the edge of the desk to steady himself, and shouted, "Sloane! What are you doin' here?"

"Came to talk, Butler." Ritter moved into the room, waving the barrel of his rifle in the older man's direction. Butler tugged at the top drawer on his desk, and Ritter added quietly, "Don't go looking for a gun, man."

The big man stopped dead. Huge hands balled into tight fists, Butler dropped into his chair. He pulled in a deep breath, glared at the intruder, and snapped, "Gunfighter, huh? This how you got that reputation of yours? Sneak into an old man's house—get the drop on him—and then what? Shoot me?"

Shaking his head, Ritter crossed the room and sat down in the leather chair on the "poor man's" side of Butler's desk. "If that was the idea, you'd already be dead and I'd be talking to myself."

The older man relaxed slightly, but the expression on his face told Ritter that Butler was no more ready to talk now than before. He watched as the rancher picked up his glass of whiskey in a none too steady hand and tossed a mock salute at him. "Drink?"

"No." Ritter crossed his legs, right ankle over left knee. Then he took off his hat and perched it on his upraised knee. "I came to talk to you. Not help you drink yourself into a stupor."

"I'm through talkin'!" Butler swallowed the liquor in one gulp and poured himself another.

"That's not what it sounded like a minute ago."

The rancher frowned into his glass. Ritter watched him flick a quick glance at the portrait before mumbling, "What'd you mean?"

"About what?"

"When you said Devlin *had* to leave!" He slapped the desktop, upsetting an uncapped bottle of ink. Staring at the spreading pool of black liquid, Butler asked again, more quietly now, "Dammit, man, tell me what you meant."

Ritter's gaze moved over the other man. Butler was a far cry now from the arrogant bastard who'd been pushing his weight around the last few weeks. Turning his head, he looked over his shoulder at the portrait behind him.

A nice-lookin' boy, he told himself. Steady, proud—

and young. Too young to know what he was gettin' into by going to war. Ritter straightened in his chair and inhaled slowly. No one knew, he acknowledged silently, until he'd been there and seen the misery firsthand. He shook himself mentally and forced his concentration on the man in front of him.

Hamilton Butler was so much like Ritter's own father, it was eerie. Strong, bullheaded, arrogant as hell, and too damned proud to back down an inch. Remembering all the times he'd tried futilely to talk to his father, Ritter thought the chances of reaching Hamilton Butler were slim indeed. But he *had* to try. Quietly he answered the older man.

"He had to go to prove himself."

Butler snorted. "Prove *what*?"

Ritter shook his head and gave the man opposite him a rueful smile. "To prove he was Devlin Butler. Not *just* Hamilton Butler's son."

Staring down at his huge hands, as if wondering why his strength was no help to him, Butler mumbled, "That don't make sense."

"No? Didn't folks always refer to him as Butler's boy? Didn't he have to earn respect from the hired hands? From you?"

Tired, angry eyes snapped up to challenge Ritter's steady gaze. "You sayin' his leavin' was *my* fault? I *drove* him off?"

"No. I'm saying he had to go to prove to himself that he was his own man. Not *just* your son."

A long, tense minute followed. Except for the soft shifting of embers in the hearth, the room was silent. Ritter watched the older man and hoped that he'd said the right things. The rancher's broad shoulders were hunched, as if expecting a blow. He was so still, he hardly seemed to be breathing.

The gunfighter could only imagine what the man might be thinking. After all, he'd never been on Butler's side of the situation before. But he knew all about Devlin's side. Only too well. When he himself went to war, his own father had pretty much acted the same as Butler.

Sloane Senior hadn't wanted his only son to march off to an inglorious end on some nameless battlefield. No—he'd wanted to buy his son out of the army so that Sloane Shipping could be safely handed down to the next generation, as it had been in their family for years.

In the quiet room Ritter allowed himself to remember that last bitter quarrel with his father. Somehow he just hadn't been able to make his father see that he *had* to go. That if he bought his way out of the war, he'd be haunted forever by what might have happened to the man sent in his place.

And in the end Ritter'd gone into the army, with his father's angry words still echoing in his ears. Only it hadn't been Ritter to die during that goddamned war, but his father. The old man dropped dead of a heart seizure in the third year of the conflict. They'd found him slumped over his desk, his fingers clutching a daguerreotype of his son.

With his father dead, he had no reason to return to Boston after Lee surrendered. Competent managers ran the shipyard and kept him informed by mail. Instead of returning to a world that had seemed almost alien to him, Ritter turned West.

He took the skills he'd developed with guns and hired himself out to causes he believed in The shipyard provided more than enough income for a wandering man, and so he'd never had to sell his gun hand just to live.

Now, after so many years of lonely living and the threat of death always close, he looked back at his early life in Boston and felt as though it had all happened to someone else.

"You think so?"

Ritter shook himself mentally, shattering old memories. "What?"

"I *said*"—Butler took a long, shuddering breath and asked in a hesitant voice—"do you reckon that's why? It wasn't due to me? Or Caleb's ol' battle tales?"

Nodding slowly, Ritter glanced at the portrait behind him again. "I'm sure of it. His decision had nothing to do with you *or* Caleb Benteen." Turning back to the older man, he saw the rancher's teary gaze locked on his son's face. "If there hadn't been a war, he would have found another way to test himself."

Butler's jaw worked furiously as he fought to get a grip on his obviously reeling emotions. Ritter watched the pain and relief mingle on the man's face and waited silently for him to go on.

"You're most likely right." He smiled sadly. "Dev always was a stubborn one."

"A lot like you, huh?"

His gaze shot to Ritter, then reluctantly he nodded. "Yeah. Yeah, he was." Cocking his head, he looked carefully at Ritter and asked, "How'd you know so much about it?"

"Let's just say you weren't the *only* stubborn, powerful father in the country."

Butler nodded again, accepting the explanation, and reached for the rosewood humidor on the corner of his desk. After lifting the intricately carved lid, the older man first offered a cigar to the gunfighter, then took one himself. As matches flared and streamers of smoke swirled in the still air, Butler asked quietly, "Why'd you come here tonight, Sloane? I know it wasn't just to tell a foolish old man about his own son."

Leaning back in his chair, Ritter studied the glowing end of his cigar. "I want to talk about the Benteens—and you—and this war you started." Deliberately he paused and took a long drag on his cigar. Blowing the blue smoke toward the ceiling, he looked Butler square in the eye. "First off, where are all your gunhands, Butler?"

Hallie opened the door and looked outside for the third time. She squinted into the distance, trying to see down the long, dark road that stretched out away from the ranch. But there was nothing. Finally she closed the door against the night air and asked, "What d'ya suppose he's doin'?"

Jericho's gaze flicked from Micah to Shad before he offered, "Maybe he's talkin' to one of his new friends. Way I heard it—everybody in town tried to buy him a drink this morning."

"Uh . . . yeah." Micah looked back at Jericho, then added, "Seems folks in town are thinkin' mighty highly of him right now."

Hallie smiled and walked to the table to join her brothers. Oily rags, kerosene, brass cleaning rods, and a still-steaming kettle of boiling water lay scattered over the old table.

Shad reached for a patch of cloth, tied a string around it, and drew it down the rifle barrel. Absently Hallie dipped another patch into the gun oil and handed it to him. She grinned suddenly. "Isn't that somethin'? Him savin' little Jonathan that way, I mean? And all the folks in town takin' on so after him?" Looking from one to the other of the boys, it took her a moment to realize that *she* was the only one smiling.

Well, for heaven's sake, she asked herself as she walked to the settee and plopped down. What does the man have to do to prove himself? She'd thought that Jericho and Shad at least would be more accepting. Micah always *was* the toughest nut in the bunch.

Her gaze flicked up to her brothers, then just as quickly slid away again. She stared instead into the fire. Surely, she thought, even *Micah* had to admit that Ritter'd done more than his share around the place. And now, after saving Jonathan, even the *sheriff* was lookin' a little kinder on her husband.

Husband. She smiled inwardly. She'd never have believed that she could get so fond of a husband. Hell, Hallie'd never *wanted* another man around the house all the time. And now . . . with Ritter gone—the place seemed downright *empty*.

Strange to think that in another three weeks or so, Ritter'd be leavin'. Though they hadn't spoken of it in some time, Hallie remembered their agreement very well indeed. And to give him his due, he'd more than lived up to his side, too. She wrapped her arms around herself and let the memories of Ritter's loving flood her.

Silently Hallie acknowledged that she hadn't been thinking of making babies lately, either. No. She was enjoying her time with Ritter for its own sake. Because of him.

But was he still plannin' on leavin'?

Of course he was. Why wouldn't he? They'd never talked of anything else. But everything had changed, hadn't it? It surely had for her. Hallie didn't want him to leave. She didn't want *a* baby. She wanted *lots* of babies—and Ritter right beside her to help ride herd on 'em.

He couldn't know that, though. Hell, she thought, grinning, she'd just now admitted it to herself! And for the life of her, she couldn't understand why it had taken her *this* long to figure out what she wanted! It didn't matter, though. They still had time. And as soon as Ritter came home, she'd tell him so. Home. Husband. Strange how those two little words fitted so right together.

She glanced over at her brothers and pushed herself to her feet. Might as well start with them, she thought firmly. They'd best start treatin' Ritter more like a brother, 'cause if she had anything to say about it—they would all be a family for some time to come!

"Y'know, boys," she said as she strolled over to the table, "when Ritter gets back from town, I want you three to start right in on makin' him feel more welcome round here."

"What?"

She looked at Micah. "You know what I mean. Like for one thing, stop lookin' at him with that evil eye of yours, Micah."

He frowned, but she leaned her palms on the table and went on. "See, he's your brother now, and you'd best get used to it. 'Cause he ain't leavin' anytime soon."

Micah's gaze shifted from Hallie to Jericho. Jericho avoided looking at Hallie entirely and turned to Shad.

Uneasiness stirred in Hallie. Something was wrong. Something was goin' on that she knew nothing about. And she felt in her bones that whatever it was, it boded no good for Ritter.

Looking at the *one* brother who'd never been able to lie to her, Hallie said quietly, "Shadrack?"

He looked up almost guiltily.

"What's goin' on here? What do you know about Ritter that you ain't tellin'?"

His guileless green eyes locked on hers. Even when his brothers murmured warnings, his gaze didn't waver. When she thought she couldn't stand his silence another minute, Shadrack took a deep breath and said softly, "He went to Butler's, Hallie. Alone."

"Well, Butler," Ritter asked again, "are you going to tell me what happened to those warriors you had strutting around here a while back . . . or are you just gonna sit there?"

"I fired 'em."

"What?"

"I *said*, I fired 'em."

That was something Ritter hadn't been expecting. He stared at the older man. Though he wanted to shout out more questions, he forced himself to be quiet and wait for the explanation he knew was coming.

"It was after the, uh . . . fight at Dixie's." Butler shoved his cigar in his mouth and clenched his jaw around the end of it.

"From what I hear, fighting in the saloon is nothin' new.

And you were all for the Benteen boys getting pushed around. So why—"

"Hallie." He spoke around the cigar, and his voice sounded tight.

"What about her?"

"Dixie told me that Jed tried to . . ." He snatched the cigar free and shook it at Ritter. "Hell! You should be able to understand that!"

Anger filled him again as he recalled the cowboy's rough handling of Hallie, but Ritter tamped it back down. He wanted the old man to keep talking. Maybe there would be a way out of this mess after all. "Yeah. *I* understand. But she's my wife. What the hell did it matter to *you*?"

"Your wife!" Butler snorted and stood up, sending his chair skittering back into a bookcase. He jabbed the red tip of his cigar at Ritter's face like a pointer and shouted, "What is it to me? Hell, I've known that girl since—well, since *forever*! Like my own, she is . . . and I'll not have some man pawin' at her like she was a common . . ." He stopped abruptly, walked around the edge of his desk, and marched to the fireplace. Hands curled around the mantel, he leaned forward and stared into the dead fire. "I near went crazy when I found out that a man workin' for *me* would lay a hand on that girl."

"All right." Ritter stood up and walked over to stand beside the rancher. "So you fired Jed. Why the others, too?"

Butler raised his head slightly and looked at Ritter from the corner of his eyes. "The rest of 'em were no better than him. Just trail trash more ready to shoot a gun than handle a branding iron or a rope. If I'd kept them on, it woulda just happened again." He straightened abruptly. "I won't have it. Not from men workin' for me."

His gaze locked on Butler's face, Ritter saw the truth etched plainly in the older man's expression. It had cost him a lot to admit his mistake. Nodding slowly, he asked, "So. This mean you're callin' off the war?"

The man pulled in a deep breath and tilted his head back to look up at the portrait of his son. He seemed more at peace as he stared into the young man's face. In fact, he was more composed, more calm than Ritter'd ever seen him.

"Yeah," the man finally said with a sigh. "Yeah. I reckon it does."

"And what about Nathan Pine?"

Butler turned to look at him. "Dixie told you?"

"Yes."

He smiled. "A good woman, Dixie. Shoulda known she'd tell you folks as soon as she could." He met Ritter's steady gaze unflinchingly. "Yeah, I sent for him. Shames me to admit it now . . . but dammit!" He frowned at the gunfighter. "You quit on me. Made me look like a damned fool. I had to do something!"

"And you think what you did makes you *not* a fool?"

Butler's ruddy skin flushed a deep red, and the veins in his thick neck stood out. Ritter stood his ground, waiting for an answer.

"Does it matter now?" Butler threw his cigar into the cold ashes and propped one boot up on the hearth. "Hell, does any of this matter now? Pine's on his way, and I can't call him off."

"When's he coming?"

"I don't know." The man shoved one hand through

his unruly gray hair and muttered viciously, "It could be anytime now. Got a wire a few days ago. Said he was on his way."

"From where?"

"Cheyenne."

Ritter cursed silently. Cheyenne. Pine could arrive any day. Maybe tomorrow. Maybe next week. There was no way to tell. Nathan had been champing at the bit for a try at Ritter for years. But he told himself, it would be just like Nathan to draw out his journey, hoping to make his opponent nervous.

"What about when he gets here, Butler? What then?"

"What d'ya mean?"

"First thing Pine will do is report to you. You're the man who hired him. You're the one who'll pay him." Ritter leaned one hand on the mantel and stared at the other man. "When he shows up here . . . at your door . . . then what?"

"I . . . uh . . ." Butler ran a hand over his jaw, and Ritter watched him try to think. To find a way out.

"What are you gonna say to him?"

"I don't know!"

"You best think of something! You said yourself a minute ago that the war was over." Leaning closer, Ritter said, more quietly this time, "It's up to you, Butler. Are you gonna set your hired gun on the Benteen family? Or not?"

Butler's knuckles whitened as he gripped the mantel. His jaw clenched, he shook his head. "No," he finally ground out. "I'm not." He looked over at Ritter. "When he gets here, I'll pay him off and send him on his way. The war's over."

Ritter nodded slowly. At least *this* part of the trouble was finished.

"What's the matter?" Butler snorted. "Don't believe me?"

"Oh, I believe you, man," Ritter countered. "I just hope it's enough to pay him off."

"What d'ya mean?"

"I mean, nobody sends Nathan Pine on his way if he don't want to go." Butler's eyes narrowed, and Ritter nodded again. "That's right, Ham. You called on the Devil. Now he's comin,' and there's gonna be hell to pay."

Chapter
※
Sixteen

HALLIE RAN into the yard and slammed the front door behind her. She got no more than a few feet from the house, though, before the door was thrown open again.

"Hallie!" Micah shouted. "You wait a damn minute! Where the hell do you think you're goin'?"

"Butler's." She kept walking, her gaze fixed on the barn. "If you bunch are scared and willin' to sit around waitin' to see what's gonna happen next—I *ain't!*"

"You can't do that," Jericho called out. She heard his running steps and tried to hurry, but he cut her off. Grim-faced, he stopped right in front of her, blocking her path to the barn—and her horse.

"Get outta my way, Jericho." She moved around him, but suddenly Shad was there, and she came up short.

"Now, Hallie . . ." Shad started.

"How could you let him go ridin' off alone like that?"

"How was we s'posed to stop him?" Jericho asked, his arms spread wide.

"Besides," Micah added as he took a stand on the other side of her. "It was a good idea."

The night sky blanketed by clouds, there was no moonlight or even starlight to see by. She had to strain to see her brothers' expressions. And the arrogant tilt of Micah's head lit a fire under her already simmering anger.

"Good idea?" Hallie shoved at Micah, and he staggered off-balance. "Lettin' him ride in *alone* into a nest of hired guns?"

"He said he could *sneak* in easier alone," Shad countered.

She whipped around and sneered at him. "And what was *your* job? Lyin' to your sister? Your own *blood*?"

Shad flinched, but Jericho said quickly, "We didn't *want* to, Hallie. But sometimes you get up a full head of steam and do things that folks might call . . ."

"Stupid!" Micah finished for him.

She swung her fist back to take aim, but Jericho grabbed her arm. "Now, Hallie, why don't we all go on in and . . ."

She raised her arm and snapped it back down, shaking him loose. Then she took a half step in one direction, and when the boys shifted, she quickly sidestepped the other way and headed for the barn.

Micah was too fast for her, though. He grabbed her from behind, his big hands encircling her waist. Lifting her off the ground, he shouted, "Dammit, Hallie—I ain't never been fond of that fella! But he *does* know what he's doin'!"

Hallie's fingers pulled ineffectually at her brother's hands. She couldn't budge him. With Micah practically shouting in her ear, she tried swinging and kicking her legs out and gave silent thanks she was wearing her buckskins.

"Right now," Micah was saying, "he knows where his enemies are. But *you* go thunderin' in there and . . . *Ow!*"

He dropped her abruptly and fell to the ground himself when her bootheel connected with his shin. Leaping up almost immediately, Hallie took off again, still determined to reach her horse.

Jericho snatched her hand as she ran past and swung her around. But with her free hand, Hallie grabbed the rope handle of the nearby wooden milking bucket. Bringing it high, she bounced it off Jericho's forehead, and he staggered back, loosening his grip.

Micah yelled, "Catch 'er, Shad!"

Before Hallie knew what was happening, she was facedown in the dirt, struggling to recapture the breath knocked out of her when Shad tripped her. Now Shadrack was sitting on her backside and obviously had no plans to move real quick.

Hallie blew her hair out of her eyes and smiled slyly. She'd wrestled with the boys for years. In fact, she hadn't stopped until she'd developed bosoms and started embarrassing her brothers. Every time they'd grabbed her in the wrong spot, they'd dropped her like a hot rock.

Now she used a trick she hadn't pulled in years. Quietly she began to sniffle and take short, gasping breaths. At the same time Shad slipped to one side of her, Hallie heard Micah shout, "She ain't cryin'! Don't move!"

But it was too late. She rolled over, hooked one leg around Shadrack's neck and threw him clear. Then she was up and running again. Just as her fingers curled around the barn door latch, though, her feet left the ground.

"Damn you, Jericho!" she screamed as he tossed her over one shoulder. Her head hung down to the middle of Jericho's back, and he held her legs in a viselike grip next to his chest. "Let me down, or so help me Hannah . . ."

"Hang on to 'er, Jericho," Micah said as he limped up to them. Hallie pushed against her brother's back to hold herself upright enough to see.

"Leg hurt, Micah?" she asked sweetly.

"You nasty-tempered—" Micah broke off suddenly and studied her backside thoughtfully for a long minute.

Hallie saw what he was thinking and immediately began to squirm and twist, trying to get free. "You lay a hand on me, Micah Benteen, and I swear there ain't enough country in Wyoming for you to hide from me!"

Micah shook his head and glared right back at his sister. "No—I ain't gonna spank you. Though, Lord knows, it's a temptin' thought . . ."

"Ain't it just," Shad echoed as he pushed himself to his feet.

"Shad!"

"Sorry, Hallie. But that cryin' trick wasn't fair. And 'sides"—he rubbed one side of his head, sending his bushy auburn hair into a wild halo framing his face— "You about busted my head open when you slammed me into the ground like that."

Jericho tossed her into the air, and the wind rushed out of her when her abdomen landed once again across his shoulder. Jericho laughed and urged, "Don't pass this chance up, Micah! God knows when we'll get her hogtied like this again."

Hallie punched him in the middle of his back and nodded victoriously when she heard him groan.

"Cut that out, Hallelujah!" Micah stepped up closer to her. He ignored her flashing eyes and grabbed her hands with both of his. Shaking his head, he said, "Y'know, sometimes I think Papa done wrong by you."

She blew at her hair, trying to clear her vision. "What d'ya mean?"

"I mean lettin' you run wild with us boys your whole life. Nobody bothered to teach you different. Not even Mama. Hell"—he sighed heavily—"I reckon it was easier to teach you how to fish and hunt than it woulda been to teach you how to be a lady."

"Hah! Who woulda taught me that? *You*?"

"Lord save me from foul-tempered females!" Micah got right down in her face, nose to nose. "You know, I'd rather be shut up in a cage with a grizzly than married to a hardheaded, sharp-tongued woman like you!"

Hallie's eyes narrowed.

"Yessir," Micah went on, "at first, I was so damned mad at that gunfighter for havin' his way with ya, I'd as soon as shot him as made him marry you. Now I think shootin' him woulda been *kinder*!"

"Perhaps," a deep voice agreed, "but far less interesting."

"Well, thank the Lord," Micah muttered and straightened up to face the man who'd just ridden up.

"Ritter!" Hallie shouted, snatching her hands away from Micah and pushing frantically at Jericho's broad back. "Goddammit, lemme go!"

Jericho obediently loosened his hold, shrugged his shoulders, and let his sister tumble to the ground. He gave her a satisfied smile as he watched her get up, rubbing her backside. Then, speaking to his brother-in-law, Jericho said, "You watch out for her, man, she carries quite a punch!"

Shad started for the house, still rubbing his head. "Yeah, and her kicks ain't bad, either."

Micah looked up at the shadowy figure, then glanced

at his sister. "Reckon we'll wait to hear what you got to say till after she's through with ya." He turned away, muttering, "If there's anything left of ya."

When they were alone in the yard, Ritter swung down from his horse and walked to Hallie's side. It wasn't until he was right next to her that he could read her expression. And then it was too late. She hit him hard, flush on the jaw, and before he could react, she'd thrown her arms around his neck and was squeezing the life out of him.

"Butler's men didn't shoot ya!" she whispered frantically and hugged him even tighter.

Ritter's arms closed around her, and he buried his head in the soft curve of her neck and shoulder. It was so good to have her hold him. To feel her pleasure at his return. Even the punch she'd given him was welcome. He wiggled his jaw slightly. Painful, but welcome.

Lord, he was going to miss her. She kissed his neck, and Ritter tried desperately to hang on to that feeling. To remember exactly what the touch of her mouth against his skin felt like so that he could draw up the memory on cold, lonely nights.

And if he lived to be a hundred, he would never forget the scene that greeted him on his return from Hamilton Butler's ranch. He'd actually stopped in the shadows for a moment or two, to watch his wife best her brothers in a wrestling match. Ritter squeezed her tightly, pressing her body close. He wanted to be able to recall everything about her. From her temper to her laughter to her open eagerness in bed.

From where he stood, there were far too many lonely years ahead.

Hallie leaned her head back and stared up at him. "I'm sorry I hit ya, Ritter. Are ya all right?"

"Yeah." He raised one hand to smooth her hair back from her cheek. "I'm fine."

"Good." She pushed away from him, put her hands on her hips, and yelled, "Don't you *never* do something like that again, y'hear?"

He opened his mouth, but she rushed on.

"Dammit, Ritter, I ain't your child. I'm your wife. You shoulda told me what was goin' on!"

"I didn't want you worried." It sounded like a lame excuse even to his own ears.

"Y'mean you didn't think I was worried anyway? Or you just plain didn't think at all?" She leaned in close and grabbed the lapels of his fleece-lined coat. "Worryin' is part of carin', husband. If ya don't give me one, then ya can't give me the other. Don't ya see that?"

He nodded, unable to speak.

"All right then, we'll say no more about it." She leaned her forehead against his chest. "Just don't lie to me, Ritter. I can't abide lyin'."

Ritter rested his chin on the top of her head and stared blankly at the darkness. Her arms slipped around his waist, and she held him tightly. Perhaps for the last time, he allowed himself to enjoy her closeness. Knowing he would soon be leaving added a bittersweet edge to her touch, but he couldn't deny himself.

She was right about the lies. She deserved the truth, and she would get it. Tonight.

"I won't lie to you again, Hallie." He pulled in a deep breath of the cold night air and felt it settle around his already heavy heart. "I promise."

"Then I promise not to hit ya again." Her voice was muffled, but she snuggled in closer to him. "Now, tell me what happened with Ham."

Quietly Ritter told her everything about his visit with the older rancher. She was silent for the length of time it took for him to tell his story, but when he was finished, she leaned back in his arms and grinned.

"That's wonderful, husband! You did it! You talked Ham into calling off the war—and even got him to swear to sending Pine on his way when he turns up!" She reached up and cupped his cheek with her hand. "Everything's fine now. With Ham comin' to his senses, our worries are over!" Hallie rose up on tiptoe and pulled his head down to hers. Slanting her lips across his mouth, she whispered urgently, "Let's us go on to bed and celebrate, shall we?"

"No." He watched disappointment fill her eyes as she slowly lowered herself back down. She didn't understand about Pine. She didn't know yet that nothing was finished. She didn't know that her husband would be leaving her in just a few days.

He sighed heavily. As much as he wanted to go into their room and close the rest of the world out, he couldn't do it. Not yet. He wanted to put off telling her goodbye just as long as he could.

"No?" she asked.

"I mean, uh . . . I've got to tell the boys all the news first, Hallie. They've been waiting, too."

She chewed at her bottom lip before nodding abruptly. "All right. You go on ahead and talk to them. I'll be waitin' on ya, though. So don't take too long."

He watched her walk to the house, and when she opened

the door, lamplight shone on her briefly, illuminating the soft smile she gave him before slipping inside.

Alone, Ritter turned for the barn. First, he would stable his horse, then talk to his brothers-in-law . . . then he would have to face Hallie.

Nathan Pine sliced into his well-done steak, smiling absently at the clean cut of a sharp blade. He could feel the stares from the other diners in the tiny restaurant. He heard the muted whispers and knew the people were talking about him. Speculating about the gunfighter's next job and pitying his next victim.

Deliberately he ignored them all. Signaling the waitress, he held his empty coffee mug up. She hurried over to him, and Nathan read the wariness in her brown eyes. Slowly he gave her a smile and watched as some of her fear was replaced by curiosity.

He let his gaze move over her well-rounded curves, and when she preened a little, he hid a satisfied smile. With very little effort Nathan was sure he could convince her to "keep him company" for the night. Most women, he'd found, were more interested in gunfighters than they pretended. And he suspected that for years afterward they remembered their one night with a *dangerous* man very fondly indeed.

Nathan's gaze lingered on the swell of the woman's breasts a moment longer than was proper, then looked up into her eyes. The fascination was there. All he had to do was feed it a bit.

And why not? He would be in Stillwater in two or three days. Why not enjoy the trip as much as he could?

He stood and held out the chair beside his. Smiling at

the waitress, he said smoothly, "Won't you join me? It's much too lonely, eating alone."

Slowly the woman sat down, her gaze locked on the notorious gunfighter who behaved like such a gentleman.

Ritter'd almost hoped that Hallie would fall asleep while waiting for him. But she hadn't. And in her arms he'd enjoyed for the last time, he was sure, what most men took for granted. The simple joy of making love with his wife.

His breathing still ragged, Ritter lay on his back, Hallie curled up beside him. Idly he ran his hand up and down her spine and told himself that he couldn't wait any longer. He had to tell her.

"Hallie," he whispered, "you asked me not to lie to you anymore . . ."

"Yeah?"

"There's no easy way to say this, so I'll just get it out and over with. I'll be leaving soon, Hallie."

She went absolutely still. He couldn't even feel her breath on his chest anymore. "When?"

"I won't leave until after Pine gets here. But once that's settled, I'll be going." He paused for a shaky breath. "It's better this way, Hallie."

She didn't move. She didn't speak. For a long moment Ritter wondered if he'd been wrong. If she really didn't care one way or the other about his being there.

"Better for who, Ritter?"

"You, of course."

"Me." Hallie pulled back from him and rose up to her knees. "And just who decided what was best for me? You? My brothers?"

"Hallie . . ."

"No!" She pushed her hair back out of her eyes and glared at him.

Ritter tried to keep his eyes locked on hers, but her naked flesh, still damp from their loving, distracted him.

Quickly she grabbed the quilt from the end of the bed and threw it around her shoulders. Lifting her chin, she told him, "If you ain't fixin' to be my husband anymore, you can damn sure keep your eyes to yourself!"

Ritter sat up and reached for her. "Hallie, try to understand,"

"Oh, I *understand* just fine, Ritter." She rolled off the edge of the bed and began to pace furiously. "You had enough of playin' house, and now you're ready to take off."

"That *was* the original bargain we made. Remember?"

"The hell with that!" She clutched the quilt with one hand and shook the other fist at the naked man on her bed. "You know good and well we gone way past that bargain. Don't you go throwin' *that* up at me now!"

He sighed. "You're right. This has nothing to do with the bargain."

"Then why?"

"Because of *me*." He rolled off the bed and walked to her. "Can't you see that as long as I stay here, *none* of you would be safe?"

"No, I don't." She tilted her head back to look at him. "Butler's gonna fire Pine as soon as he shows up. If he ever does!"

"Oh, he's comin', Hallie." Ritter grabbed her shoulders. "Count on it. And it doesn't matter if Butler fires him or not. Pine doesn't care if he gets *paid* for killing me. Hell, he's been achin' to do that for years!"

"Well, if he's comin' here to get you, why're you stayin'? Wouldn't we be *safer* if you left now?"

He paid no attention to her sarcasm. "I thought about that. But I don't think so. I think Pine will come in here and find out about you."

"So?"

"So, once he knows I have a wife, he'll be able to use you to get to me. And don't think he won't do it, either!"

"Don't make much sense." She turned her back on him. "How can he get to you by doin' something to a body you don't care nothin' about?"

He wanted to pull her into his arms and tell her he loved her. Promise to stay with her always. He wanted to tumble her back down onto that mattress and plunge his body so deeply into hers that they would never be free of each other. But he couldn't. He couldn't risk her life by staying with her. But he couldn't let her think he didn't give a damn, either.

Hesitantly he laid his hands on her shoulders. "I *do* care, Hallie, it's just—"

"Not enough?" Her voice shook and Ritter clenched his jaw tightly at the sound. "Tell me somethin', Ritter. What about the boys? You figure things've changed for them, too? You figure that they ain't gonna hunt you down?"

His hands dropped to his sides. "I don't think they will, no. But even if they do, I'll have to take that chance."

She snorted and walked to the window, keeping distance between them. "Rather take a chance on gettin' yourself shot than stay with me, huh?" She pulled in a deep breath. "Well, don't you give the boys another thought, *husband.*

They won't come after ya. I'll see to it. I'll just tell 'em I don't *want* ya back."

"Hallie—"

"Don't talk anymore, Ritter." She grabbed the edge of the curtains and tugged it out of the way. "Tell ya what. Since you're so dead set on leavin', why don't you just go on and get out now? Tonight."

"No, Hallie. I have to wait for Pine."

"If you're wantin' to do what's best for me here, Ritter, you'll go."

"I can't."

She dropped the curtain and spun around to face him. In the half light Ritter saw one tear roll down her cheek.

"Then you wait for him somewheres else."

She lifted her chin and stared at him unblinkingly. With the quilt pooled around her feet, she looked much as she had that first morning when the boys burst in on them unannounced. He could hardly believe so much had changed in such a short length of time.

"What?" he asked.

"I *said*, you go somewheres else to wait. You won't be doin' it in my bedroom. Not anymore."

"I see." Ritter nodded briefly. He turned and snatched his clothes off the chair in the corner of the room. "Where do you want me to go, Hallie?"

"I want you to go to hell, Ritter."

Chapter

Seventeen

HALLIE GAVE the eggs another stir, then picked up the coffeepot and set it on the table. Turning back to the stove, she opened the oven door to check the biscuits one more time. As she performed all the familiar morning chores, her mind went back over the scene with Ritter the night before.

What in the hell had happened? When did he decide to leave? And why? Oh, she didn't believe any of that nonsense about it bein' safer for her and the boys if he was gone. For God's sake, the Benteens had been standin' up to trouble for more years than she'd been alive.

Hell, everybody who lived west of St. Louis had more trouble than they could shake a stick at. That was all part and parcel of livin' where they did. Folks accepted it as such, too. Even with Ritter gone, it didn't mean they'd be any safer! It only meant they'd have one less gun around to defend the place in time of trouble. Dammit, why couldn't he *see* that?

Unless, she told herself thoughtfully, it had nothing to do with any of that. Could it be that he was really leavin' 'cause she just wasn't good enough? Self-consciously Hallie looked down at her worn buckskins. Maybe, she thought, he just didn't want a wife who wore pants more often than skirts. Maybe he didn't like a woman who could shoot her own meat better than most men. And he prob'ly didn't care for women cussin', either.

She sighed and glanced at the shiny copper bottom of a pan hanging on the wall. Her own indistinct reflection stared back. Maybe he liked his women with long hair, too.

Well, shit! She could let it grow. And dresses might be all right once in a while. . . .

Oh, stop it! she told herself and grabbed a towel. She opened the oven door and took out the sheet of golden brown baking powder biscuits. Slamming the iron door shut again, Hallie slid the biscuits onto a plate, then tossed the towel to the table.

No matter how many dresses she wore or how hard she tried to stop cussin' or how long she grew her hair, she just would never be the kind of *lady* Ritter Sloane wanted.

Dry-eyed and angry, Hallie dropped onto the closest bench and propped her elbows on the table. What she wanted to know was, how come the first man she ever wanted didn't want her?

Micah snatched another biscuit and broke it open. He slathered butter on the still-steaming inside and glanced covertly at Ritter and Hallie. Casting a quick look at his two brothers, Micah shook his head. He didn't know what was goin' on any more than they did. But whatever it was, it didn't look like it was gonna end any time soon.

Edgy, he shifted position on the bench and wished to hell someone would say something. He'd never sat through such a quiet breakfast in his life.

"Say, Micah," Jericho said too loudly, "what d'ya think we ought to do about that bay mare of Trib's?"

"Huh?" Micah shook himself.

"I say, you think we ought to break Trib's mare or wait and let him do it?"

"Uh, best wait for Trib, I reckon."

"Yeah." Jericho looked uneasily around the table. "Yeah. Guess so."

Ritter knew they were wondering what was going on. They kept looking at him out of the corner of their eyes. Everyone, that is, but Hallie.

He risked a glance at her. She'd only looked at him once, when he first came to the table. And in that one look Ritter'd seen the hurt and the anger in her eyes. He'd wanted to do something, *say* something . . . but he couldn't.

She hadn't been crying, he told himself. Her eyes weren't red and puffy. They were clear and sharp, and they looked right through him as if he weren't there. He took another sip of coffee and silently admitted that Hallie wasn't the kind to cry her heart out all night.

No. It was much more likely that she'd shoot him. And he wouldn't blame her.

"Now, who the hell's that?" Jericho leaned back and pulled the curtain out of the way. Staring outside, they saw a lone rider approach the house at a fast trot.

Shad stood up. "I'll go see."

He crossed to the door and opened it. The others heard a brief, subdued conversation, then the door was closing again and Shad approached the table. They heard the messenger ride away at a gallop.

Face grim, Shad held a telegram in his right hand.

Holding it out to his oldest brother, he said softly, "It's for Micah."

Micah rubbed one hand over his bearded jaw before reaching out for the folded paper. He looked up at Hallie and the boys. "It don't *have* to be bad news, y'know."

"Why the hell else would somebody be sendin' us a telegram?" Jericho countered.

"I don't know." Micah's thumbs moved over the crisp folds uneasily.

Ritter took a deep breath and stared at each of them in turn before saying, "Why don't you open the damn thing and find out?"

"Yeah." Micah unfolded the paper and stared down at the block letters for a long, quiet moment. Finally he looked up. "It's from Trib. He needs help. Wants Jericho and me to come quick and Shad to stay here with Hallie."

"Let me see it," Hallie said and grabbed the paper. Her gaze moved quickly over the message. "What do you suppose is wrong?"

"No tellin'." Micah stood up and shoved his hands in his pockets. "But we can't go."

Jericho's eyes snapped up to meet his brother's. "What do you mean we can't go? *Course* we're goin'!"

"How?" Micah waved one hand at Ritter. "Trib don't know a damned thing about Sloane here, or what's been goin' on. If he did, he wouldn't a sent for us."

"Point is," Shad commented, "he did. And you know Trib. He wouldn't ask for help unless he really needed it. You got to go."

"Yeah? And what about Nathan Pine, Shad?"

"*I* can handle Pine," Ritter spoke up quietly and waited

until the others were looking at him to continue. "As long as Shad's around to protect Hallie."

Shad smiled. "There you go."

"Just a damned minute!" Hallie shouted out. "I don't need a damned one of you bunch protectin' me. I been takin' care of myself for years."

"Nobody said you couldn't, Hallie," Shad said quietly.

"*He* did!" She pointed at Ritter. "You just take care of yourself, gunfighter. You got no call to worry about me. Not anymore."

Anger rushed through Ritter as he stared at his hardheaded wife. He felt her brothers' curious eyes on him and fought for control of his temper. It wouldn't do any good to get into another argument with Hallie right now.

After a long, tense moment Micah said, "When you figure Pine'll get here, Sloane?"

Ritter's gaze never left Hallie. "Anytime now."

"Well, if we leave right now," Micah said thoughtfully, "we could be back in about a week, maybe. What do ya think, Jericho? Two days goin', two days there, and two days back?"

"Seems about right."

"Done." Micah nodded abruptly. "We'll take two horses each so we can ride straight through, switchin' animals when they get tired."

"I'll get our blanket rolls packed up," Jericho offered and headed for their bedroom. "The quicker we get gone, the quicker we'll be back."

"I'll help with the horses," Shadrack offered and followed Micah out the front door.

*　　*　　*

Ritter watched Hallie as she moved quickly and competently about the kitchen. She didn't spare him a glance, and yet, Ritter was sure she was aware of his presence. The stiff way she held her shoulders and how she managed to avoid looking anywhere in his direction proved it.

He let his gaze move over her, and he realized he was glad she hadn't taken to wearing dresses very often. He liked the way the soft buckskin clung to her body like a lover. She moved with an inner grace that made each of her movements smooth, liquid. Her shining clean hair just touched the edge of her shirt, and it was all he could do to keep from going to her and threading his hands through the auburn curls.

Suddenly he closed his eyes and drew a long, shaky breath. This idle daydreaming was accomplishing nothing. Except making it even harder for him to think about leaving.

"Why don't you go, too?"

He shook his head. Hallie *spoke* to him? "What?"

She spun around and faced him. Hands curled around the counter behind her, Hallie looked him square in the eye and said again, "Why don't you go now, too?"

"What do you mean, go? With the boys?"

"No!" She breathed deeply and cast one glance at the closed door to her brothers' bedroom. Lowering her voice so Jericho wouldn't hear her, she said, "Of course not with the boys. I mean why don't you just leave like you want to?"

"I've already told you . . ."

She raised one hand to stop him from continuing. "I know. But this is your best chance. With Micah and

Jericho gone, Shad won't leave me to track you down. You can get good and clear of the Benteens' once and for all."

"And what about Nathan Pine?" Ritter countered, taking a step closer to her. "What kind of man do you think I am, Hallie? You really think I'm gonna walk away from my *wife* when I know that trouble is coming?"

She snorted and sidestepped slightly. "*Wife*, is it? For how much longer? No, don't say nothin'. I don't need you to worry about me, Ritter Sloane. Besides, maybe when you leave, Pine'll chase after you."

"It's possible. But I can't risk it."

"*You* can't risk it? Hah!"

"That's right. I can't risk it. If I left and he didn't follow me—"

"Oh, yes, he'll *use* me to get to you." She smirked at him.

"Yes! He will." Ritter closed the gap between them quickly. "Don't you think if there was an easier way to handle this, I would do it?"

Hallie shook her head, and a bitter smile curved her lips. "You should listen to yourself sometime, Sloane. All you talk about is you."

"What?"

"Yeah. About what you want. What you think. What you hate to do. How Pine is comin' after *you*. How he'll use me to get at *you*." She laughed shortly and stared up into her husband's eyes. "Do you think everything in this whole damned world centers on *you*? Believe it or not, gunfighter, folks all over the damn country have problems and manage to *fix* 'em without *you*!"

"That's not what I—"

"*You* again! Well, I heard enough about you, Sloane. Now it's *your* turn to listen!" She poked his chest with her index finger. "Us Benteens have been gettin' into and out of messes for generations . . . all without your help. And we'll go right on takin' care of our own long after you're gone."

He grabbed her elbows and pulled her to him. Lowering his head, he argued, "This has nothing to do with the Benteens. Whether you want to hear it or not, this is between Nathan Pine and *me*. It's been comin' for years, and now it's here. Can't you understand that I'm only trying to protect you?"

Hallie shook her head slowly. "You still don't see, do you, husband? In this family, we protect each other. And don't try to tell me that you're leavin' here to keep me safe. I know that ain't so. Hell, even a fool would know that walkin' away only means you're leavin' us with one less gun for when trouble starts. And trouble comes, Ritter, whether you're here or not. Besides"—she lifted her chin proudly—"I know why you're really tryin' to get shut of me."

He sighed. "Why's that?"

"Because I ain't good enough for ya."

"What?" His jaw dropped and he stared at her, wide-eyed.

"Don't make it worse by pretendin'." She pulled free of him and stood up straight. "Oh, I know what you think of me."

He crossed his arms over his chest, cocked his head at an angle, and asked quietly, "Why don't you tell me what I think?"

"All right. You like me fine for warmin' up your bed

and such . . . but the way I dress and talk"—she shook her head—"just ain't ladylike enough for you."

Through clenched teeth he said, "How do you figure that?"

"Well, why else would you buy me all them new clothes? And why else would you be sneakin' off?"

"I *enjoyed* buying you gifts, Hallie. And as for sneaking off . . . we had a bargain."

"Six weeks was the bargain. It ain't been but three or so."

He pushed one hand through his hair. "Things changed."

"I'd say so." She turned her back on him. "Why don't you leave now? *Please?*"

Ritter reached for her but stopped himself before touching her. He'd already hurt her enough. Maybe she was right. Oh, not about what he thought of her. Lord, could anyone be more wrong than *that*? But maybe he *should* leave. Maybe Pine *would* follow him.

His gaze lingered on her a moment longer, and he knew he couldn't risk it. If he left and Pine hurt Hallie . . . Abruptly Ritter spun about, crossed the room, yanked the door open, and slammed it hard behind him.

Hallie glanced over her shoulder to make sure he was gone, then ran for the solitude of her room.

When everything was quiet again, Jericho opened his door. Cautiously he looked around before stepping into the empty room. He shook his head and clutched the two blanket rolls tightly. For the first time since the telegram arrived, he was glad of Trib's message. Nathan Pine or no, Jericho knew he didn't want to be anywhere *near* the home ranch while Sloane and Hallie were at each other's throats.

He almost felt sorry for Shad.

* * *

Shad tugged at the strip of rawhide until it was good and tight, then sliced off the excess length with his knife. He'd been repairing the bridle for over an hour. More than twice the time it usually took him. But then again, he was in no hurry to leave the peaceful barn and face his sister and her husband again.

Shaking his head, he leaned back against the barn wall and remembered that last conversation he'd had with Micah and Jericho before they left.

"Somethin' mighty strange is goin' on between them two," Jericho said, after telling his brothers all about the argument he'd overheard. "Seems like Hallie was tryin' to get Ritter to take off, but he don't want to go. At least not yet."

"Don't make sense," Micah mumbled. "I been expectin' Sloane to head for the high country for the last few weeks, and he ain't made a move. And Hallie's been happier than I ever seen her since he come here. Now she wants him to go?" He shook his head. "No. Don't make sense a'tall."

"Sense or not, something's goin' on," Jericho said again. "It don't feel right, leavin' only Shad here to watch 'em. 'Specially with Pine headed in."

"I reckon I can do as good as you."

Micah ignored Shad's insulted expression. "You'll do fine. I don't think Ritter's gonna be goin' anywhere . . . leastways, till we get back."

Jericho snorted. "Since when are you thinkin' so high of Sloane?"

"Since the man's been workin' hard every day. Since our sister's got no complaints. . . ." Micah frowned. "Hell,

I didn't expect to *like* him, but—"

"Yeah." Shad nodded. "Me, too."

"Look," Micah cut in quickly, "we'll get back home as soon as we can. We'll have Trib along, too. You just try to hold things together as best you can."

He watched them ride out and fervently wished he was going with them.

Snorting a laugh, Shad told himself that he wished he was going *anywhere*. All day Ritter'd gone from one chore to the next. The man never stopped. Never rested. The gunfighter carried a look on his face that was enough to stop a train and more than enough to keep Shad from asking any questions.

Hallie was just as bad. In and out of the house, she clearly had a devil ridin' her. The looks she'd been shooting her husband were black as sin and when Shad tried to talk to her, she about tore the hide right off him.

Shadrack sighed heavily and picked up the bridle again. He wished to hell he knew what was goin' on. Hallie'd been happy for weeks, and now she was miserable. Ritter Sloane was more closed-up and tight-lipped than he was when he first arrived.

"Supper's on!" Hallie yelled from the house.

"Lordy," Shad mumbled and pushed himself to his feet. He wasn't looking forward to sitting across a table from the two silent, angry people. He stepped out of the barn and saw Ritter walking from the corral to the house. Slowly Shadrack followed him.

Something was gonna break soon, he told himself. Neither one of them would be able to keep this up much longer, Shad knew. Especially Hallie. She just wasn't naturally a peaceful person. Her tryin' to keep hold of her temper couldn't last long. As he stepped through the open doorway, Shad only hoped that when the lid finally blew off, he was nowhere around.

Hallie lay on her back, staring at the ceiling. She'd just heard the clock in the main room chime twelve, and she was no closer to sleep than when she'd first gone to bed. She couldn't seem to get comfortable. Shifting position again, she realized for the first time that she was lying on the very edge of the bed, unconsciously leaving room for Ritter.

She ground her teeth together and deliberately slid to the very center of the mattress. Crossing her arms across her chest, she fumed silently. Even when she wasn't thinkin' of him, she was thinkin' of him. Hell, she even made room for him in her bed the night after she threw him out of her room!

A tiny voice in the back of her mind whispered slyly, *Well, why not? You want him in your bed, don't you?*

"No, I don't," she mumbled to the empty room.

Sure you do, that voice argued. *You want him back. You just don't want to go tell him is all.*

"Well, why the hell should *I* have to go get *him*?" She shook her head and told herself aloud, "*He's* the one wants to leave. I ain't about to go ask that man to stay *again*." Hallie squeezed her eyes tightly shut. She would *not* go to Ritter. She had *some* pride left. Hell, she'd practically thrown herself at him for the last few weeks! Just thinkin' about what the two of them had done in that very bed was enough to make her cheeks flush! And now he don't want her?

No. Hallie rolled to her side and slipped one hand under

her pillow. She wouldn't ask him to stay. Not again.

Stay or leave—it had to be his choice.

She bit her lip. So far, though, she didn't much like his decision.

Ritter lay in Jericho's bed, one arm behind his head. From the bed across the dark room came another ear-shattering snore. Ritter eased up and glared at Shadrack. How the hell was he supposed to get any sleep with that racket going on all night?

Abruptly he flopped back down. His sleeplessness had nothing to do with the snoring, and he knew it. He couldn't sleep, because he'd become too accustomed to Hallie curled up next to him. He missed the weight of her head on his shoulder and her leg tossed across his. His solitary bed felt cold, empty. Just like him.

Dammit. He didn't want it to be like this. At that moment he would have given *anything* to be beside Hallie.

He stared into the darkness and gave free rein to his busy mind. What could happen if he stayed? Couldn't he find *some* way to work out the problems he knew his reputation would cause them? Wasn't *he* entitled to a little happiness?

Or had he given up any right to a normal life when he started selling his gun? Jesus, when had it all become so complicated? When had he stopped thinking like a gunfighter and started thinking like any other man?

When he fell in love with Hallie.

The windowpane beside his bed rattled suddenly and in seconds Ritter was on his feet, his pistol in hand. He held his breath and waited for the sound to repeat itself. When it did, Ritter's shoulders slumped with relief.

The wind. Only the wind against the glass.

He dropped down onto the bed and stared at the gun in his hand. It had been instinct to reach for it. He couldn't even remember grabbing it. Sighing, Ritter told himself he'd spent too many years living at the edge of danger. It was no use. He couldn't stay.

If he did, he'd be sentencing Hallie to a lifetime of jumping at the wind.

Chapter

✳

Eighteen

HAMILTON BUTLER stood on the wide porch of his home and watched one of his ranch hands ride a wildly bucking horse in the corral. A satisfied smile crossed his face at the sound of the good-natured teasing and catcalls from the other men as their friend got the ride of his life. When the cowboy was thrown into the dirt, Butler snorted a half laugh and turned away.

He propped one hand on a porch post and let his gaze wander over his property. It was good to be back to normal. No more strutting gunhands littering up the yard, no more pangs of worry or guilt chewing at his insides. Even Dixie was talking to him again.

Grinning, he straightened up and pulled in a deep breath. Just thinking about the night before at Dixie's place was enough to make him feel like a youngster again! Yessir, everything seemed just about right. There was only the one problem yet to be faced.

Nathan Pine.

He frowned suddenly. It had been four days since Ritter Sloane had come to see him. Four days since he'd called a halt to the war. And in that time he hadn't heard another word from the infamous gunfighter he'd hired.

What the hell was taking the man so long? Why didn't he come? All the waiting was about to drive Butler out of his mind. And since his visit to the Benteen place the day before, Butler knew what it was doing to them. He'd never seen Hallie strung so tight. As jumpy as a cricket on a hot rock, she barely sat still long enough to talk.

And Ritter Sloane looked like a man who hadn't been getting any sleep. Every line of the gunfighter's body screamed with tension and fatigue. Somehow, Butler'd expected the man to be more in control. After all, Sloane was used to the expectation of battle.

Poor ol' Shad looked about done in, too. Of course, worrying over what Trib had got himself into probably wasn't helping any, either. He hoped that the boys got back quick. He'd hate to see trouble come before they were ready for it.

Trouble. Butler mumbled a curse and turned for the door. No one had to remind him that all of this was *his* fault. If he hadn't sent for that damned Pine, none of this would be happening.

From the corner of his eye he noticed a lone rider heading for the ranch house. He squinted into the distance trying to study the man out, but his eyes weren't what they used to be. Moving to the edge of the porch, Butler crossed his arms over his barrel chest and waited. As the rider came closer, a twinge of worry began to work its way through him.

The stranger was tall, thin, and dressed completely in black. Of course, that description could fit *anyone*, but Hamilton knew in his bones that Nathan Pine had finally arrived.

A few feet short of the house, the man pulled his horse

to a stop and dismounted. Stepping up to the hitch rail, he tossed the reins over the well-polished wood, propped one foot on the lowest step, and looked up at the older man. "You Butler?"

He nodded.

"Well, I'm Nathan Pine. You sent for me?"

Hamilton's gaze moved over the other man quickly, from his sharp, almost feral face to the gun in a hand-tooled holster strapped to his thigh. Absently the rancher noticed that the noise from the corral had stopped. He flicked a glance at his men and saw them all watching him and the gunman.

"We'll talk inside," he said gruffly and led the way into the privacy of his house.

Once seated in the library, Butler poured himself a drink and hoped the other man wouldn't notice that his hands were shaking. "Drink?" he asked offhandedly.

Pine shook his head and carefully removed his hat.

Butler's mind worked feverishly. This was a hard man. There was no telling how he'd take to being fired. But, he told himself as he tossed the whiskey down his throat, he'd gotten himself into this, and he was the only one who could get him out.

He reached into the desk drawer and pulled out the small leather poke that he'd had ready for the last week. It was heavy, and the gentle clink of the gold inside reminded him of just how much his mistake was costing him. He stretched his arm out and set the poke down in front of Pine. "That's one thousand dollars there. Half the money we agreed on."

Pine nodded and reached for the sack. "Fair enough. Half now, half when the job's finished."

"No."

The gunfighter's eyes snapped up. "No?"

"No. I, uh . . ." Butler ran one hand through his hair. "I made a mistake. Turns out I won't be needin' you after all. That money there I figure I owe you for your time and travel."

Nathan picked up the sack of gold coins thoughtfully.

"In fact," Butler went on in a rush to fill the ominous silence, "with the troubles around here over, it'd prob'ly be best for everybody if you just . . . left."

The gunfighter's lips curved in a half smile that never reached his eyes. "You telling me to leave the county, Butler?"

A stab of fear sliced through Hamilton. He was no match for a gunfighter. Pine could shoot him dead in the time it took him to *think* about going for a gun. "No, I got no right to *tell* you anything. I just thought—"

"Don't think." Pine hefted the sack as if testing its weight, then slipped it into his coat pocket. "It just so happens, Butler, that I'm not ready to go anywhere. I came here for one reason. Ritter Sloane. Your money was just an added—*bonus*." He stood up, his legs spread wide, and looked down at the older man. "If you'll just tell me where I can find Ritter, I'll be on my way."

Hamilton Butler's hands closed into helpless fists. He'd brought this down on all of them. And now he was unable to stop the very force he'd started. But, he told himself with a sudden surge of determination, he'd be *damned* before he'd hand *any* man over to Nathan Pine.

"I don't know," he said quietly, avoiding the man's hard stare. "I called off the war with that other family a few days back. Don't suppose there's any reason for Sloane to stay around, do you?" He finally risked a quick glance at the man towering over him. The faint, mocking smile did nothing to ease Ham's fears.

"Well, I suppose that's something I'll have to find out for myself." He set his hat gingerly on his head and cocked it at the right angle. Then he smiled again. "With or without your help, Butler. I *will* find Sloane."

Hamilton sank back in his chair as the other man left the room. He poured himself one more drink, but then couldn't bring himself to swallow it. It wasn't over. *Nothing* was over. Ritter had been right. Nathan Pine had no intention of leaving until he'd faced Ritter Sloane.

As soon as his legs were steady again, Ham told himself, he'd ride over to the Benteens and tell them that the wait was over.

"I'm not ashamed to admit it, Sloane," Ham said and picked up his cup of coffee. "That man Pine scared the pants off me. He ain't normal. He's . . ."

"A gunfighter?" Ritter asked, a wry smile on his face.

"No, dammit, that ain't what I meant at all. It's . . ." He struggled for a minute, searching for the right word. "It's as if he's all empty inside. There's no light in his eyes. They're . . . ah, hell. *You* know what I mean! And how in thunder do ya reason with a man like that?"

"You don't." Ritter leaned his elbows on the table and propped his head in his hands. Looking from Shad to Butler, he said, "That's what I was tryin' to explain to you. I knew Pine would come. And he won't leave without meeting me."

"If he's as bad as Ham says," Shadrack put in, "maybe Hallie's right. Maybe you *should* just leave."

"Wouldn't solve anything. Pine's a patient man. Besides, I've never run from anyone before, and I don't intend to start now."

"It wouldn't be runnin'. . . ."

"I'm not goin' anywhere, Shad."

"Then we best come up with some kind of plan." Butler looked at the other men steadily. "It won't take him very long to find out where you are."

"Yeah." Ritter glanced at Hallie's closed door, then turned back to the men. "All right, then, here's what I think we should do."

Hallie straightened up and walked over to the bed. Idly she rubbed her neck to relieve the crick she'd gotten eavesdropping on the men's conversation.

Nathan Pine was finally here. In a strange way it was almost a relief. Like the feeling you got when you finally pulled a sore tooth. She knew Ritter and Shad felt the same. She'd seen the expressions on their faces when Ham rode up. The last few days had been hard on all of them. She couldn't remember a time when she'd been so mad and sad all at once. Every time she saw Ritter, she was torn between throwing herself into his arms and throwing a fist into his face.

But now that Nathan Pine was here, it was almost over. Once things were settled between them, Ritter would be leaving. Forever.

Her stomach churned suddenly, and she sucked in a deep breath and swallowed heavily. The last week or so, she'd spent more time queasy than not. And it seemed as though she just couldn't get enough sleep.

Running one hand over her mouth, Hallie shook her

head resignedly. She had a sneaking suspicion what was wrong with her. Usually, you could set a watch by her monthlies, but now she was runnin' a couple of weeks late. And her breasts were so tender, her heavy coat was uncomfortable.

She was pregnant.

Hallie tossed a glance at the door as if she could see her husband on the other side. Just a week ago she'd have been tickled to death with the knowledge, and she'd have gone running to Ritter with the good news. Now she knew she wouldn't tell him. There was no reason to. He'd made his choice. He was leaving.

Besides, she told herself with a sigh, she'd gotten exactly what she'd bargained for on their wedding day. A baby. With no husband clutterin' up the place.

Instinctively she touched her still-flat belly. Well, they'd be just fine without Ritter. As a matter of fact, she thought suddenly, why not help him on his way? If he was gonna be leaving after meeting Pine, it would be a helluva lot easier on her if it all happened quick.

Besides, she was mighty damn tired of everybody doin' her thinkin' for her. Determinedly she stood up and tossed another glance at the door. It was likely that the three men would sit there for hours, figurin' out exactly what it was they planned on doin'. With never a thought for her, either beyond tellin' her what to do and what not to do!

She'd had enough of that, by God, and now was as good a time as any to let them know it. Quietly she moved around her bedroom. Grabbing up her coat and hat, she walked carefully to the window and slid it open. Noiselessly Hallie slipped outside and cautiously made her way to the barn. If she was careful, she could get to

town, see Pine, and be back before any of them noticed
she was gone.

Dixie saw her coming and tried to head her off. "Hallie,
for heaven's sake, go home."

"Is he here?"

"Hell, yes, he's here." Dixie looked over her shoulder
warily as if the notorious gunman could hear her from
across the room. "And he's not the kind of man you want
to be talkin' to."

"Maybe not," Hallie said and took off her hat. Giving
her short hair a shake, she added, "But he *is* the one I've
got to talk to." She looked around the fairly crowded
saloon and was just about to ask her friend to point the
gunman out when her gaze settled on a dark man alone
at a table in the corner. His back was to the wall, and
he seemed to be staring at her. "Is that him?" she asked
unnecessarily.

Dixie looked. "Yeah. That's him. Hallie, I'm asking
you not to do this."

"Don't worry, Dix." Hallie forced a smile she didn't
feel. "I'll be fine."

The saloon was warm after the cold afternoon air. The
mingled odors of men, cigar smoke, beer, and the cheap
perfume favored by a couple of Dixie's girls hung over
the tables like mountain fog. Tinny piano music started,
stopped, and started again as the drunk piano player hunted
for the proper keys.

Hallie threaded her way through the forest of tables,
and chair legs scraped against the wooden floor as folks
moved out of her way. It took every ounce of courage she
possessed to lock her gaze with Nathan Pine's. Each step

she took was an effort because every nerve in her body was urging her to turn and head back home.

Instead, she went on and tried not to notice that Ham was right about the man's eyes. They were soulless. Flat, black, and cold. How could anyone ever take Nathan Pine and Ritter for the same kind of man?

By the time she reached his table, she could feel sweat rolling down her back beneath her buckskin shirt. She pulled her heavy coat off and almost sighed her relief. Maybe, she told herself, she should have worn one of those dresses Ritter'd bought her. Then she noticed Pine's gaze moving lazily over her body, and she was glad she'd worn the old familiar clothes. It gave her an extra shot of confidence.

She would need all she could get.

Nathan waved one hand at the chair opposite him. "Sit down?" He watched the woman as she took the chair and saw the wariness in her eyes. She knew who he was. She was scared, but still she came over to him. Sought him out.

Why?

He reached for the bottle of whiskey in the center of the scarred table. "Would you like a drink?"

She shook her head. "No. But you go ahead."

He nodded and poured himself another. It was only his second. Lifting the glass to his lips, he tossed the liquid down his throat, then looked at her expectantly.

"You're Nathan Pine?"

"That's right." He leaned back in his chair, crossed his arms over his chest, and began to rock on the chair's back legs. "Who're you?"

"Hallie . . . Benteen."

He stopped rocking and slowly lowered the chair to the floor. Benteen. Wasn't that the name of the family Butler'd hired him to drive out? Is *that* what this was about? He almost smiled. Fool woman. Didn't even know her own war was over.

"Benteen," he said thoughtfully. "I suppose you know that I was hired by Butler?"

"Yes, but—"

"But you don't know that he canceled the job?" He shook his head. "Go home, Miss Benteen. I have no reason to come after your family. Never did. It was just business."

"I know that."

The woman set her coat down on the table and leaned toward him. He saw the nervousness in her eyes and thought he detected a slight shake in her hands.

"Then why are you here?" he asked.

"I came to find out when you're leaving town."

She said it in a rush, and a stab of irritation grabbed at Pine. What the hell was going on here? Didn't she know if a *man* had said that to him, he'd have called him out? Nathan stared at her, trying to figure out what she was up to.

Why was she so interested in gettin' him out of town? For God's sake, he wasn't coming after her family anymore. What difference could it make to her if he stayed or went? Nathan Pine didn't like puzzles. He liked things neat. Orderly. He liked things to make sense.

And so far, none of this woman's talking had done *that*.

Something was going on. Something he didn't know

about. But before he left town, Nathan promised himself he would find out.

His long fingers toyed with the empty whiskey glass, and he let his silence torment her. He could see the effect it was having on her. Her eyes shifted nervously, and her teeth pulled at her bottom lip fitfully.

"Why would that concern you?" he asked quietly.

"I, uh . . ." She looked down at her hands, clenched tightly together. "I only want things around here to get back to normal." She pulled in a shaky breath and raised her gaze to his. "As long as you're here, my family will always be thinkin' about you. Worryin' about what you're up to."

Nathan Pine smiled and shook his head. "No reason to. Your family doesn't interest me any longer. I have some unfinished business to deal with here in Stillwater. There's a man I have to see about an old debt."

"Who?" The word was hushed, hesitant.

"Ritter Sloane."

Hallie's breath caught, and she barely managed to repress a shudder. Even though she'd known exactly who Pine had been talking about, she'd had to ask. And hearing the man say Ritter's name with such a cold finality made the hair at the back of her neck stand on end. Her unsteady stomach rolled, and she swallowed convulsively.

Somehow, she *had* to get Pine to leave. Just sitting across a table from the man had been enough to convince her that she would do whatever it took to keep the two men apart. She couldn't bear the thought of Ritter facing this man. She couldn't risk her husband being killed by Nathan Pine.

No matter *what* Ritter'd said in the last few days, Hallie

loved him. If he was going to leave, she couldn't stop him. But she *could* do everything possible to keep him alive. Quickly she said, "Sloane's gone."

Pine's hard, black eyes flicked up to hers. "What?"

"Ritter Sloane. He's gone."

"When?"

She swallowed heavily and fought down the tremor in her voice. "A few days ago. When Butler told us the war was over and that he'd be sendin' you on your way." His eyes narrowed suspiciously, but Hallie kept her gaze locked with his and lied through her teeth. "I remember he said there wasn't no reason for him to stay anymore."

"Did he say where he was goin'?"

"Uh . . ." She closed her eyes and pretended to think about his question. "New Mexico," she finally blurted out.

"New Mexico."

"That's right." Hallie looked at him again. "So, if you was waitin' on him, I reckon you can be goin' now."

"It appears so." Pine leaned back in his chair, rubbed his clean-shaven chin with one hand, and watched her thoughtfully.

Her insides jumping around nervously, Hallie tried to keep her expression blank, innocent. She'd done the best she could. Now she could only hope that he believed her and left quickly before he found out she'd lied to him.

"Afternoon, Hallie!"

Hallie turned in her chair and watched Sheriff Tucker walk up to the table and stop beside her. The older man was smiling down at her, but his eyes looked angry. He held a shotgun cradled in his arms, and his right hand was dangerously close to the trigger.

"Hello, Sheriff," she answered softly.

He looked away from her and frowned at Nathan Pine before turning back to Hallie.

She felt the tension between the two men, and she sensed the sheriff's anger at her. But truth to tell, she was so glad to see Tucker, she didn't even care that he was mad. She'd begun to feel a little trapped under the watchful gaze of Nathan Pine, and she hadn't had any idea of just how she was going to get away from him. Thankfully, the sheriff gave her just the excuse she needed.

"Guess I'd better be gettin' on home now, Sheriff. It's about suppertime, and the boys'll be worryin' over their stomachs."

She stood up and shoved her arms through the sleeves of her coat.

"Well, you tell that husband of yours that there's still plenty of folks in town would like to buy him a drink!"

She glanced at Pine and saw his eyebrows lift curiously. Of course, she'd told *him* her name was Benteen. "I'll do that, Sheriff." As quickly as she could, Hallie moved through the crowd. She'd almost reached the door when a voice called out, "Mrs. Sloane!"

Hallie came to a dead stop and slowly turned to the speaker. It was the man from the telegraph office. "Yes?"

"If you want to wait just a minute here," he said and drank down the last of his beer, "there's a package for you over to the office. We can get it now."

She nodded, and as the little man walked past her, she sneaked a look at Nathan Pine. Any hope she might have had about him not overhearing the telegrapher died when she met his hard gaze. His flat, black eyes drilled into hers until she felt a cold chill spread through her body.

Forcing herself, she broke free of his icy stare and walked woodenly to the batwing doors.

He'd heard. He knew she was Mrs. Ritter Sloane.

She didn't even want to *think* about what Ritter would say when he found out.

Chapter

Nineteen

"MRS. *SLOANE*," Pine mumbled thoughtfully.

Sheriff Tucker looked down at the dark gunfighter and swallowed back the curses he wanted to hurl at the damned telegrapher. He'd heard the tail end of Hallie's lies to Pine, and he was willing to bet she'd about had the man convinced that Ritter was gone. Until that yahoo opened his mouth.

"You never mind about her," Tucker said in a tight, low voice.

"Why, Sheriff"—Pine smiled, his eyes wide in mock innocence—"I have no interest in Mrs. *Sloane*. It was *she* who spoke to me. My *business* is with her husband."

Tucker hitched the shotgun higher in his arms and cleared his throat. "Your 'business' in this town is finished, Pine. We don't want your kind litterin' up the streets."

The gunfighter's eyes narrowed. He cocked his head slightly and met the sheriff's gaze. "My 'kind'? I expect you're talking about gunfighters?"

"That's right."

"And what about Ritter Sloane? Have you asked *him* to leave as well?"

"No, I haven't." The older man lifted his chin and

looked down on the dangerous gunman. "Sloane hasn't given me any problems."

"Neither have I."

"You will. It's in your blood. You can't help bringin' trouble to wherever you are any more than you can help breathin'."

Pine snorted. "And Sloane is a model citizen?"

"That ain't none of your business, Pine." Tucker bent lower, looked his opponent dead in the eye, and added, "But since you asked, Ritter Sloane's different. The man's made friends here. *Good* friends." He straightened up and ran his right hand slowly over the trigger guard. "They wouldn't much like it if you brought him grief."

Pine's gaze slipped away from the sheriff's. He felt the stares of at least a dozen men who were close enough to have overheard what Tucker'd been saying. A little uneasy, Nathan shifted position in his chair and noticed that the small creaks of the wood screamed out into the unnatural silence of the saloon.

"Now, Mr. Pine," Tucker was saying, "I don't believe in rushing a man. So, I'll give you till tomorrow to be out of this town and on your way."

"And if I'm not?"

"Well, then, I'm sure you're wanted *somewhere* for *something*. I'll just lock you up and go through my stack of posters." He smiled. "Shouldn't take me more than a couple of months."

Long after Tucker'd left the saloon, Nathan Pine sat at his solitary table trying to figure out what was happening. First, Butler fires him. Then some woman in buckskins tries to get him to leave town. *Then* he finds out Ritter Sloane is *married* to the woman!

But the most startling thing was the sheriff. A town *sheriff* taking up for a gunfighter? Nathan shook his head wearily. He simply couldn't understand any of this.

What the hell kind of town is this? his brain screamed.

For the first time in many years, Nathan Pine reached for the whiskey bottle and poured himself a generous third drink.

Dusk, and the light was fading quickly. Hallie walked her horse directly to the barn. She'd been gone so much longer than she'd planned, she had no doubt that Ritter and Shad were both sittin' inside just waitin' to tear into her.

Well, she told herself, they could just wait awhile longer. She needed a little more time to think before facing the two of them. As she stripped the saddle and blanket off her horse and gave the animal a brief rubdown with a handful of straw, Hallie thought about the small package she had yet to open.

Leaning back against the side of the stall, her right hand slipped into her coat pocket. Her fingers toyed with the brown-paper-wrapped parcel, and she remembered the telegrapher's excitement when he'd given it to her.

"Imagine! All the way from Boston!" His watery eyes shone with fanciful notions. As he handed her the small, square package, he waved a piece of paper with his other hand. "This here says there's somethin' else comin', too. Be here in a day or two."

Hallie stared at him, confused.

"And," he went on, "it says right here that I should tell you to bring a wagon to pick it up!" Laughing and shaking his head, he speculated to himself, "Now, don't that set you to wonderin'. What all could be comin' for you from

Boston that's so big you need a wagon to tote it?"

The front door slammed across the yard and jolted Hallie back into the present. Deliberately she released the package, keeping it out of sight in her pocket. She straightened up tiredly and faced the barn's double doors.

Her husband marched in, with Shadrack close on his heels. At first sight of Hallie, Ritter came to an abrupt stop and Shad crashed into him, sending them both staggering.

"Where have you been?" His heart pounding, Ritter stared at the woman who'd had him about worried to death.

"Town."

One word. She'd taken off without even leaving a damned note . . . after he'd *told* her not to leave the ranch again without him . . . and all she had to say was *one word*? Open-mouthed, he watched as she walked across the barn, clearly headed for the house. When she got close enough, Ritter grabbed her arm and spun her about to face him.

"Now, listen you two . . ." Shad started. He looked first at his sister's mutinous face, then at his brother-in law's furious expression. Silently the triplet turned on his heel and left the barn, closing the double doors behind him.

When they were alone, Ritter took a tight grip on his rising temper and ground out, "Why did you leave without telling us?"

Hallie yanked her arm free. " 'Cause if you knew I was goin', you woulda tried to stop me."

"Wrong," he said, his nose just inches from hers. "I wouldn't have 'tried.' I *would* have stopped you."

Her lips curved in a smile that told him what she thought his chances were of that. "Don't matter now," she said. "It's already done, so let it go."

Ritter understood clearly now why she'd punched him in the jaw the night he'd returned from Butler's ranch. He was absolutely torn between wanting to strangle her and wanting to hold her so tightly she'd never escape him again. He did neither. Instead, he *tried* to find out what she'd been up to.

"I'm not about to let it go, Hallie. Why did you go to town? What did you do there?"

She lifted her chin slightly and in a few brief sentences told him about her little chat with Nathan Pine.

"I don't *believe* this!" Ritter clapped one hand to his forehead, turned his back on her, and laughed. He couldn't help it. It was either laugh or kill her.

The whole time he, Shad, and Ham had been calmly making plans, his own *wife* was sitting with his enemy telling him to get out of town!

"What's so damn funny?"

He shook his head and glanced at her over his shoulder. "You, Hallie. *You're* so damned funny!"

Her face flushed, her blue eyes blazing with sudden anger, she shouted, "I'll thank you not to laugh at me, Ritter Sloane."

"Hell, Hallie, what d'ya *expect* me to do?" He turned around to face her and threw his hands up in the air. "You want me to *thank* you?"

She lifted her chin and squared her shoulders. "You might at that."

"For what?"

"Well, for tryin' to . . ."

"Yeah?" He took a step closer to her. "Trying to what? Fight my wars for me? Chase the bad men away so poor little Ritter doesn't have to get hurt?"

"That's not what . . . "

"That's exactly what you were doing, Hallie." He grabbed her upper arms. "I'm a grown man, Hallie. I fight my own battles. Have for years. How do you think it looks for a gunfighter to have his *wife* out tryin' to save his hide?"

Her eyes filled with tears, and she blinked to keep them from falling. Angrily she pulled free of him and snapped, "I wasn't tryin' to *save* you, Sloane. I was only tryin' to get you leavin'."

"What?"

"You said as soon as Pine was gone, you'd be movin' on. Well, I only figured to help you on your way."

He stared down into the shimmering blue of her eyes and felt something cold and hard settle around his heart. As she continued, every word she uttered added strength to the icy chill swallowing him.

"I finally decided you was right, Ritter. Be best for both of us if you take out. No sense in pretendin' somethin' is there when it ain't."

The pain in Hallie's eyes cut him so deeply it hurt to look in them. He'd done that to her, and he hated himself for it. Slowly he raised one hand and touched her cheek. Her eyes squeezed shut, and he let his hand drop to his side.

Somewhere deep inside him a well of misery broke open. Even knowing he had to leave her, Ritter'd been hoping against hope for some other answer. For something to change his reality. He'd hoped that against all reason, he'd be able to stay and enjoy her love.

But now, watching the rigid set of her shoulders and

knowing the chance she'd taken just to be rid of him sooner . . . He told himself that it looked as though he'd managed to kill her love for him, too.

"All right, Hallie," he said softly, his shoulders slumped in defeat. "We'll say no more about this. It's over. You're safe."

"Well, of course I'm safe," she mumbled. "I admit that man is a mite frightening and all . . . but I think I coulda convinced him to leave if it wasn't for that telegraph fella."

Ritter looked at her suspiciously. "What about him?"

She took a half step back. "Well, I was leavin' the saloon, and he started tellin' me about a package he had for me . . ."

"Yes?"

"And . . . he called me Mrs. Sloane."

"What?" Ritter's heartbeat pounded in his ears. He grabbed her arms again and gave her a little shake. "Did Pine hear?" When she didn't answer right away, he shouted, "Did Pine hear him?"

"Hell, he'd have had to be stone deaf *not* to hear him!"

"Goddammit!" He pulled her close, squeezed her tightly, then set her away from him almost at once. "This changes *everything*!"

"What d'ya mean?"

"Now that Nathan Pine knows we're married, you're in more danger than ever."

"Don't see how it makes much difference either way."

He snorted a half laugh and shook his head. "I tried to tell you this before. He'll use you to get to me."

"He can't do that, Ritter."

"What's to stop him, Hallie?"

"I'll just let it be known around town that you're leavin'." Her eyes met his and held them. "I'll tell everybody I see that you just don't give a good goddamn." She turned away and started for the door, then stopped suddenly. She reached into her pocket and pulled out the mysterious package. Looking over her shoulder, she tossed it to him. "Since I ain't *really* Mrs. Sloane no more, don't reckon I'll be needin' this."

She slipped through the doors, and Ritter stood alone in the center of the barn, staring down at the little package. His thumbs moved over it slowly, and he swallowed back the regrets rising up inside him.

Whether she wanted it or not, the package belonged to her. And he would see that she accepted it. If it was the last thing he did.

Nathan paid the woman and sent her on her way. Just before she slipped through the door, the redhead looked back over her shoulder and gave him a sultry smile. Pine nodded his thanks for a pleasant hour but wasn't sorry to see her leave.

He stuffed an extra pillow behind his head, reached for a cigar, and lit it. He inhaled deeply, then exhaled in a rush, hoping the rich, smoky aroma would overpower the too-sweet perfume smell the woman'd left behind. Why was it, he wondered, that most whores used such strong scents that the odor lasted for hours on the flesh of their customers?

Sighing, Nathan closed his eyes and mentally compared the woman who'd just left to Hallie Benteen Sloane.

An image of Ritter Sloane's wife rose up before him,

and he knew immediately there was no comparison. The whore's carefully made-up face and flowery perfume were no match for Hallie Sloane's clean, fresh beauty. He took another drag at his cigar and told himself that the woman was more than good-looking. She had nerve. Despite her fears, she'd faced him and even tried to bluff him.

One corner of his mouth lifted in an admiring smile. Took a lot of guts to tell a gunfighter to leave town, he told himself. His eyes opened and he stared straight ahead at the garish, flowered wallpaper. She must really care for Sloane, Pine thought and felt an unfamiliar stab of envy.

A "good" woman had never given Nathan Pine a second glance.

His gaze moved around the small room, which was over the saloon. His clothes lay neatly piled on a chair. His pistol lay beside him on the quilt. From downstairs came the sounds of drunken laughter and the badly tuned piano. Rooms just like this one were all he'd known for most of his life. Women like the one who'd just left were all he could hope for. All *any* gunfighter could hope for.

Yet somehow, Ritter Sloane had found a way to make a *real* woman love him. He wondered idly if Sloane loved her, too. Probably.

Briefly he considered the possibility that Ritter would dismiss the challenge Nathan had sent him. Was it possible that Sloane himself was behind his wife trying to get his enemy out of town?

No. Whatever else he might be, Ritter Sloane was no coward.

But he *was* a husband now.

Nathan pursed his lips around the end of his cigar. Slowly he smiled. A man in love—especially a gunfighter—had lost his edge. The only way a man stayed alive in *this* business was to keep his mind strictly on his opponent. If he was distracted . . .

The gunman folded his arms over his chest and crossed his feet at the ankles. It was a real shame that poor ol' Ritter'd finally found love. Just before he died.

Hallie sat straight up and stared at the door. Someone was knocking, and she had a feeling who it was.

"Yes?"

"Hallie? Can I come in for a minute?"

"Go away, Ritter," she said softly. "Please."

"Just for a minute." The doorknob turned, and Hallie wished that she'd had the sense to put a lock on that door. But it was too late now. He was standing in the open doorway, and she knew she couldn't keep him out. Quietly he entered the room, and closed the door behind him.

In the glow of her bedside lamp, Hallie let her gaze move over him hungrily. His blond hair tussled, it lay across his forehead, stopping just above his eyes. There was a faint stubble of blond whiskers along his jaw, and Hallie conquered the urge to go to him. To hold him. It seemed like years since they'd been together in that room.

Suddenly a wave of cold washed over her as she realized that after he left, it really *would* be years, if ever, before she saw him again.

Her hands tightened into fists, and she pulled her bare feet up under the hem of her nightgown. He sat down on the edge of her bed, just an arm's reach away, looking down at his hands. It was only then Hallie noticed he was holding the package she'd brought from town.

"I wanted you to have this, Hallie."

"Told you, Ritter," she said, her voice breaking slightly, "since we're not *really* married, I'd rather not."

He chuckled harshly and looked up at her from the corner of his eyes. "No matter how you want to think of it, Hallie, we are *really* married."

"Not much longer."

"No." He sighed and tapped the package against his fingers. Lamplight fell on his hair, and Hallie found herself ridiculously thinking that it needed trimming. Just a bit. Just to the top of his collar. She let her gaze move over him and almost missed it when he said, "At least, we won't be together. Legally, we'll still be married." He turned to face her. "Unless you want to get a divorce."

Looking into his pale blue eyes, that was the *last* thing she wanted. But she ignored the hunger filling her and said only, "No, I guess not. Not if you don't want one." She forced a smile. "Remember, I told you once that I never did want a husband. Reckon if I got one already, nobody else'll come 'round botherin' me."

His lips twisted, but he nodded. "Then, this *is* yours." He held the package out to her and waited until she finally accepted it. "I wired my lawyer to send it."

"Lawyer? You got your own lawyer?"

"The family's lawyer." He shook his head. "It's a long story, and it really doesn't matter now, anyway. The point is, I wanted you to have this, and I wanted my lawyer to know that I'm married."

Her brows drew together, and she cocked her head. "Why? It ain't any of *his* business. Hell, I don't even know this fella you're tellin' our business to!"

Ritter smiled sadly. "Open the package, Hallie. Please. Then I'll explain."

She didn't like the look in his eye. It had all the signs of goodbye in it, and she wasn't ready yet for that. And why wasn't he tellin' her about that durned lawyer?

"C'mon, Hallie. Open it."

Almost unwillingly her fingers moved over the paper. She pulled and yanked until it finally tore, revealing a square, flat, black box. Glancing up at him, she saw him smile again.

Hallie took a deep breath, turned the little gold latch, and opened it. She exhaled on a sigh and felt her mouth drop open. Gingerly her fingers moved over the prize inside while her eyes questioned her husband.

"They were my mother's," he said softly.

The square-cut emerald ring set in a dainty gold band shimmered in the lamplight. A delicately wrought gold chain necklace dotted with tiny emeralds and diamonds lay on the black velvet base, encircling the ring.

Her index finger smoothed over the cool stones gently. "They're real pretty, Ritter . . ."

"And they're yours."

Hallie's gaze snapped up to his. "Mine?" She shook her head, closed the box, and held it out to him. "No. It wouldn't be right. 'Sides, how would I look, wearin' them and my buckskins?"

He grinned and Hallie's heartbeat staggered.

Ritter opened the box, and lifted the emerald ring free. Then he picked up her left hand and slid the jewel over her knuckle. "I think they'd look fine with buckskins." Still holding her hand, he looked at her solemnly. "And as my wife, I want you to have them."

Hallie started to speak, but he cut her off.

"Just listen for a minute, Hallie." He took a deep breath and continued, a half smile on his face. "Who knows? maybe you got your wish and you *are* pregnant now and don't even know it."

She looked away, afraid he'd see the truth in her eyes.

"And if you are, it *could* be that girl you wanted." He squeezed her hand. "If so"—his voice thickened—"you can give the emeralds to my daughter. But either way, Hallie, they're yours now. You can do as you like with them."

Her fingers still held in the warmth of his hand, Hallie stared down at the emerald ring Ritter's mother had worn before her. Her brain taunted her silently. All of her ridiculous notions about Ritter not thinking she was lady enough for him went right out the window. A man didn't give just *any* woman his mother's jewelry. He wanted her, then his daughter, to have them.

Lord, maybe she *should* tell him about the baby. Maybe he had the *right* to know. Maybe he'd *stay* if he knew. But, her mind chided, do you *want* him to stay just because of the baby?

No. He had to stay because he *wanted* to be with her. Tears filled her eyes, and even furious blinking couldn't keep them from falling this time. Silently, helplessly, they rolled down her cheeks and splashed near the green stone on her hand.

Without a word, Ritter pulled her into his arms. Resting his chin on top of her head, his hands moved up and down her back, comforting, soothing her in the only way he could. Hallie listened to the steady beat of his heart beneath her ear and willed herself to remember the warm strength of him.

The feel of his arms around her. His breath ruffling her hair. Everything. She wanted to remember everything.

"There's one more thing, Hallie," he said, and she smiled as his voice rumbled through his chest. "The lawyer I told you about . . ."

"Yeah?"

"Starting next month, he'll be sending you money regularly."

"What?" She pulled back from his arms and stared at him.

"Once a month you'll get a bank draft from my bank in Boston."

"I don't want your money!"

"I know you don't. Nevertheless, it's coming."

She scooted back from him.

Ritter sighed and stood up. "You can't stop it, Hallie. It's all taken care of."

"But—"

"Just listen." He held one hand up and looked down at her. "There's more. I've told my lawyer that if he doesn't hear from me for one year, he's to assume I'm dead and transfer all my properties to you."

"What?"

"Don't argue, Hallie. It's done. Finished."

"No, it ain't." She rose up on her knees. "You don't want to stay with me, but you're givin' me your *money*? Am I s'posed to be *happy* about this?"

Ritter pushed his hair up off his forehead, then rubbed one hand across his jaw. "No. You don't have to be happy, Hallie." He snorted a laugh. "Guess I really didn't expect that. But you *do* have to know what I've done to take care of you."

"Take *care* of me?" She cocked her head and lay her balled fists on her hips. "That's what you're s'posed to be doin' here? You're hopin' *money* will do what you don't want to?"

Ritter reached out and grabbed her. Pulling her close, he squeezed her so tightly, she thought her ribs might break. Then he lowered his head and kissed her, putting all of the pent-up passion of the last few lonely days into it. Hallie's arms snaked up to encircle his neck and answered his need with her own. Desperate to make him change his mind, she poured her soul into the kiss, trying to tell him without speaking what his leaving was doing to her.

When he finally broke away, she was breathless, and his voice was strained and harsh. "It's not that I don't *want* to stay. I *can't.*" He ran his fingers lightly down the line of her face and stared at her as if committing her to memory. "I love you, Hallie. No matter what else happens, I want you to know that." Gently he bent, kissed her forehead, then straightened up. "You don't know how much I wish I was a different kind of man. The kind who could stay with you forever."

Hallie blinked away the tears in her eyes, trying to see him clearly.

"But I'm not," he continued, "and I can't stay and bring danger down on you."

"Ritter . . ."

Whatever she might have said was lost in the thunder of hooves approaching the house. Ritter turned and ran for the door with Hallie only a step behind him. In the hall Shad was waiting with two guns. He handed one to Ritter, then slowly opened the door.

A boy of about fourteen sat on a restless, prancing horse. The slash of light from the house outlined him distinctly.

"What d'ya want?" Shad called.

"Got a message for Ritter Sloane," the boy answered in a surprisingly deep voice.

"I'm Sloane."

"Nathan Pine says he'd be pleased to meet you in town tomorrow. Ten o'clock."

Hallie's heart dropped to her feet, and she sneaked a glance at her husband's face. She watched him answer softly, "Tell Pine I'll be there."

"Yessir!" The boy took off like a shot, and in seconds, the yard was empty again. Like nothing had happened. But it had.

"Y'see, Hallie," Ritter said sadly. "*This* is what it would be like. *Always.*" He lifted one hand to touch her cheek but thought better of it and let his hand drop to his side. Silently he went back inside to clean and load his guns.

To prepare for battle.

Hallie's mind raced. He loved her. He didn't *want* to leave—he thought he had to. She looked down at her left hand, and the emerald winked up at her. There had to be some way to convince him. She had to *do* something!

And suddenly a glimmer of an idea sparked in her brain and quickly took hold. If it worked, then Ritter would face a clear choice. Hallie had to take the chance that he would choose her.

Grabbing Shad, Hallie pulled him outside and closed the door. She had a lot of talking to do, and she didn't want Ritter to hear a word of it.

Chapter

※

Twenty

RITTER STEPPED out of the boys' bedroom, dressed, shaved, and ready for his appointment with Nathan Pine.

He'd slept much later than he'd planned to, and already the sun was climbing into a bright, clear sky. It had taken hours to fall asleep the night before. He'd stared unblinking into the darkness so long, his eyes still ached. And it was because of Hallie. Of course, there was always a sense of edginess before a gunbattle, but this time he'd found his thoughts centering not on his enemy but on his wife.

He snorted and tugged at the hang of his black coat. Thinking like that would only get him killed. He *had* to concentrate on Pine.

The silence of the house finally reached him, and he looked around the main room. There was no sign of Hallie or Shad. Curious, he walked across the floor, knocked on Hallie's door, then threw it open. The room was empty.

Puzzled, Ritter went back to the great room. Fresh coffee bubbled on the stove, but otherwise, there was not a sign of life. A glance out the window showed no one in the yard, either. Quietly he grabbed a cup and poured himself some coffee. As he sipped the hot liquid, he told

289

himself that Hallie and Shad were simply trying to avoid saying goodbye. And maybe it was just as well.

He gulped at the coffee and realized he was relieved. After the long, almost sleepless night, he didn't think he'd be able to handle any tearful farewells. A wistful grin creased his face. He *surely* didn't want to be faced with one of Hallie's angry tirades, either.

Tossing a glance at the clock on the mantel, Ritter sighed and set his cup down on the table. One last time he let his gaze roam over the Benteen house. No matter what happened later that morning, Ritter would always be grateful to Hamilton Butler for hiring him. He wouldn't have missed the last few weeks for anything.

Reluctantly he crossed the room and snatched his hat off the peg by the front door. Then he stepped outside and left his new life behind him.

Stillwater looked like a ghost town in the morning sunshine. Not a soul on the street. Even the horses at the hitch rails had been moved to safety. A tiny devil wind picked up dust and pebbles and danced them across the wide road. A rawboned dog wandered down the empty boardwalk, jumped off the end, and curled up under the edge for a nap.

Ritter rode his horse up the middle of the street, stopped in front of the Silver Spur, and dismounted. Flipping the reins over the closest railing, he stood alone and waited.

Uneasiness crept up Ritter's spine as his gaze moved over the lonely-looking buildings. Were the citizens of Stillwater hiding behind their curtains, waiting to see who would win and who would die? He felt the stares of unseen eyes and knew he must be right.

And though it had happened before, in too many towns, he felt an odd swell of disappointment. He'd thought that he had friends in Stillwater. He'd begun to believe that the folks in town had ceased looking at him as a gunfighter and had accepted him as a man. But he was wrong. Even now they waited in safety to watch him shoot or be shot.

Knowing that they were no different than any other townspeople he'd encountered over the years destroyed that last glimmer of hope he'd been carrying with him.

The saloon doors swung open. Steady boot steps echoed in the stillness, and without turning, Ritter knew that Nathan Pine was there. Behind him.

Pine took the steps slowly, and when he stood in the dusty street, Ritter turned around to face him. Separated by only a few feet, Nathan smiled victoriously. Ritter's expression didn't change, but inside he found himself wishing that he'd been able to see Hallie one last time. He stifled a sigh of regret. No matter what happened here today—whether he lived or died—he wouldn't be going back to the ranch.

Still smiling, Nathan sidestepped to the middle of the street and stopped. Ritter nodded briefly and walked out to meet his enemy, while widening the distance between them. He saw Nathan tuck the right-side edge of his coat behind his back and watched as the gunfighter's fingers moved delicately through the air above his pistol.

Ritter's lips twisted into a half smile. It was all so familiar. So simple. *This* was his life. It didn't matter that he was tired to the bone of gunshots and empty streets. It didn't matter that he no longer felt like the same man who lived with death at his shoulder. Nothing mattered beyond surviving this encounter and then the next and the next. There was no way out of the hole he'd dug for himself so long ago. And it was just as well that he get used to that notion now.

An image of Hallie flashed through his brain, and Ritter's chest tightened briefly at the thought of what might have been. But he resolutely pushed the dream out of his mind when Nathan Pine spoke.

"Been a long time comin', Sloane."

"Yes, it has, Nathan." Slowly Ritter moved his right hand and tucked his coat behind his back. Even knowing it was useless to try, he heard himself say, "We don't have to do this, y'know."

Pine's eyebrows shot up, and he cocked his head. "What's wrong, Sloane? Too busy with that pretty little wife of yours to want to do business?"

"She's out of this," Ritter's teeth ground together.

"Agreed," the gunman said with a grin. "For now, she's out of it. But I want you to know I'll be happy to look in on your widow from time to time. . . ."

Anger rushed through him. Wild, unreasoning anger, and Ritter knew in an instant that he would probably die in the coming gun battle. His old detachment was gone. His concentration was shattered. And as he realized all this, he knew with a certainty that before he died, he *had* to kill Nathan Pine. Otherwise, Hallie might never be safe.

"You stay the hell away from my wife," he finally said softly.

Pine laughed. "You'll have nothin' to say about it, man. You'll be six feet under and *finally* out of my way. So what do you say we take care of business now? Just between you and me."

"I don't think so, boys." Sheriff Tucker's calm voice grabbed at the two men, and as one, they turned toward his voice.

The older man stood under the overhang in front of Elmira's store. He held a shotgun casually in his arms, and it was pointed at Nathan Pine.

"Pine, I thought I told you to leave town today."

"Well, now," the gunman returned easily, "I'm gonna do just that, Sheriff. As soon as I finish my business."

"Look, Sheriff," Ritter broke in, "I appreciate what you're tryin' to do, but—"

"You hush, Sloane." Tucker only glanced at him before turning his steely gaze back on Pine. "Mister, your business here *is* finished."

As if at a silent signal, gun barrels began appearing. From half-opened windows, behind curtains, through doorways . . . There were even a few people on the rooftops, holding rifles aimed at the street. Ritter turned his head quickly, trying to understand. Everywhere he looked, one of the townspeople was stepping forward, holding a gun.

Shotguns, pistols, rifles. Homer Triggs, the barber, stepped out on his porch, staggering under the weight of a Spencer .50. Glancing over his shoulder, Ritter watched Dixie lift a double-barreled derringer and aim it at Nathan. Behind her, her girls and the bartender spread out in a semicircle, armed and ready.

From the alley between the Silver Spur and the Feed and Grain, Hamilton Butler and four of his ranch hands walked into the street and took position behind Nathan. Their rifles were aimed at the gunfighter, too.

Ritter shook his head and snapped his jaw shut. He

looked back at the sheriff. Right behind him was Elmira Huggins. Her short, round body and usually smiling face were dwarfed by the size of the Colt revolving shotgun she held. Quick, light steps caught his attention, and he looked to see Rose, little Jonathan's mother, hurrying down the boardwalk, an old army pistol clenched tightly in her fist. She smiled at Ritter and took her place by the sheriff.

"What the hell's goin' on here?" Nathan yelled out. "What kind of town *is* this?"

Ritter grinned and kept turning this way and that, looking in stunned surprise from one face to another. The only one missing was Professor Adams, since he hadn't returned from his trip to Denver.

"This is *our* town, Pine," Sheriff Tucker said. "I told you yesterday that Ritter Sloane had friends here. Friends who wouldn't take kindly to you bringin' trouble down on him." He waved his shotgun at the still-growing crowd. "Reckon now you see what I mean."

Hallie's voice rang out, and Ritter spun around, trying to locate her in the mass of people.

"All you have to do, Mr. Pine," she said, "is ride out. Because if you don't . . . the minute you lay a hand on your gun"—she chuckled—"well, there won't be enough left of you to bury."

Sheriff Tucker cut her off in a dangerously low voice. "There's no place for you here, Pine. And the time is comin' when there won't be a place for your kind anywhere. Gunfighters are goin' the way of the buffalo. Folks just ain't gonna put up with your nonsense anymore. They want peace. They want their kids to grow up safe from flyin' bullets."

Ritter only half heard the sheriff, though he agreed

with the man's statements. But right now he was more interested in locating Hallie. She was there. *Somewhere.* He couldn't find her. She had to be standing behind somebody. Though hiding wasn't usually Hallie's way. As he searched the crowd, Ritter saw Shad and smiled at the triplet's easy grin. *No one* had ever done anything like this for him before. He couldn't believe it. In fact, if he hadn't seen it with his own eyes, he *never* would have believed it.

Glancing back at Nathan, he saw that the gunfighter had turned a pale, sickly greenish color. Ritter could hardly blame him. Being the target of at least fifty guns would do that to any man.

"Well, Pine," Tucker shouted, "what's it gonna be?"

Ritter waited a moment and watched Nathan carefully. The man was frozen into position. He was obviously terrified to make the slightest move. Slowly Ritter walked toward his old enemy.

"Nathan, we can let it end, right here."

Casting a doubtful eye on the sheriff, Nathan swallowed heavily when the shotgun Elmira was holding slipped, and she lurched to grab it. Beads of sweat dotted Pine's forehead, and he didn't breathe until the woman had her weapon under control again. He looked at Ritter out of the corner of his eye. "What do you mean, let it end?"

Ritter hid a smile. "Nathan, you've been wanting to be rid of me for a lot of years."

"True," the man answered with a nervous twitch.

"Then how about I get out of the business and leave you to it?"

Pine's gaze snapped to the other man. "For good?"

"For good." Hope swelled in Ritter's chest. He really

had a chance to get away from the life he hated. If only Nathan would settle for never knowing which of them was the fastest.

"How do I know you'll stay out?" Nathan asked, then jumped when Elmira started losing her grip on the shotgun again. This time Sheriff Tucker took the big weapon away from her. Nathan sighed in relief, then groaned when Tucker handed the little woman a pistol.

"You've seen my wife," Ritter said with a smile. "Why would I want to leave her and go back to hiring my gun?"

"Well . . ."

"Look," Ritter said quickly, afraid to lose his advantage, "with me out of the way, you'll get all the big jobs. Folks'll be coming to you from all over the country."

"Hmmm . . ." Carefully, as slowly as he could manage, Nathan lowered his right arm, still keeping it wide of his gun. "Would it be all right with you if I told folks you was dead?"

Ritter laughed out loud and clapped Nathan's shoulder. "Hell, yes, it's all right with me! Shoot, tell everybody you beat me to the draw!"

Pine smiled, thought a moment, then shrugged. "All right. It ends here."

The last knot of tension in Ritter's chest loosened and dissolved. He was free. The killing was over.

"You know somethin', Sloane?" Nathan cocked his head and looked at him.

"What?"

"I *would* have beat ya."

Ritter looked into the cold, dark eyes for a long, silent moment. Maybe he would have. Now they would never know. And that didn't bother Ritter in the slightest. But he knew it would *always* bother Pine.

He glanced around him at the crowd of people who'd put their lives on the line for him. Their smiles, their nods meant more to him than anything he'd experienced in years. But gunfighting was all Nathan Pine had. All he would *ever* have. And so Ritter gave the gunman one last gift.

"You know, Nathan? You're probably right. I believe you *would* have won."

Nathan Pine smiled, satisfied, and turned away. Tucker stepped down from the boardwalk to escort the man to his horse, and everyone else in town swarmed around Ritter Sloane.

Talking, laughing, patting each other on the back, the people surrounded him. Though grateful beyond measure, he shook the hands extended to him absently, his gaze continuously moving over the crowd. Eagerly he looked all about him but couldn't find the one person he was searching for.

Somebody grabbed him and Ritter spun around. He couldn't help returning Shadrack's delighted grin. "So, brother, you about ready to go home now?"

"More than you'll ever know, Shad," Ritter had to shout to be heard over the mass of people. "But first, where's Hallie?"

Shad's brow wrinkled, and he glanced over the heads of the townspeople. "You know, I ain't seen her since we hit town." He looked back at Ritter and winked. "She's been busy."

Ritter laughed. "Yeah, I can see that! But I have to find her."

"Then let's us get through this bunch and do it," Shad offered.

As if in answer to a prayer, the two men heard Dixie shout, "Free beer, everybody! On the house! Coffee for the ladies!"

Ten o'clock in the morning or not, there wasn't a single man in the crowd who would turn down a free drink. Quickly the crowd melted away until only a few women were left in the street, already gossiping over the morning's activities.

From the corner of his eye, Ritter saw Ham Butler walk into the saloon, Dixie on his arm. The older rancher smiled, but Ritter didn't have time to do much more than nod in return. He and Shad split up, each of them taking one side of the street.

In fifteen minutes the town had been searched, pillar to post, with no sign of Hallie. Where the hell is she? Ritter asked himself. And why'd she disappear? You'd think after going to all the trouble to save his hide, she'd at least have waited around to let him thank her!

He stood in the shade of the overhang and rubbed his jaw thoughtfully. Unless, he told himself, she'd decided she wanted no part of him anymore.

No. That wasn't it. It couldn't be the reason. He straightened up. Even if it *was* the reason, it made no difference. He wasn't goin' anywhere. At least, not without her. She could just get used to *that* idea right now!

Fine, he snorted. How can you *threaten* her when you can't even *find* her?

Shad walked up shaking his head, but before he could speak, they heard it. A woman, yelling and cursing in

Spanish and a disgruntled male voice shouting, "Woman, will you shut up!"

They walked into the street and met Micah, Jericho, and a huge man Ritter took to be Tribulation Benteen riding into town. Seated behind Micah was a pretty woman with waist-length night-black hair, wearing a leather riding skirt, heavy coat, knee-high moccasins and cussing the air blue!

"Jesus! Woman, don't your jaws never get tired?" Micah turned in the saddle and glared at her.

She hissed right back at him, muttering a Spanish oath that made Ritter laugh out loud.

Micah looked at him quickly. "You understand Mex?"

"Yeah," he answered on a laugh. The woman, he noticed, was watching him, a smile in her startlingly blue eyes.

"Well, what the hell is she sayin'?" Micah swung his right leg over his horse's neck, jumped to the ground, then pulled the woman down after him. "She's been goin' on at me for the last hundred miles!"

"Well," Ritter said, looking from Jericho's laughing face to Trib's interested expression, "near as I can translate, she says you're the bastard son of a mule and a coyote and . . ." He stifled his laugh when Micah's lips pressed together tightly.

"And?" the triplet urged.

"And you lack the brains to be either one."

Jericho exploded in laughter.

Trib chuckled behind one huge hand.

Shad looked down at his feet to hide his grin.

Micah snatched his hat off and flung it to the ground. "If that ain't the beatinest thing . . ."

The woman laughed delicately, lifted her chin, and planted her fists on her hips defiantly.

"Who *is* she?" Shadrack finally managed to ask.

The woman turned to him and proudly announced, "I am Julietta Maria Rosaria Duffy y Santos."

"Duffy?" Shad repeated.

"Yeah." Micah frowned at her. "Her pa's Irish, her ma's Mexican. And that's *some* kind of mix, I'm here to testify. We're s'posed to be takin' her back to her pa. . . ."

She smirked at him, and Micah added, *"If* I don't kill her first!"

"Hah!" Julietta Duffy spat at him.

"You must be Hallie's husband." Trib's voice was much deeper than his brother's. When he spoke, Micah quieted with only a glare directed at the woman.

"That's right." Ritter looked up at the man and realized just what a *huge* man the oldest Benteen really was.

Trib nodded. "The boys told me. Also said there was some trouble? Nathan Pine?"

"It's over, Trib," Shad said. "Pine's gone. Won't be back."

"What?" Jericho sounded stunned. "You mean we *missed* the fight? Hell, we liked to killed ourselves gettin' back here."

"Wasn't no fight."

"What happened?" Trib demanded.

"Later," Ritter spoke up quickly. "Right now we're tryin' to find Hallie."

"What's wrong?"

"Nothin'." Shad shook his head. "She's fine. Just up and took off somewhere. Hidin'."

"Well," Micah put in, "she ain't at home. We just come from there."

"Hidin'? Hallie?"

"It's a long story, Trib."

"Did ya ask Dixie if she seen her?" Jericho's soft voice grabbed both Shad and Ritter.

"No." They stared at each other sheepishly.

Jericho snorted. "Can't do a damned thing without us. C'mon. We'll have a beer, you can tell us everything."

Ritter didn't wait. He hurried ahead of the Benteen boys and entered the saloon. Ignoring the welcoming shouts, he walked straight to Dixie and Ham.

"Do you know where she is?"

"Who?" Ham asked, and Dixie slapped his arm.

"Yes, I do," she answered.

"Dix," Ham thundered, "I promised not to tell."

"You ain't tellin' him. *I* am." She looked back at Ritter and smiled. "She's at Ham's place."

Ritter turned to leave, and Dixie shouted, "She says she's gonna *stay* there."

"That's what she *says*," Ritter countered with a knowing grin and pushed past his brothers-in-law in the doorway.

"Say, is Mr. Sloane leavin'?" the telegrapher said as he struggled through the crowd. "I got that other package for him down to the depot."

"What package?" Shad asked.

"Says on the box it's a telescope." The little man rubbed his nearly bald head. "Come all the way from Boston. What you figure he wants one of them for?"

The Benteens looked at each other and smiled. Clearly, Hallie's husband knew just what kind of gifts to buy his wife.

"Don't fret," Jericho told the man. "We'll pick it up on the way home." He looked up. "First things first, though. Dixie, how 'bout a beer?"

*   *   *

Hallie wasn't even surprised when she heard a horse gallop up to the house. She'd figured Dixie would tell Ritter where she was. But just because he'd found her didn't mean that she would be going anywhere with him.

That depended entirely on what the man had to say.

Deliberately she put her feet up on the low footstool in front of the settee and tried to look relaxed.

The front door crashed open, and she flinched at the sound of glass breaking. Had to be the tall vase in the entryway. She crossed her arms over her chest and listened to his heavy steps going into and out of the rooms as he looked for her. Shaking her head, she told herself that naturally a man would look in the most logical place last.

When the door to Ham's study flew open, she managed to sit still, though what she wanted to do was run to the man standing there. It had taken every ounce of will she possessed to leave town before he could speak to her. But she'd had to.

She didn't want him promising to stay with her out of gratitude any more than she wanted him to stay because of the baby. She'd had to give him a few minutes to think about what it was he wanted. If that was *her*, then he had to find her and tell her.

"I've been lookin' everywhere for you," he said softly.

"I been right here," she countered and picked up a nearby book. She opened it and pretended to read, even though the words all ran together in a blur. Her every sense was concentrated on her husband.

"Why'd you leave?"

"The way *I* remember it, it was *you* doin' the leavin'."

He stepped farther into the room. "That was different."

"Leavin' is leavin'."

"Hallie . . ."

She watched him take a deep breath and knew he was getting angry. Good. Lord knew, it was *his* turn.

"What?"

"About what you did today . . ."

"I didn't do it—the whole town did."

He came closer. "But *you* started it. I don't even know quite how you pulled it off . . . ." She opened her mouth, but he went on quickly, "And it doesn't matter."

She shrugged and returned her eyes to the book.

He was beside her now, and when he knelt down and took the book from her hands, she was forced to look at him. He wasn't angry. Her breath caught. His pale blue eyes held nothing but tenderness. She felt his gaze move over her as surely as a touch, and she shivered slightly with the force of her love for him.

"Hallie," he whispered, "let's go home."

"For how long, Ritter? Till the next gunman shows up?" She shook her head. "What if folks don't believe Nathan Pine? What if someone finds you anyway? What then?" Her eyebrows rose, and she cocked her head. "Will you leave then, too?"

"No."

He said it quickly, decisively. Reaching out, he cupped her cheek with one hand, and Hallie bit her tongue to keep from saying anything. She wanted to hear him out before she welcomed him back home.

"Whatever happens, Hallie, I'm here to stay, if you'll have me."

She wasn't convinced, and it must have shown on her

face, because he added quickly, "See, I finally realized you were right about something."

"What?" She had to force the word out past the lump in her throat.

"When you said families protect each other. Well, I've been alone so long, it never occurred to me to count on anyone's help." He leaned toward her and kissed her forehead. "But you showed me different. And even if I spend the rest of my life lookin' over my shoulder"— he held up one finger—"*which* I don't believe I'll have to do once Nathan starts talking . . . it'll be worth it." He held her shoulders and pulled her closer. "God knows, I'll always wonder if I've put you in danger somehow—but I think I finally understand that living with worry would be easier than living without you."

She shook her head gently and ran one hand over his jaw. "*Everybody's* got worries, husband. The trick is to get somebody to *share* 'em with ya."

He smiled and Hallie noticed that for the first time, there wasn't a hint of shadows in his eyes.

"All right, then." Ritter pulled in a deep breath before asking, "Hallie Sloane, will you share my worries and let me share yours?"

She grinned and couldn't help questioning, "For how long, Ritter Sloane?"

"Forever and then some, ma'am." He pulled her up against him and lowered his lips to hers in a gentle kiss full of promise. It seemed as though she'd been waiting for that kiss for a lifetime. When he broke away smiling, Hallie answered, "I think I'd like that, *husband*."

"Then, *wife*"—he chuckled—"can we go home now?"

"But don't you want to go back to town to join in the

celebration?" She couldn't hide the teasing note in her voice. There was nothing she wanted more than to be at home in their own bed, shut away from everyone. For at least a while.

He shook his head and stood, pulling her to her feet. "Nope. Your brothers are back. Trib with them. And a Mexican woman giving Micah fits. . . ."

"What?"

"Hey! I just realized something!" He grinned and added, "I had no trouble at all telling the boys apart!"

"I knew they'd grow on ya." She cocked her head. "Ya say Trib and some woman are with 'em?"

"Yep. And I figure they'll be in town for quite a while yet . . . so why don't you and I go home and have a private celebration. Just the two of us?"

It only took her a moment to agree. With all her brothers home, privacy would be hard to come by soon enough. And who was the woman with them?

Suddenly, though, her stomach churned, and she remembered that there was still one more thing she hadn't told Ritter yet.

"Wait," she said firmly and swallowed.

"What is it?" Ritter looked down at her. "Did I forget something?" He slapped his forehead. "I should've said it straight off." His voice softened. "I love you, Hallie."

She slapped his chest playfully. "Hell, I know that. I love you, too."

"Then what is it?"

"What you said just then . . . about the two of us?"

"Sounds good, doesn't it?" he shot back and began to lead her out of the house eagerly.

"Yes . . ."

He stopped. Looking at her suspiciously, he asked, "What?"

"Oh, it's just that I forgot to tell *you* something." She snaked her arms around his neck and smiled up at him. "You remember that bargain we made?"

"How could I forget?"

"Well, Ritter, you was true to your word."

"What d'ya mean?" He leaned his head back and looked at her questioningly.

Hallie shook her head and grinned. Grabbing one of his hands, she laid it gently on her flat belly and said, "Husband, meet your daughter."

In a heartbeat his expression changed from desire, to astonishment, to pride, then back to desire. Carefully he slid his hand over her abdomen, wonder in his eyes.

He snorted a half laugh. "You *forgot* to tell me?"

She covered his hand with her own and added softly, "Well, I thought it best to wait a bit before lettin' you in on it. Though I got to warn ya, Ritter, there might be more than one in there. Us Benteens run to twins and triplets and such."

He swallowed heavily. "Just promise me one thing, Hallie."

"What's that?"

"Promise me that every daughter we have will be just like her mother."

She pulled his head down to hers, and just before she kissed him, Hallie whispered, "I always knew you was a brave one, husband."

If you enjoyed *Shotgun Bride*, watch for Micah and Julietta's story in *Runaway Bride*, coming in April 1994.

Diamond Wildflower Romance

A breathtaking new line of spectacular novels set in the untamed frontier of the American West. Every month, Diamond Wildflower brings you new adventures where passionate men and women dare to embrace their boldest dreams. Finally, romances that capture the very spirit and passion of the wild frontier.

__RIVER TEMPTRESS by Elaine Crawford
   1-55773-867-X/$4.99

__WYOMING WILDFIRE by Anne Harmon
   1-55773-883-1/$4.99

__GUNMAN'S LADY by Catherine Palmer
   1-55773-893-9/$4.99

__RECKLESS WIND by Bonnie K. Winn
   1-55773-902-1/$4.99

__NEVADA HEAT by Ann Carberry
   1-55773-915-3/$4.99

__TEXAS JEWEL by Shannon Willow
   1-55773-923-4/$4.99

__REBELLIOUS BRIDE by Donna Fletcher
   1-55773-942-0/$4.99

__RENEGADE FLAME by Catherine Palmer
   1-55773-952-8/$4.99

__SHOTGUN BRIDE by Ann Carberry
   1-55773-959-5/$4.99

__WILD WINDS by Peggy Stoks
   1-55773-965-X/$4.99 (December)

For Visa, MasterCard and American Express orders ($15 minimum) call: 1-800-631-8571

FOR MAIL ORDERS: CHECK BOOK(S). FILL OUT COUPON. SEND TO:

BERKLEY PUBLISHING GROUP
390 Murray Hill Pkwy., Dept. B
East Rutherford, NJ 07073

NAME_____

ADDRESS _____

CITY_____

STATE _____ ZIP_____

PLEASE ALLOW 6 WEEKS FOR DELIVERY.
PRICES ARE SUBJECT TO CHANGE WITHOUT NOTICE.

POSTAGE AND HANDLING:
$1.75 for one book, 75¢ for each additional. Do not exceed $5.50.

BOOK TOTAL $ _____

POSTAGE & HANDLING $ _____

APPLICABLE SALES TAX $ _____
(CA, NJ, NY, PA)

TOTAL AMOUNT DUE $ _____

PAYABLE IN US FUNDS.
(No cash orders accepted.)

406

FROM THE AWARD-WINNING AUTHOR OF
RIVERS WEST: THE COLORADO, **HERE IS THE SPRAWLING
EPIC STORY OF ONE FAMILY'S BRAVE STRUGGLE
FOR THE AMERICAN DREAM.**

THE HORSEMEN

Gary McCarthy

**The Ballous were the finest horsemen in the South, a
Tennessee family famous for the training and breeding of
thoroughbreds. When the Civil War devastated their home
and their lives, they headed West—into the heart of Indian
territory. As a family, they endured. As horsemen, they
triumphed. But as pioneers in a new land, they faced
unimaginable hardship, danger, and ruthless enemies...**

__**THE HORSEMEN   1-55773-733-9/$3.99**

__**CHEROKEE LIGHTHORSE 1-55773-797-5/$3.99**

__**TEXAS MUSTANGERS 1-55773-857-2/$3.99**

__**BLUE BULLET 1-55773-944-7/$3.99**

For Visa, MasterCard and American Express ($15 minimum) orders call: 1-800-631-8571

FOR MAIL ORDERS: CHECK BOOK(S). FILL OUT COUPON. SEND TO:	POSTAGE AND HANDLING: $1.75 for one book, 75¢ for each additional. Do not exceed $5.50.
BERKLEY PUBLISHING GROUP 390 Murray Hill Pkwy., Dept. B East Rutherford, NJ 07073	BOOK TOTAL $ _____
NAME———————————————	POSTAGE & HANDLING $ _____
ADDRESS—————————————	APPLICABLE SALES TAX $ _____ (CA, NJ, NY, PA)
CITY———————————————	TOTAL AMOUNT DUE $ _____
STATE ——————— ZIP————	PAYABLE IN US FUNDS. (No cash orders accepted.)

PLEASE ALLOW 6 WEEKS FOR DELIVERY.
PRICES ARE SUBJECT TO CHANGE WITHOUT NOTICE.

440

If you enjoyed this book, take advantage of this special offer. Subscribe now and...

Get a Historical

No Obligation

If you enjoy reading the very best in historical romantic fiction...romances that set back the hands of time to those bygone days with strong virile heros and passionate heroines ...then you'll want to subscribe to the True Value Historical Romance Home Subscription Service. Now that you have read one of the best historical romances around today, we're sure you'll want more of the same fiery passion, intimate romance and historical settings that set these books apart from all others.

Each month the editors of True Value select the four *very best* novels from America's leading publishers of romantic fiction. We have made arrangements for you to preview them in your home *Free* for 10 days. And with the first four books you

receive, we'll send you a FREE book as our introductory gift. No Obligation!

FREE HOME DELIVERY

We will send you the four best and newest historical romances as soon as they are published to preview FREE for 10 days (in many cases you may even get them before they arrive in the book stores). If for any reason you decide not to keep them, just return them and owe nothing. But if you like them as much as we think you will, you'll pay just $4.00 each and save at *least* $.50 each off the cover price. (Your savings are *guaranteed* to be at least $2.00 each month.) There is NO postage and handling—or other hidden charges. There are no minimum number of books to buy and you may cancel at any time.

FREE
Romance

(a $4.50 value)

Send in the Coupon Below

To get your FREE historical romance and start saving, fill out the coupon below and mail it today. As soon as we receive it we'll send you your FREE Book along with your first month's selections.

Mail To **True Value Home Subscription Services, Inc. P.O. Box 5235**
120 Brighton Road, Clifton, New Jersey 07015-5235

YES! I want to start previewing the very best historical romances being published today. Send me my FREE book along with the first month's selections. I understand that I may look them over FREE for 10 days. If I'm not absolutely delighted I may return them and owe nothing. Otherwise I will pay the low price of just $4.00 each, a total $16.00 (at *least* an $18.00 value) and save at least $2.00. Then each month I will receive four brand new novels to preview as soon as they are published for the same low price. I can always return a shipment and I may cancel this subscription at any time with no obligation to buy even a single book. In any event the FREE book is mine to keep regardless.

Name _____

Street Address _____ Apt. No _____

City _____ State _____ Zip Code _____

Telephone _____

Signature _____
(if under 18 parent or guardian must sign)

Terms and prices subject to change. Orders subject
to acceptance by True Value Home Subscription
Services Inc.   959-5

AWARD-WINNING AND NATIONAL
BESTSELLING AUTHOR

JODI THOMAS

__CHERISH THE DREAM 1-55773-881-5/$4.99

From childhood through nursing school, Katherine and Sarah were best friends. Now they set out to take all that life had to offer–and were swept up in the rugged, positively breathtaking world of two young pilots, men who took to the skies with a bold spirit. And who dared them to love.

__THE TENDER TEXAN 1-55773-546-8/$4.95

Anna Meyer dared to walk into a campsite full of Texan cattle-men and offer one hundred dollars to the man who'd help her forge a frontier homestead. Chance Wyatt accepted her offer and they vowed to live together for one year only...until the chal-lenges of the savage land drew them closer together.

__PRAIRIE SONG 1-55773-657-X/$4.99

Maggie was Texas born and bred. The beautiful Confederate widow inherited a sprawling house of scandalous secrets. But more shocking was her newfound desire for a Union Army soldier.

__NORTHERN STAR 1-55773-396-1/$4.50

Hauntingly beautiful Perry McLain was desperate to escape the cruel, powerful Union Army captain who pursued her, seeking vengeance for her rebellion. Yet, her vow to save Hunter Kirkland plunged her deep into enemy territory...and into the torturous flames of desire.

For Visa, MasterCard and American Express orders ($15 minimum) call: 1-800-631-8571

FOR MAIL ORDERS: CHECK BOOK(S). FILL OUT COUPON. SEND TO:

BERKLEY PUBLISHING GROUP
390 Murray Hill Pkwy., Dept. B
East Rutherford, NJ 07073

NAME_____

ADDRESS _____

CITY_____

STATE _____ZIP_____

PLEASE ALLOW 6 WEEKS FOR DELIVERY.
PRICES ARE SUBJECT TO CHANGE WITHOUT NOTICE.

POSTAGE AND HANDLING:
$1.75 for one book, 75¢ for each additional. Do not exceed $5.50.

BOOK TOTAL	$ _____
POSTAGE & HANDLING	$ _____
APPLICABLE SALES TAX (CA, NJ, NY, PA)	$ _____
TOTAL AMOUNT DUE	$ _____

PAYABLE IN US FUNDS.
(No cash orders accepted.)

361